Fragile Hearts

PAT NICHOLS

Fragile Hearts by Pat Nichols
Published by Armchair Press
ISBN: 979-8-9912411-5-1

Cover Design by Elaina Lee
Edited by Sherri Stewart

Available in print from your local bookstore or online.
For more information on this book or the author visit:
https://patnicholsauthor.blog
Printed in the United States of America
Fragile Hearts is a work of fiction. Names, characters, and incidents are all products of the author's imagination or are used for fictional purposes. Any mentioned brand names, places, and trademarks remain the property of their respective owners, bear no association with the author or Fragile Hearts/ Pat Nichols

Books by

Pat Nichols

Blue Ridge Series

Blizzard at Blue Ridge Inn
The Inheritance
The Wedding
Christmas at Hilltop Inn
The Promise
Summer of Second Chances
Whispers of Hope
Fragile Hearts
Road to Forgiveness

Willow Falls Series

The Secret of Willow Inn
Trouble in Willow Falls
Starstruck in Willow Falls
Bridges, Books, and Bones

Butler Family Legacy Series

Big Secrets, Little Lies
Truth and Forgiveness
New Beginnings

For Freya Diane Graw, my closest high school friend, proof that even after losing contact for decades, true friendship endures.

Chapter 1

Amanda Smith's pulse pounded in her ears while she rushed down Hilltop Inn's front stairs to the foyer then out to the porch and down to the front sidewalk. Halfway to the driveway, she froze mid-step, her chest heaving as if she had run a mile. Drawing in deep breaths, she glanced up at the three story Victorian-style inn. Was the young woman from New Orleans who had checked in twenty minutes earlier watching from her suite window?

Millie Cunningham caught up with her. "I didn't know you could move that fast."

Amanda blinked, lowering her gaze to the first-floor turret window. What if the young woman from New Orleans had told her the truth? A November gust of cold wind sent a shiver racing through her limbs. Regretting not taking the time to retrieve her jacket from the inn's kitchen, she resumed scurrying toward the driveway, then across the side yard and through the carport to the ranch house kitchen. Dusty, the resident golden retriever, padded in from the den, her wagging tail creating a breeze.

Millie followed Amanda inside and pushed the kitchen door closed. "Tonight our mystery club will find out what sort of scam our new check-in is trying to pull."

"Look, I appreciate your intentions." Amanda tossed the inn keys in the bowl on the counter. "At the same time, I don't want anyone else to know about Savannah Landry's outrageous claim. Which is why your little band of sleuths needs to focus your efforts on her mother."

Millie propped her hand on her hip. "How do you expect me to explain digging into some random dead woman's past?"

"You're our company's chief information officer. You'll figure out a way." Amanda grabbed a bottle of water from the fridge. "If you don't mind, I'm not in the mood for company."

"Before I go, do you mind if I offer a word of advice?"

Amanda twisted the cap off her water bottle. "What if I say no?"

"I'll give it to you anyway."

Amanda rolled her eyes. "Why did I bother to ask?"

"I don't have a clue." Millie placed her hand on Amanda's arm. "Anyway, I suggest you spend the afternoon reading a book or watching a movie to avoid working yourself into a tizzy."

"At least this time I agree with your unsolicited advice." She pulled her arm away from Millie. "I'll see you tonight."

"My house. Six o'clock sharp." Millie waved over her shoulder while heading out to the carport.

Amanda schlepped to the den and dropped onto the sofa. She gulped down half the water to ease her parched throat. After wiping the back of her hand across her mouth, she set the water bottle on the end table then collapsed against the back cushion and closed her eyes. Within seconds a gut-wrenching memory she'd kept buried until a few weeks earlier came rushing back. The day her husband packed a bag and stormed out of their New Orleans shotgun house three months before she was due to give birth to her now twenty-two-year-old daughter. After all these years, the reason for her fight with Preston continued to escape her.

She opened her eyes, blinking rapidly in an attempt to dismiss Savannah Landry's claim that Preston was her father. She couldn't possibly be telling the truth, could she? Other than those twenty-six agonizing days before he returned home, their marriage had been close to perfect—until that drunk driver ended his life.

Dusty padded over and laid her head on Amanda's lap, her soulful eyes peering up at her. "Whatever Preston and I fought about couldn't have been bad enough to make him cheat on me." She stroked Dusty's head. "Which means that young woman who checked into Hilltop is up to no good." She scoffed. "Savannah probably isn't even her real name."

Amanda grabbed the remote off the coffee table and aimed it toward the flat-screen television above the fireplace mantel. After surfing the channels a third time, she turned off the TV, then headed straight to the hall closet and pulled out the vacuum cleaner. During the remainder of the afternoon, Amanda poured every ounce of energy into cleaning the entire house except the two bedrooms occupied by her remaining housemates—one eighteen years old, the other nineteen. Relieved Sierra and Abby had made plans to meet at a restaurant after work, she finished her house-scrubbing mission with enough time left to shower and change clothes.

Ten minutes before six, Amanda donned her heavy winter coat then pocketed Hilltop Inn's private phone. She headed out to the carport, locking the house behind her. The cold night air nipped her skin while she made her way down the driveway then turned left. Lights shining from Hilltop Inn cast a warm glow on the front lawn. Had the woman who called herself Savannah stayed in or driven to town for dinner?

Amanda scurried past the inn to the adjacent property, where she headed up Millie's driveway to the sidewalk fronting the ranch-style home. As usual, Millie's calico cat perched on the windowsill keeping an eye on the outside world.

Moments after she stepped onto the front porch and rang the bell, the door swung inward. "You're the first to arrive."

Amanda stepped into the foyer. "Am I early or is everyone else late?"

Millie pushed the door closed. "You're five minutes early."

After peeling out of her coat and tossing it over the back of a living room chair, Amanda followed Millie into the dining room. Libations and appetizers sat artfully arranged on the buffet. "Do you always serve adult beverages during your mystery club meetings?"

"That's what adults do."

Amanda pointed to five chairs lined up on one side of the dining room table. "What's with the crazy one-sided arrangement?"

Millie glared at her as if she'd asked the most ridiculous question imaginable. "How else could all of us see everything we find on the internet? We only need five chairs because Susan and Eileen can't join us tonight."

The doorbell rang, followed by footsteps. Gordon, the man Millie had finally admitted she was seeing socially, ambled in with Stanley, his neighbor who was pushing ninety. "Now I understand why you wanted me to bring this." Gordon grinned while setting his laptop on the table. "You've uncovered another mystery for us to tackle."

Stanley leaned on his cane. "What is it this time, Millie?"

"I'll explain once we're all settled."

Bernie, Millie's assistant chef and close friend, walked in. "You've obviously set up Investigative Central again."

Amanda stepped back from the table, her palms moistening while the four senior citizens headed to the buffet. Why hadn't anyone seemed surprised to see her? Had Millie already clued them in? She wiped her palms on her jeans. Despite the fact that Gordon was a retired police officer, had she made a huge mistake trusting amateurs to look for the truth?

Millie carried a glass of red wine to Amanda. "Your beverage of choice."

Especially tonight. "Thanks."

As soon as the plates were loaded and drinks poured, Millie directed Amanda and Bernie to the chairs on Gordon's left. After they were seated, she settled on his right between him and Stanley.

Gordon set his beer on a coaster. "Now that you've dictated the seating arrangements, are you planning to give us an assignment or keep us guessing?"

Amanda's shoulders tightened. What sort of explanation had Millie concocted?

Millie placed her wineglass beside Gordon's beer. "We need to find out everything we can about one Jacqueline Landry from New Orleans."

Stanley plucked a cheese ball off his plate. "Who is she, and why are we investigating her?"

"I have no idea who she is, which is the point." Millie's tone mocked. "As far as the reason goes, let's just say she might have some connection to a woman who checked into the inn earlier today."

"Slick move, Millie." Gordon fingered his thick white moustache then booted his laptop. "You've given us an assignment *and* kept us guessing."

Amanda leaned back. The tension gripping her shoulders eased a bit while Gordon's fingers raced across his keyboard. A long list of women named Jacqueline Landry appeared on his screen. Obviously a fairly common name, at least in Louisiana. He narrowed the list to New Orleans residents.

Millie nudged Gordon. "Check for that name in the obituaries."

He hesitated. "Why are you interested in a dead woman?"

Stanley leaned forward. "Knowing Millie, she wants us to solve some obscure cold case."

Millie drummed her fingers on the table. "Look for obits within the past couple of months."

"So much for a cold case." Gordon tapped his keyboard. "Pay dirt. Jacqueline Landry is survived by a daughter, Savannah."

Bernie snapped her fingers. "Savannah checked into the Dogwood Suite earlier today, didn't she?"

Amanda nodded, hoping no one would ask more questions. "Is there a way to find out how her mother died?"

"If her death was anything other than natural, I'll find it." Gordon resumed searching. Five minutes later, he tapped the screen. "There's your answer."

Amanda gawked at the headline. *Blackjack Dealer Victim of Deadly Ambush.*

Gordon scrolled to the first paragraph, reading it aloud.

Jacqueline Landry, career blackjack dealer, was shot outside a popular New Orleans casino and rushed to the hospital where she succumbed to her injury. The shooter, who was identified as a twenty-year-old Louisiana native, Marcel Guidry, continues to elude police.

Amanda gripped the table edge to steady her trembling hands.

"Good job, Gordon. Perfect time for a sweet break." Millie scooted her chair away from the table. "How about giving me a hand, Amanda?"

Had everyone noticed her reaction or only Millie? Desperate to regain her composure, Amanda grabbed her wineglass then followed their hostess to the kitchen. Her focus drifted to the potted plant on the windowsill while painful memories of another criminal raced through her mind. Gunter Benson had been illegally married to her at the same time he was married to Erica and Wendy. While both women had become family, Gunter was serving twenty-five to life for murder in a Las Vegas prison.

Millie eased beside Amanda and looped her arm around her elbow, hinting she understood the turmoil playing havoc with her emotions. "We'll find out what sort of con Savannah Landry is trying to pull."

Amanda clung to Millie's comment with hope, until a spark of reality sent a shiver up her spine. What if Jacqueline Landry's daughter had told the truth?

Chapter 2

Wendy Armstrong carried her infant daughter into the nursery and placed her in the white crib centered against the wall accented with pink and white stripes.

Seventeen-month-old Ryan followed, pointing to his sister. "Baby Cindy night night."

"You're such a smart boy." Wendy lifted the child Chris had adopted as his own son into her arms and carried him out of the nursery, leaving the door ajar. Duke, their lovable Black Lab, followed them into the great room. "Mommy has some work to finish before tomorrow's board meeting." She placed Ryan on the floor between the coffee table and the stone fireplace then settled on the sofa with her laptop balanced on her thighs.

Two years ago, she could never have imagined serving as a chief financial officer. Now, a few months from earning an online business degree, she successfully managed all the finances for the company she had formed with the two other women Gunter Benson had illegally married. Eager to begin, she pulled up an Excel spreadsheet. A smile curled her lips. Every projection she had shared with her partners about the potential income from a successful bed-and-breakfast had come to fruition. Not bad for a gal raised in foster homes who barely graduated from high school.

Responding to a familiar ringtone, Wendy set her laptop on the coffee table. "Your Aunt Kayla's calling." She swiped her finger across the screen, activating FaceTime. "Hey." She gazed into her half-sister's eyes, still sad weeks after their mother's passing. "You look a little down. Is everything okay?"

"Not really."

"What's going on?"

A flicker of sorrow distorted her features, gone in an instant but undeniable. "Dad's still sleeping on the den sofa. He's freaking out over Zach quitting his part-time job and refusing to go to school. I got a D minus on a math test. Seems Riley's the only one of us who's halfway back to normal. I guess it's easier for a nine-year-old to deal with losing a mother than it is for us older kids."

"Sounds as if you guys could use a change of scenery." Wendy paused the moment an idea bubbled up. Was it too soon to suggest? Especially since the last time the Gilmores visited, their mother had been alive. Only one way to find out. "Hilltop Inn is closed Christmas Eve and Christmas day. What do you think about the four of you celebrating Christmas here in Blue Ridge?"

Kayla's eyes lit up. "Great idea if Dad agrees to take time off from his restaurant and bar."

"Talk to him and let me know what he says. In the meantime—" Wendy lifted her little guy onto the sofa. "Your nephew wants to say hello."

Ryan fingered the screen, leaving a smudge.

Wendy smiled while the sister she hadn't known existed until fewer than two years ago carried on a conversation with her nephew. A warm sensation flowed through her. She, Chris, and their babies would forever be connected to her mother's family.

The sound of the garage door opening sent Duke scrambling to the kitchen while Ryan climbed off the sofa. Wendy wiped Ryan's fingerprints off her phone then glanced over her shoulder the same time Chris walked in. "Hi, darling. We're talking to Kayla."

Chris set his briefcase on the counter then carried Ryan to the sofa and settled beside Wendy. She aimed her phone toward him. He smiled. "Hi, Kayla. How's everything going in Nashville?"

"Better, now that Wendy invited the four of us to spend Christmas with you guys in Blue Ridge."

"Let me guess. As exclusive guests at Hilltop."

"Yeah, if Dad goes along with the plan." Kayla paused. "Um...my boyfriend just texted me. He wants to come over and help me study math."

"No kidding." Wendy's mind drifted to Kayla's description of her last boyfriend who was far too old for her. "How long have you had a boyfriend, and how old is he?"

"Sixteen and a half. Since five days ago. He's cute and really smart. Anyway, I'll call you after I talk to Dad about your invitation. Love you guys."

"We love you, too." Relieved, Wendy tossed her phone on the cushion then turned toward Chris while tucking her ankle under her knee. "I'm worried about Zach."

"Is your brother still ditching school?"

Wendy nodded. "Maybe you should reach out to him again."

"I'll try. Although the last two times I left him a message, crickets."

"Seems Kayla is the glue holding her family together."

"She's carrying a heavy burden for a sixteen-year-old. Fortunately, she has you as her big sister to help guide her."

Ryan climbed off his daddy's lap then toddled to his toy basket.

"Speaking of burdens—" Wendy propped her elbow on the back of the sofa and rested her chin on her knuckles. "What's happening with your latest trial?"

"One more day, and we'll deliver closing statements." Chris slipped out of his loafers then leaned back and planted his feet on the coffee table. "This is the last client Dad and I will defend as a team before he assumes his role as the newly elected district attorney."

"How's your firm's new hire working out?"

"After spending years prosecuting cases, Regina's adapting to her role as defense attorney. Enough about work." Chris faced Wendy. "How are you holding up caring for our baby and our rambunctious toddler?"

"Better than I expected. Taking an afternoon nap with our babies helps."

"If you ask me, you've earned a day off. Which is why I've arranged for Mom to babysit Saturday, so you and I can enjoy a day-long date." Chris stroked her cheek. "Breakfast out. Train ride in the premier coach. A candlelight dinner in one of your favorite restaurants."

Wendy leaned close, whispering. "Followed by a passionate night at home with the sexiest man on the planet."

Chris touched his nose to Wendy's. "The perfect way to end our date. Especially if you wear the cowgirl hat you bought in Nashville."

"The same day you and I created our baby girl."

Ryan toddled over and plopped a book on his daddy's lap. "Read me book."

"I've been summoned for reading duty."

"So it seems."

While Chris lifted his son onto his lap, Wendy plucked her ringing phone off the cushion. "Perfect timing. My stepmother is calling."

"Maybe Donna has news about Douglas dismissing his ridiculous lawsuit against the two of you."

"I'm not holding my breath my father will come to his senses without something dramatic happening to change his mind." While grabbing a throw off the sofa, Wendy pictured the moment she and Chris showed up at Douglas's front door a couple of months before Ryan was born. Until that moment her father had no idea she existed. She forced the memory aside then tapped her screen and headed out to the back deck. "Hi."

"How are my grand babies?"

Wendy activated the speaker before setting her phone on the railing. "They're both as sweet as ever." She wrapped the throw tightly around her shoulders. "What's happening in Hilton Head?"

"On the plus side, my boys have adjusted to their father not being around every day. Unfortunately, Douglas still blames you and me for breaking up our marriage." Donna released a sigh. "That man's ego is too inflated to admit he's a slave to his illicit desires."

"No matter how good he thinks his lawyers are, Chris and his law firm's new partner are far better."

"If Douglas doesn't figure that out pretty soon, he'll lose a ton more money to his greedy attorneys. At least there is one good outcome from his infidelity. His one-night stand in Biloxi during spring break twenty-six years ago created the child who grew up and became my step-daughter."

"A blessing for me, Ryan, and baby Cindy." While she gazed at the wooded lot sloping down to a creek, memories of that day at Hilltop Inn when she first met her stepmother drifted up from Wendy's memory bank. In Donna's mind, she had replaced the unborn daughter she'd lost years ago. "Does Douglas know my mother passed away?"

"Not as far as I know. Besides, I doubt he'd care." Donna paused for a long moment. "I'm glad I had the chance to meet Cynthia."

"I'll always remember the afternoon you and Mom became acquainted over a bottle of chardonnay."

Donna chuckled. "That day Cynthia and I both needed a little liquid courage. Especially since I had finally filed for divorce after putting up with Douglas's cheating all those years. Enough about him. My best friend from high school who moved to Atlanta a few years ago spent a few days with us. She and her husband have a son Carter's age and a daughter a year younger than Tyler. I haven't seen Tyler smile that much since before his father moved out. Anyway, my friend's daughter and Tyler promised to FaceTime each other every day."

Wendy smiled while watching a deer emerge from the woods and peer up at her before moving on by. "There's nothing sweeter than teenage romance."

"Especially with all the trauma going on around here."

While they continued to chat, Wendy's emotions volleyed between sorrow over losing her mother and heartwarming gratitude for her close relationship with her stepmother. When the conversation ended, she returned to the great room. Chris sat on the floor engaged in a delightful conversation with their son. Wendy sat beside Duke. "Before long our little guy will master enough words to carry on a conversation with any adult."

Duke's tail slapped the floor prompting Ryan to point to his canine protector. "Doggie Duke's happy."

Chris caught Wendy's eye and winked.

She smiled. Despite the ongoing challenges involving her mother and stepmother's families, life was good.

Chapter 3

Pretending she hadn't heard Bernie's question, Millie transferred a pan of her signature cinnamon buns from the oven to a cooling rack on Hilltop Inn's kitchen island. "One of our guests reserved a private dinner for tomorrow night."

"You have ears like a bat, so I know you heard me ask the real reason for Amanda's interest in Jacqueline and Savannah Landry." Bernie removed a bowl of yogurt from the fridge. "You should also know that ignoring me only adds to my curiosity."

Millie pressed her lips into a thin line while avoiding eye contact. She couldn't break her promise to Amanda…at least not yet.

"Amanda swore you to secrecy, didn't she?"

Millie hesitated. Denying would only rouse more curiosity. "It took you long enough to come to that conclusion."

"You need to know that Gordon and Stanley also believe there's more to the story than either of you are willing to admit."

Millie huffed. "As an experienced chief information officer, don't you think I know how to read the room?"

"Yeah, well, as esteemed members of our mystery club, so do the rest of us." Bernie folded blueberries and sliced strawberries into the yogurt. "How long before Amanda gives you permission to tell us the real reason for our newest investigation?"

"Until I have an answer, this subject is off the table." Assuming her curt tone would prevent Bernie from asking any more questions, Millie turned her attention to icing the cinnamon buns. Even though keeping secrets from the woman who had become a close friend and confidante didn't come easy, until Amanda gave her permission to reveal details, she'd honor her vow of silence. At least she could keep a close eye on Savannah during breakfast, then show up an hour before the staff meeting to report any unusual behavior to Amanda.

After placing two plates of scrambled eggs and toast on the island in her new home's renovated kitchen, newlywed Erica Barkley climbed onto the stool beside her husband.

Brad kissed her cheek. "Tomorrow morning I'll fix us breakfast."

Erica's lips curled into a smile. The moment she gazed into his deep blue eyes, peace enfolded her like a warm blanket on a cold winter morning. After two failed marriages, the second one illegal, she had found her soulmate.

Brad dug his fork into his eggs. "What's on your schedule today?"

"An eleven o'clock massage client and a one o'clock board meeting. Anything other than typical high school principal duties on your agenda?"

"Not as far as I know." He swallowed a bite. "Are you up for golf with Carl and Lauren Saturday afternoon?"

"Definitely." Erica took a bite of toast. "Sometimes it's hard to imagine that I had never held a golf club in my hands until I met you."

"You've come a long way since I introduced you to the game. Now every time you play you inch closer to finishing eighteen holes with only a hundred strokes."

"One day, I hope to play as well as Jan did." Erica's mind drifted to the day she agreed to play her first round with Brad's deceased wife's clubs. "Maybe because I'm still using Jan's set."

"She's smiling down from heaven, knowing how lucky we are to have found each other."

Erica placed her hand on Brad's thigh. "I imagine Jan and I would have been close friends."

"Without a doubt." Responding to an incoming text, Brad lifted his phone off the island. "Message from a parent questioning why her son's chemistry teacher gave him a D on his last test." He shook his head. "She needs to ask her kid why he didn't study."

"I imagine dealing with some parents is frustrating."

"Comes with the job. Another reason why coming home to my beautiful bride is always the best part of my day."

Erica tilted her head. "Maybe tomorrow I'll pretend I've been called to the principal's office and show up with a surprise bribe."

"Cookies or kisses?"

"If I told you, it wouldn't be a surprise."

Following another ten minutes of playful banter, Brad kissed her before heading downstairs to the garage.

Erica's phone pinged a text from Amanda to her and Wendy. "Can you come over an hour before our meeting?" She responded with a thumbs-up then set her phone aside. Amanda obviously wanted to talk to them about something important before Millie arrived.

Three hours later, Erica entered Hilltop Inn's free-standing garage converted into a spa. She walked through the reception area anchored on one end by a sauna and unlocked her massage room, leaving the door ajar. Following her normal routine, she headed straight to the waist-high cabinet anchored to the dark blue accent wall and switched on the subtle overhead lights. After lighting a candle, she reached into the cabinet to activate the CD player. Soft background music drifting from the wall-mounted speakers created a relaxing atmosphere.

Erica breathed in the subtle candle scent while heading to her office. She pulled up Hilltop's website and clicked on the reservation page identifying her eleven o'clock client as Savannah Landry. Was she young, old, or middle aged? Would she prefer quiet or conversation? Hopefully the former.

"Is anyone here?"

Responding to the soft voice, Erica returned to the massage room. "Hi, I'm Erica, your massage therapist. You must be Savannah."

The pretty dark-haired client nodded, her eyes wide. "I hope I'm not too early."

"Not at all." The young woman's demeanor hinted at uncertainty. "Is this your first massage, Ms. Landry?"

"Sort of." She glanced around the room. "At least by a real massage therapist."

"You're in for a relaxing hour." Erica explained the routine. "Call out to me when you're ready." She returned to her office. After selecting massage oil, she gazed out the window at the fence separating the deer population from Millie's English country garden. Four women who hadn't known each other two years earlier had transformed a private home into a luxury inn. Erica's eyes drifted to the Massage Institute of Cleveland diploma on the wall beside the window—her equivalent to a college degree. Partnering with Amanda and Erica and moving to Blue Ridge had been the best decision she'd ever made.

Responding to her client calling out to her, Erica returned to the main room to begin the massage. During the first fifteen minutes, Savannah remained silent. Then out of nowhere, she spoke. "You're one of the inn's owners along with Amanda Smith, aren't you?"

"Yes."

"I suppose you know her pretty well."

Erica blinked. "We're more like family than business partners."

"She seems like a good person."

Erica hesitated. Had Amanda checked her in to Hilltop? "She is."

Savannah fell silent for a long moment. "Do you know why she moved from New Orleans to Blue Ridge?"

Erica's brow pinched then released. Did Amanda's request for her and Wendy to show up an hour before the staff meeting have something to do with this stranger? "I suggest you ask her."

Savannah remained silent during the rest of the session. After she left without thanking her or giving her a tip, Erica locked the massage room then headed out of the spa. Eager to share the strange encounter with her partners, she rushed past the parking pad to the side yard as Wendy drove up the driveway to the carport. Erica greeted her the moment she climbed from the driver's seat. "Any idea why Amanda wants to meet with us before our meeting?"

"I don't have a clue. Chris's grandmother Susan is babysitting so we won't have any interruptions." Wendy followed Erica into the kitchen then on to the den.

Amanda sat on the sofa with her laptop balanced on her thighs. "Thanks for coming early."

Wendy sat beside her. "We're both eager to find out what's going on."

Erica settled on a club chair beside the fireplace. Should she mention her encounter with Savannah or wait to hear what Amanda had to say?

Amanda eyed Erica while moving her laptop to the coffee table. "Savannah Landry was your morning massage client, wasn't she?"

"Yes."

"Did she say anything about me?"

"Funny you should ask—"

The back door opened followed by footsteps striking the kitchen floor. Millie halted beside the sofa, her eyes darting between the partners. She propped her hands on her hips. "Did I miss a message about a private get-together before our official meeting, or are you intentionally leaving me out?"

"Relax, Millie." Amanda nodded toward the other club chair. "Erica's about to tell us what happened during this morning's massage session with Savannah."

"I can't wait to hear what happened." Millie lowered onto the other club chair. "Because she didn't bother to show up for breakfast this morning."

Wendy tucked an ankle under her knee. "Who is this woman, and what happened during the massage?"

Erica relayed her conversation with Savannah then eyed Amanda. "Do you have any idea why she was fishing for information about you?"

Millie crossed one leg over the other. She pumped her foot as if struggling to avoid blurting out an answer.

Amanda drummed her fingers on the sofa arm in time to Millie's foot. "Yesterday, when Savannah Landry checked into Hilltop, she claimed Preston Smith was her father."

Wendy gasped.

Erica's jaw dropped.

Millie's foot stilled. "Thanks to my mystery club's investigation, we found out a woman named Savannah Landry lives in New Orleans. Her mother was murdered outside the casino where she worked as a blackjack dealer."

Erica stared wide-eyed. "Do you have any idea if the woman I met is the real Savannah?"

Millie nodded. "We found her social media pages. She's legit. The question is whether or not her claim about Preston Smith is true."

Amanda's brows drew together in a tight knot. "When I was six months pregnant, Preston and I had a huge fight that ended with him leaving home. Every day during the twenty-six days he was gone without a word, I promised God if my husband came back, I would never question his absence." Her brows released. "Now I regret keeping that promise."

Wendy stretched her arm across the back of the sofa. "Did he ever give you some sort of explanation?"

Amanda shook her head. "He apologized six ways to Sunday and promised he'd never leave me again." She paused for a long moment, her eyes downcast. "We never spent another day apart...until the accident."

Wendy touched her fingertips to Amanda's shoulder. "What can we do to help?"

Millie scooted to the edge of her seat. "I'll tell you what the four of us should do. March straight over to Hilltop and confront that woman head-on."

Amanda glared at Millie. "What part of making a scene in front of other guests makes even a smidgen of sense?"

"What makes sense is taking action." Responding to Hilltop's ringing phone, Millie scrambled to pluck it off the dining room table. "Hilltop Inn. Chef Millie speaking." She listened then carried the phone to Amanda and propped her hip on the sofa arm. "Savannah Landry wants to talk to you."

Amanda hesitated a moment before pressing the phone to her ear. "This is Amanda."

Erica's heart ached for their partner while she zeroed in on her pinched expression. Was it possible the stranger who had checked into the Dogwood Suite had told the truth about Preston?

"All right." Amanda swiped her finger across the phone then tossed it on the cushion beside her. "Savannah wants to meet me tonight at six."

"I'll go with you. As your bodyguard."

Amanda stared up at Millie. "The last thing I need is you brandishing your gun. Besides, we're meeting in public, at Hook and Eye."

"At a bar? What if she's packing and ends up drunk?"

***

"Savannah is a potential con artist, not some crazed killer." Amanda bolted off the sofa. "The last thing I need is you butting in."

Millie scoffed. "Protecting a board member isn't butting in."

"I know you mean well, but I need to handle this alone. You three go ahead and start the board meeting. I'll join you in a couple of minutes." Amanda lifted her phone off the coffee table then headed straight to her bedroom, pulling the door closed behind her. How should she explain breaking tonight's dinner date with Gary Redding, especially since she had no idea how the meeting with Savannah would turn out? With a version of the truth, that's how. She typed a text. "Sorry for the last minute notice. I need to cancel dinner to deal with a situation at Hilltop."

He responded, "Friday night, same time?"

She hesitated a beat, then answered with a thumbs-up emoji, hoping she could keep that date.

Chapter 4

Ten minutes before six o'clock, Amanda pulled into a parking spot facing the Blue Ridge railroad track. She grabbed her purse off the passenger seat, then climbed out of the truck—the only remaining vehicle that had belonged to Gunter Benson. She waited for a car to pass then walked across the street to Hook and Eye. Inside, she glanced around. No sign of Savannah. She blinked. *Are you kidding me*? Her eyes burned with the icy edge of anger when she closed the distance to Millie and Gordon sitting at the far end of the bar. "What don't you understand about not butting in?"

Millie turned toward her. "Don't get all bent out of shape. I'm not packing."

Gordon chuckled. "Now I understand Millie's last minute invitation to join her." He faced Amanda. "You're meeting Savannah Landry here, aren't you?"

"Any minute now." Movement outside caught Amanda's eye. "She's crossing the street. If you two stay put, maybe she won't notice you and think you're spying on her."

"No need for you to worry." Gordon wrapped his fingers around his beer. "I'll make sure the esteemed leader of our mystery club behaves herself."

"Good luck keeping Detective Millie reined in." Amanda's tone mocked as she spun away and rushed to the door, arriving seconds before Savannah walked in. Hoping to prevent her from spotting the two intruders, she escorted the young woman to a table along the side wall, close to the front. Amanda chose the seat with a clear view of Millie and Gordon.

Savannah settled across from her. "Thanks for agreeing to meet with me."

Grateful the young woman's back was turned toward the sleuths, Amanda hung her purse on the back of her chair. "I didn't know I had a choice."

The waitress ambled over and laid menus on the table. "Welcome, ladies. What may I bring you to drink?"

Savannah eyed Amanda. "What are you gonna order?"

She hesitated. Should she opt for a soft drink or something stronger? Definitely the latter. "A glass of chardonnay."

"Bring me the same."

"Coming right up." The waitress stepped away.

Amanda laced her fingers on the table. Should she keep the conversation casual or bombard Savannah with questions? Better to let her take the lead.

Savannah set her keys on the table. "Do you miss living in New Orleans?"

Strange way to begin a serious conversation. "I did when I first moved here. Not anymore."

"Guess it's a lot safer here than back home." Savannah glanced around. "What's it like living in a town that's a fraction of the size of the French Quarter?"

Amanda's chest tightened. Had she cancelled dinner with Gary to engage in meaningless conversation with this stranger? "Comforting."

"Must be fun owning Hilltop Inn. Meeting all sorts of people from lots of different places."

"Managing a bed-and-breakfast has its pros...and *cons.*" Was Ms. Landry sharp enough to catch the emphasis?

"Sounds like a good job."

Apparently she wasn't all that sharp.

The waitress returned with the wine. "Would you like to order dinner?"

Savannah shook her head. "I stopped for a burger on the way over."

Ignoring her grumbling stomach, Amanda handed her menu to the waitress. "We'll skip dinner."

"Enjoy your wine, ladies." The waitress collected the other menu then left them alone.

Savannah wrapped her fingers around her wineglass stem. "Mom made a decent living as a blackjack dealer, especially when high rollers gave her big tips."

Amanda took a sip of wine. Would she reveal that her mother had been murdered, or was the memory still too raw to speak out loud?

"She left me a ten-year-old car and a few thousand dollars." Savannah paused for a long moment. "I pawned most of her jewelry, so I'd have enough money to drive here."

Amanda's attention remained focused on Savannah's body language and facial expressions. She didn't seem to act like a criminal, but then neither did Gunter—which was how he charmed three women into illegally marrying him.

Savannah swirled her wine. "Why did you leave New Orleans?"

Back to a safe subject. "The time had come for a change of scenery."

"What made you pick this town?"

"I had friends here." *Not exactly the truth.*

Savannah's eyes met Amanda's. "You mean Erica?"

How much did she already know? "Among others."

"Did Morgan move here with you?"

Amanda's posture stiffened. Idle conversation about her daughter was off the table. "No, she didn't."

Savannah took a sip of her drink. "This is the first time I've tasted wine. It's not bad."

Her patience wearing thin, Amanda clicked her fingernails against the table. "Enough with the idle conversation. What's the real reason you wanted to meet with me?"

Savannah hesitated for a long moment. "My mom and your husband were in the same high school class."

How many other of her mother's schoolmates had she tried to con?

"Before Mom became a blackjack dealer, she worked as a stripper in the French Quarter."

Amanda's jaw clenched. Preston would never have stepped foot in a sleazy strip joint, much less ending up with a stripper.

Savannah tilted her head, her eyes trained on Amanda. "You don't trust me, do you?"

"You show up out of nowhere claiming my husband was your father, and you expect me to trust you?" Anger narrowed Amanda's eyes to slits. "What sort of con are you trying to pull?"

Savannah's fingers tightened around her wineglass stem. "I didn't know about Preston being my father until I read Mom's journals...after she died."

Amanda stiffened, every muscle locked in place the moment memories of another dead woman's words popped into her head. Her eyes drifted to Millie, who had confirmed that everything Eleanor Harrington had written in her journals had been true. "If your mother's so-called journals exist, why don't you have them with you?"

Savannah broke eye contact. "Why is Hilltop's chef here, and who's the guy she's with?"

So much for Millie and Gordon remaining unnoticed. "Around here we have each other's backs." Amanda tapped her fingernails on the table. "What do you want from me?"

Savannah slumped back in her chair, her eyes downcast. "I told you the truth about my father."

Amanda bristled, hoping the young woman sitting across from her was an accomplished liar. "Forgive me if I don't believe a word you're saying." She pulled a twenty from her purse and slapped it on the table. "Unless you have proof about Preston being your father, don't bother to contact me again." Amanda bolted from her chair and made her way to the end of the bar.

Millie's eyes flicked to her. "What did you learn?"

"She claimed her mother left behind journals proving what she's claiming. Considering she showed up empty-handed, I question their existence. One more thing you'll find interesting—Savannah knows you're here."

Gordon chuckled. "Seems we need to work on being inconspicuous."

"No kidding. I suggest you two settle up and leave before she corners you." Amanda headed straight to the exit. Outside, she dashed across the street and climbed into the truck. A quick glance in the rearview mirror confirmed what she'd assumed might happen. Millie and Gordon had failed to follow suit.

Seconds after Amanda walked out, Millie slid off her stool. "I'm going to have a word with that woman."

"Hold on a minute." Gordon grasped her arm. "Are you certain you want to get involved?"

Millie scoffed. "In case you haven't noticed, we're already involved."

"At this point, only as observers."

"Are you coming with me or staying put?"

"You roped me into this so-called date, so I might as well join in all the fun." Gordon released her arm. "Besides, someone needs to play Watson to your Sherlock."

"Hmph." Millie headed straight to their target with Gordon following close behind.

Savannah's eyes seemed to carry the weight of words unspoken. "I didn't come here to cause trouble."

"Good. Because you need to know two important facts. First, Amanda is like a daughter to me." Millie looped her arm around Gordon's bicep. "Second, Mr. Davenport—who's a retired police detective—and I are members of an elite investigative organization."

Gordon cleared his throat, obviously stifling a laugh.

Savannah fingered her keys, her eyes downcast. "I didn't lie about Preston Smith being my father." Her voice rose barely above a whisper.

"You seem like a decent young woman." Gordon's tone hinted of compassion. "However, unless you have proof to back up your claims, I suggest you enjoy your visit then return to New Orleans. Until such time, we'll leave you in peace." He placed his hand over Millie's and guided her out the exit before she had a chance to add her two cents' worth.

The second they crossed the street and headed toward his car, Millie thumped Gordon's arm. "What was that all about?"

"An elite investigative organization?" He smirked then grasped the passenger door handle. "Talk about stretching the truth."

"Savannah needed to know she can't fool us with her nonsense." Millie slid onto the seat.

Gordon leaned down, his arm stretched across the top of the doorframe. "You know, it's possible she's telling the truth."

Millie pulled her seatbelt across her chest. "One way or the other, we need to find out the truth."

By the time Amanda parked in the ranch house driveway, she had replayed the past half hour over and over in her mind. If Jacqueline Landry's so-called journals existed, Savannah would have brought them with her. Didn't the fact that she showed up empty-handed prove she'd lied? Of course, it did.

She climbed out and walked into the kitchen. Conversation along with the succulent aromas of tomato and pepperoni drifted from the den. She tossed her keys on the counter then joined her housemates. "Pizza smells delish."

As usual, Erica's daughter, Abby, had moved from her wheelchair to her regular seat. "There's plenty left if you're hungry."

"Thanks. I'm starving."

Sierra sat beside Theo, her nine-month-old son, secured in his highchair. She pointed to the bowl beside the pizza. "I made enough salad for three." It was hard to believe this doting mother had once abandoned her baby before she turned her life around.

"I'll grab a plate." Amanda returned to the kitchen while marveling at how close Abby and Sierra had become during the past few months. She carried a plate and fork back to the table and sat across from Abby. "Have you talked to your mom today?"

Abby swallowed a bite. "Not since yesterday. Tommy and I are going to Mom and Brad's for dinner Saturday night."

Amanda made a mental note to call Erica and ask her not to mention Savannah to Abby. If the young woman was a fraud, Erica's daughter didn't need to know about her baseless accusation. Amanda plated a pizza slice. On the other hand, if Savannah ended up presenting some sort of proof about Preston being her father, she would need to break the news to her own daughter before bringing Abby and Sierra into the loop.

Chapter 5

Millie carried the last of the dishes from Hilltop's dining room to the kitchen sink. "Little Miss Landry didn't show up for breakfast this morning because she knows we're on to her."

Bernie set the empty coffee carafe on the island. "It seems to me if Savannah was trying to pull some sort of scam, she'd pick a target closer to home."

"You obviously don't know how con artists think."

Bernie raised a brow. "And you do?"

"Based on all the stories I've heard about Gunter Benson's scams, I have a doggone good idea. Why do you think he conned Amanda, Erica, and Wendy into marrying him, when they lived in three different states?"

"I suppose because he wanted to avoid any chance of them running into each other."

Millie snapped her fingers. "Bingo. The con artist who checked into the Dogwood Suite doesn't want her target to come across anyone who knows the truth about her, so she chooses a victim who moved hundreds of miles away from New Orleans."

Bernie's head tilted. "Your theory doesn't pass the make-sense test."

Millie leaned back against the counter, her arms crossed. "Exactly how do you figure my assumption fails to make sense?"

"Amanda moved here nearly two years ago, right?"

"What's your point?"

"If Savannah didn't already know something about Amanda, how do you suppose she picked her as a target?" Bernie's head straightened. "From some random moving company or rental truck list?"

Millie tapped her fingers on her biceps while her mind raced with unanswered questions. "I need you to go upstairs and knock on the Dogwood Suite."

Bernie's brows pinched. "Why?"

"Some detective you are. I want to find out if Savannah's here."

"What do I do if she answers?"

Millie rolled her eyes as if Bernie didn't have a clue. "Ask her an innkeeper-type of question, such as does she need towels."

"If she doesn't answer?"

"I'll fulfill my duty as Hilltop's chief information officer and gather intelligence."

"You mean go snooping for evidence."

Millie scoffed. "What you call snooping, I call obligation. Until our little company we call Awesam has a computer technology system, my responsibility as CIO is to identify actions that place my partners or our guests at risk." She lowered her arms to her sides. "Savannah Landry qualifies as a legitimate suspect."

"Maybe Amanda should add a warning on Hilltop's website: Criminals, beware! Wannabe police detective on site."

"Don't you think big city hotels have security guards?" Millie's tone mocked.

Bernie shot her an incredulous look. "Blue Ridge is a small Southern town, not some crime-ridden metropolis. Besides, I can't imagine any of your Awesam partners approving of you spying on guests. If you do go snooping in her room, what do you expect to find?"

"Her mother's journals, if they exist." Millie propped her hands on her hips. "Are you going to help me with reconnaissance or keep offering unsolicited comments?"

"Don't expect me to do this with every guest." Bernie shook her head while heading toward the back stairs.

"Text me if the coast is clear." After moving the dishes from the sink to the dishwasher, Millie plucked her phone off the island. What was taking Bernie so long? She paced. A ping. *About time.* Seconds after reading the text, she pocketed her phone and hastened up the back stairs to the hall spanning the full length of the inn. She headed straight to Bernie standing outside the Dogwood Suite. "Are you sure she's not here?"

"I knocked three times. No response."

"All right then." Millie glanced around. "Keep watch downstairs and text me if Savannah comes back."

"I'm only going along with your crazy idea because I care about Amanda." Bernie turned away then made her way to the stairs.

Millie stepped inside, closing the door behind her. Where would a criminal hide incriminating evidence? She moved around the neatly made bed to the luggage stand and unzipped the suitcase. Empty. A peek in the closet and dresser drawers hinted of organization. The bathroom was equally neat. Toiletries lined the vanity and towels hung neatly on racks. She returned to the bedroom and leaned down to check under the bed. Nothing. Millie straightened then moved to the middle of the room and turned in a slow circle.

Her phone pinged a text from Bernie. "Escape. Fast."

Millie rushed out to the hall. Relieved no other guests were around, she headed straight to the back staircase.

Bernie met her in the kitchen. "Let me guess. You don't know anything more than you did before invading our guest's privacy?"

"This is only the third day of her week-long reservation. Our mystery club still has plenty of time to find out what she's up to."

"You don't give up, do you?"

"Not when someone in my family is threatened." Millie pocketed the ranch house key, then made her way through the den and out to the back patio. She stopped to gaze at the English country garden she'd designed to honor the building's original owner. A cardinal landed on the wrought-iron bench facing the three-tier, bronze fountain. If Eleanor and her husband were still alive, the inn wouldn't exist and she would never have met Amanda, Erica, and Wendy. Even though she'd lost her closest friend, she'd acquired a family.

Eager to share what she hadn't found in the Dogwood Suite, she rushed across the driveway and side yard then through the carport and into the ranch house kitchen.

Responding to footsteps striking the kitchen floor, Amanda looked up from her laptop balanced on her legs and glanced over her shoulder. She'd given up long ago on expecting Millie to knock before barging in. "Where's the fire this time?"

"I don't believe Savannah told you the truth about Preston being her biological father."

Amanda tilted her chin toward Millie. "Dare I ask how you came to that conclusion?"

"Let's just say I fulfilled my duty as Awesam's Chief Investigation Officer."

"Exactly when did our board change your title from information to investigation?"

Millie shrugged. "I made an executive decision." She lowered onto the sofa beside Amanda. "Anyway, I engaged in a little first-hand investigating—"

Amanda gawked at her. "Please tell me you didn't rummage through our guest's belongings."

"All of a sudden she's a guest instead of a suspect?" Millie crossed one leg over the other. "For your information, experienced detectives are perfectly capable of observing without disturbing the scene."

Feigning outrage, Amanda aimed her finger at Millie. "B and B chefs don't invade guests' privacy."

"You can put your trigger finger back in your holster, Madame President. I'm on to your fake anger."

So much for playacting. Amanda lowered her hand. "Don't think for a minute that I condone your tactics."

"Are you going to continue playing the role of good cop, or do you want to know what I discovered?"

Amanda rolled her eyes. "You might as well go ahead and give me the scoop."

"You'll be pleased to know that Savannah's suite was devoid of even a shred of evidence justifying her claim about her mother's journals."

"All you managed to do is confirm my conclusion." Hoping Millie's curiosity would play into her plan, Amanda turned her attention to her laptop.

Millie leaned close. "You're working on the Savannah case, aren't you?"

"Calling what's going on a case is a stretch."

"Stop pretending you don't want me to know what you're up to."

Amanda cleared her throat. "Given Gunter Benson's destructive gambling habit, I wondered if there might be a connection between him and Jacqueline Landry."

Millie's brows raised. "Did you find any?"

"Not yet."

"You obviously need professional help." Millie pulled her phone from her pocket and tapped her keypad. A moment later her phone pinged. "Gordon's on the case."

Stifling a grin, Amanda stared at her. "When did I give you permission to call in the troops?"

"The second you spoke about Gunter without telling me to mind my own business. Clever move." Millie thumped Amanda's arm. "Which is why I'm declaring you an official member of our mystery club."

"Lucky me. Now I belong to two distinguished groups," Amanda playfully mocked while setting her laptop on the coffee table. "The Victory Sorority Sisters—formerly the Exclusive Wives Club—and Millie's meddling bunch of senior citizens playing detective."

"As president of the mystery club, we need to celebrate your new membership."

"What do you have in mind? Some ridiculous sleuthing assignment to prove I'm worthy?"

"Not a bad idea, but no. A trip to town to indulge on cupcakes from our favorite Sweet Shoppe while we wait for an update from Gordon."

"Know what?" Amanda stood. "Every once in a while, I actually agree with the way you think."

"For good reason." Millie uncrossed her legs then lifted off the sofa. "If I had a daughter—except for your red hair—she'd be exactly like you."

"Highly intelligent?"

"More like stubborn and opinionated."

"Both noteworthy characteristics." Amanda rolled her eyes while heading to the kitchen. She lifted her purse off the counter then stepped out to the carport. "Since this is your idea, you're paying for the cupcakes."

"Not a problem. I'll charge it off to business expenses." Millie followed Amanda out to the carport and climbed into the truck's passenger seat. "Now that we're close to solving the Savannah Landry mystery, it's time for an update on our 'Who will snag a guy first' competition."

Amanda shifted the truck into reverse. "Based on the way you and Gordon stole not-so-subtle glances at each other during last night's meeting, I'm guessing you're a lot closer to becoming the winner than I am."

"Who do you think you're kidding? You were too stressed-out to pay attention to anything other than Savannah's claim." Millie buckled her seatbelt. "Tonight's dinner date at Gary's house is still on, right?"

No point denying it. Millie had an uncanny way of recognizing when she fudged the truth. Amanda backed onto the driveway.

"Stop!"

Amanda slammed on the brakes. "Why? Am I about to run over a squirrel?"

"Don't be ridiculous." Millie thrust her thumb toward the side window. "Look who just walked out of the inn."

Savannah hustled across the inn's driveway to her car. With her fingers on the doorhandle, she paused and glanced in their direction.

Millie jerked her head toward the windshield. "Do you think she saw us?"

"Unless she's as blind as a bat, yeah."

"In that case, I suppose following her is out of the question."

"You think?" Amanda gripped the steering wheel, relieved and at the same time disappointed they had been spotted. She backed down to the street. At least spending the afternoon sparring with Millie would help pass the time before tonight's date with Gary.

Chapter 6

The sun had dipped below the horizon by the time Amanda drove into a gated community a short distance from downtown. Her phone's navigation app guided her around a corner. She turned onto a short driveway leading to a single-car garage and turned off the engine. While continuing to grip the steering wheel, her eyes drifted to the townhome's rustic façade and cozy front porch. Was this the home Gary had shared with his ex?

Amanda peeled her fingers off the steering wheel and silenced her phone then dropped it into her purse. Her pulse accelerated the moment she stepped onto the concrete.

An older woman walking her dog stopped at the end of the driveway. "I live two houses down from Gary. He's such a nice young man." Her head tilted. "You look familiar. Are you a friend of his?"

How should she explain? "Gary and I worked on Keith Armstrong's campaign together."

The woman snapped her fingers. "Of course. You're Amanda Smith, aren't you?"

"Yes, ma'am."

"As far as I know, you're the first woman Gary has invited over since he moved in. After the despicable way his wife treated him, he deserves to have a good woman in his life."

Did everyone in Blue Ridge know the story about his wife cheating on him? "Gary and I are still celebrating our victory over defeating Richard Watson."

"You tell Gary that his nosy neighbor, Lila, approves of his pretty lady friend."

Sensing her cheeks were seconds from turning as red as her hair, Amanda closed her car door. "I'll give him the message." The moment the self-proclaimed nosy neighbor resumed walking, she headed straight to the porch and pressed the bell.

Gary eased the front door open. His expressive blue eyes twinkled when he held his hand out to her. "Welcome to my home."

"Thank you." A tingle radiated through Amanda as she placed her hand in his. She stepped across the threshold and breathed in the subtle scent of musky cologne.

He kissed her cheek, his salt-and-pepper beard soft against her skin. In addition to his distinguished good looks, Gary's muscular body made him appear more like an athlete than a bank president.

"I met your neighbor, Lila, a couple of minutes ago."

"Our neighborhood self-appointed mayor and matchmaker." He chuckled while escorting her past the staircase toward the elevator-style music drifting from the back of the house. "Did she tell you I needed a new wife?"

"In a roundabout sort of way. She wants you to know that she approves of tonight's guest."

Gary squeezed Amanda's hand. "Did she also tell you she's attempted to set me up on three blind dates? *Attempted* being the key word."

"She failed to share that detail." They entered the great room anchored on one end by a rustic-style kitchen and a screened porch on the other. Amanda's eyes shifted to the combination stone and wood fireplace stretching to the vaulted ceiling, flanked by nearly empty wood shelving units. A beige sofa, loveseat, and recliner formed a U facing the flatscreen television anchored above the mantel. "I like your style." Amanda ran her fingers along the kitchen island's granite counter. "Not an antique in sight."

Gary pulled the cork from a bottle of cabernet sauvignon then filled a wineglass and handed it to her. "I assume antiques aren't your thing."

Amanda's mind drifted to the day she and Morgan moved into Gunter Benson's house on Saint Charles Avenue. Years later, after learning of his deception, she'd been forced to sell nearly everything he'd owned to raise money toward paying the back taxes on Eleanor Harrington's home. "Let's just say I had my fill of real and faux antiques back in New Orleans."

Gary removed a beer from the fridge. He twisted off the cap then clicked his bottle to her glass. "To homes free of old relics. Unless they're flesh and blood."

Amanda's eyes remained locked on his while she took a sip. "Excellent choice."

"In wine or women?"

"Not to brag, but I'd say both."

A grin tugged at the corners of his mouth. "I don't know about the wine, but I definitely agree about the women." He removed two filet mignons from the fridge, releasing mouthwatering garlic and rosemary scents.

"Those smell delicious." Amanda swallowed another sip. "In addition to all your other talents, are you also an accomplished chef?"

"Other than grilling, I manage to muddle through. Come with me." Carrying the steaks, the wine bottle, and an empty wineglass, Gary led the way out to the screened-in porch. On one end a fire crackled in a stacked stone fireplace; a grill stood on the other end. In between, two flickering candles and a salad bowl laid on a round table set for two. A dimly lit rustic chandelier added to the romantic setting. Gary set his beer and the empty glass on the table then pulled a chair out for her.

"Do you eat out here often?"

"Tonight's the first time." He leaned down, his breath soft against her cheek, his voice low. "I wanted to share the experience with a beautiful woman."

Amanda's chest rose and fell with satisfied beats. What could possibly have led his ex to cheat on this charming man? "This is the perfect setting to celebrate our campaign's success."

"And our relationship."

Amanda wrapped her fingers around her wineglass stem. She could no longer deny reality. For the second time in her life, she was falling in love.

"Now for an all-important question." Gary straightened. "How do you like your steak?"

"Medium rare, leaning a bit more toward rare."

"Perfect choice."

Amanda swirled her wine while Gary lifted the grill lid. Everything about him appealed to her. The way he moved. His delightful sense of humor. His sharp mind. "How long have you lived here?"

He placed the steaks on the grill then tapped his smart watch. "Since the month after my ex fled town with her lover." Gary spun around and lifted his beer off the table. "New location, new life."

"Those are the same reasons I moved from New Orleans to Blue Ridge."

Gary's expression softened, as if he'd been touched by a heartwarming thought. He placed his hand on her arm. "I believe you and I were destined to meet."

A sensation akin to a gentle spring rain washing everything fresh and new flowed over Amanda. "So it seems." Her voice was low, almost reverent.

His hand lingered a moment before he pulled it away.

Amanda took another sip of wine while peering at the privacy fence enclosing the small backyard. In a strange sort of way, the townhouse seemed like a larger version of the shotgun house she had shared with her first love. Except for the missing few weeks, she'd spent her happiest days in that home.

"How do you like condo living?"

"It works for a single guy. One day, when the time's right, I'll sell this place and buy a house on a wooded lot." His phone buzzed. "Time for step two." He strode to the grill, flipped the steaks, then returned to his seat. "Five more minutes."

"What do you need me to do?"

"Relax, enjoy your wine, and let me do all the work."

He tossed dressing into the salad then transferred the greens to individual bowls while Amanda imagined spending many more evenings with him. Following a second buzz, Gary plated the steaks and baked potatoes then sat beside her. He reached for her hand. "Do you mind if I return thanks?"

"Please." Amanda closed her eyes, listening to the short, heartfelt prayer. He really was one of the good guys. When he finished, she whispered, "Amen."

Gary topped off her wine before pouring himself a glass.

"I thought beer was your adult beverage of choice."

"Not when I'm dining on steaks with a beautiful, sophisticated woman." He tipped his glass to hers before taking a sip. "You're right, this *is* a good choice." He lifted his knife off the table. "Let me know if your steak needs to cook a little longer."

Amanda cut into her steak. "Perfect." She tasted. "Oh my gosh, this is delicious."

"Does that mean I qualify as a half decent grill master?"

"Way better than half." Amanda dipped her fork into the potato. "I imagine it's convenient living this close to downtown."

Following a conversation about the benefits and disadvantages of living within walking distance to the heart of Blue Ridge, Gary wrapped his fingers around his wineglass. "Anything unusual happening at Hilltop?"

Amanda's eyes drifted to a log splitting in the fireplace, sending sparks swirling up the chimney. Savannah hadn't come to mind since she pulled into Gary's neighborhood. Revealing her accusation would spoil what up to this point had been a perfect evening. Besides, unless something changed, in a few days she would leave Blue Ridge without presenting a shred of evidence backing her ridiculous claim. "Same routine every day. We check some guests in and others out."

"Who's been your most interesting guest thus far?"

"There have been so many." Amanda reached for her wine. "Near the top of the list were the delightful honeymooners in their late eighties. They met at a senior living complex in Ellijay..." Should she take a chance and finish the sentence? Why not? "They proved it's never too late to fall in love a second time."

Candlelight flickered in Gary's eyes as he reached across the table and wrapped his fingers around her hand. "Or a first time."

The world seemed to stand still when she gazed deep into his eyes. Years ago she believed she would journey through life with Preston by her side. Tonight, for the first time since meeting Gary, she imagined growing old with him.

Chapter 7

Abby rolled her wheelchair out of the therapy center with Anna, her therapist, following close behind. She aimed her key fob toward the trunk while zipping to the driver's side. After pulling the door open, she moved her chair into position then maneuvered onto the driver's seat. While gripping the steering wheel with her left hand and the specially installed hand controls with her right, she glanced into the rearview mirror. Would she ever be able to climb into her car without relying on someone to stash her chair in the trunk?

After loading her wheelchair and closing the trunk, Anna moved beside the driver's door. "I don't mean to come across as insensitive, but your lousy attitude isn't helping your progress."

"Easy for you to say. You're able to stand without being strapped into a ridiculous contraption anchored to the ceiling." Abby drummed her fingers on the steering wheel. "Even better, you can park anywhere, anytime, without having to wait for someone to put your wheelchair into or take it out of the trunk."

"Here's a news flash. If you abandon your bout of self-pity, one day so will you."

Abby's gaze slid to Anna. "I thought therapists were supposed to exercise patience."

Anna leaned down, her eyes level with Abby's. "Not when their patient, who by the way is also a close friend, acts like an immature child."

Fighting to suppress a grin at the sight of Anna's mock-serious expression, Abby raised a brow. "Is this your version of tough love?"

"Yeah. Is it working?"

Losing the battle to remain angry, the corner of Abby's lips curved slightly upward. "I suppose without a box of Sweet Shoppe cupcakes, my little pity party is a big fat flop."

"There you go. Tough love works." Anna's face lit with a smile. "Even with the most stubborn patients."

"Stubborn? I prefer the term brilliantly dramatic."

"Not quite worthy of an acting award, but effective." Anna stepped back. "I'll see you in a couple of days." She pushed the door closed.

Grateful for her friend's honesty, Abby backed out of the parking spot. By the time she pulled into the ranch house carport beside the empty space, her bout of self-pity had waned. She pulled her phone from her pocket and called Sierra. "I'm here."

"I'm on my way." Moments later Sierra stepped out from the kitchen and hastened to the trunk. She repositioned Abby's ride beside the driver's door. "Amanda's out to dinner. Which is probably why Millie brought us mac and cheese. A couple more minutes, and it'll be done."

"One of my favorite comfort foods, right up there with pizza." After sliding onto her chair, Abby wheeled across the sidewalk then up the ramp and into the foyer. Responding to Dusty's enthusiastic tail wag, she stroked her dog's muzzle. "I'm happy to see you too."

While breathing in the mouthwatering aroma of cheese, Abby moved to the den. She stopped beside Theo sitting in his highchair fingering a teething ring and tickled his tummy, triggering a full-belly laugh. "After everything Little Pip has been through, he's a happy baby."

Sierra wiped a bubble from her son's chin. "Funny how being born with a cleft lip ended up being a blessing for both Theo and me."

Abby glanced up at Sierra. "I'm glad you've become part of our family."

"So am I." A timer buzzed. "Supper's ready." Sierra scurried to the kitchen. Moments later she returned and set plates of bubbly hot mac and cheese beside bowls of tossed salad.

"Everything looks delish." Abby maneuvered onto her dining room chair. Following a blessing, she tasted the main dish. "Scrumlicious. You should have invited Millie to join us."

"I did." Sierra swallowed a bite of salad. "She had other plans."

"No telling what she's up to." Abby speared a cucumber slice. "How are you enjoying your job at the high school?"

"I'm loving it. Would you believe the students treat me way better than the kids did back in Chattanooga?"

"Were you bullied in school?"

"I was mostly ignored. Even by other kids who lived in our trailer park." Sierra placed small pieces of macaroni on Theo's tray. "Everything changed after you and Tommy helped me earn my GED."

"All we did was help you study. You passed the tests because you're smart."

"At least I proved one important fact. With a little hard work and help from friends, it's possible to break free from generational welfare." Sierra sighed. "Too bad my mother never had anyone to motivate her to end the cycle. Hopefully, it's not too late for my siblings."

During the remainder of the meal and after cleaning up the kitchen, they settled in the den to continue chatting as if they'd been lifelong friends. Two hours after sunset, Sierra lifted Theo from his playpen. "Time for you to turn in for the night, sweet boy." Before she took a step, the doorbell rang, sending Dusty bounding to her paws and racing to the foyer.

"Go take care of Theo." Abby moved back into her wheelchair. "I'll find out who's here."

"You sure?"

"Positive." Abby moved into her wheelchair then wheeled through the foyer and switched on the porch light. She eased the door open then stared at a dark-haired young woman with expressive brown eyes. "Can I help you?"

"I'm a guest at the inn. Amanda checked me in a couple days ago."

Dusty moved closer to the stranger, sniffing, her tail wagging.

"Is everything okay? Do you need fresh towels?"

"Actually—" The young woman patted Dusty's head. "I was hoping I could talk to one of the inn's owners."

Abby kept a close eye on the stranger. *Why did she show up at our house instead of calling like every other guest who needed something*?

"In case you're wondering, I'm not here to complain."

Abby craned her neck to peer around the guest. "Are you alone?"

She nodded. "I drove to Blue Ridge by myself."

"I'm our company's vice president, and my dog seems to trust you. So you might as well come on in."

"Thanks." The young woman stepped into the foyer, nodding toward the living room turned into an office. "Is this the inn's headquarters?"

A strange question. "It serves as Awesam's office." Abby pushed the door closed. "What's your name and where do you live?"

"Savannah Landry." She paused. "I'm from New Orleans."

"No kidding. That's where Amanda was born and raised."

"Really?" Savannah followed Abby into the den. "How long has she lived in Blue Ridge?"

"All of Hilltop's owners moved here a couple years ago. Some of us from Asheville; others from Gulfport." Abby motioned for the young woman to take a seat.

Savannah settled on the sofa. She crossed her right leg over her left as her eyes darted around the room. "I hope I'm not interrupting anything important."

"You're not."

Sierra ambled in from her bedroom. "Theo's down for the night."

Abby nodded toward their guest. "Sierra, meet Savannah. She's staying at the inn."

"Hi." Sierra appeared to eye Savannah with suspicion as she lowered onto the opposite end of the sofa. "You're the first Hilltop guest to show up at our home since I've been living here."

Abby positioned her wheelchair across the coffee table from Savannah. Dusty sprawled on the floor beside her. "You said you want to talk to a Hilltop owner. What's on your mind?"

She hesitated, fingering her hoop earring as if trying to figure out what to say. "I've been thinking about maybe opening a bed-and-breakfast, and I want to find out what sort of training I might need."

Not believing a word she'd said, Abby laced her fingers on her lap, her eyes locked on the strange young woman sitting across from her. *What does she really want*? "Managing an inn is more about experience than training."

Savannah tilted then straightened her head. "What sort of experience?"

"First, you'd have to know how to deal with all sorts of people. Plus you'd need skills such as managing a budget and marketing."

Sierra turned toward Savannah, stretching her arm across the back of the sofa. "It takes a lot of money to start any sort of new business. Especially a luxury inn."

"Not a problem. I have some money to invest."

Abby's gaze flicked to Sierra, then back to Savannah. "If you're eyeing Hilltop, you need to know that our inn isn't for sale."

"I'm not. It's just...well...Amanda seemed really nice when she checked me in. Ever since, I've wondered what sort of experience she had before owning Hilltop. You know, to figure out if maybe I qualify."

Abby unlaced her fingers. Her back remained ramrod straight. No way she'd share personal information about any of her Awesam partners. "I have a better idea. Tell us about your experience, and we'll let you know if you might have what it takes to successfully manage a bed-and-breakfast."

Savannah fidgeted, as if she'd suddenly been caught in a lie.

Dusty bolted off the floor. She faced the stranger, her tail tucked.

"Easy, girl." Abby stroked Dusty's back, her eyes riveted on the intruder.

"Now that I think about it..." Savannah slowly lifted off the sofa, obviously avoiding any sudden movements. "I probably don't have the right kind of experience. But I appreciate you taking the time to talk to me."

"If you want to know about Amanda's experience, I suggest you ask her."

"Thanks for the advice."

Sierra stood. "I'll show you out."

Following Savannah with measured movements, Sierra disappeared around the corner. After the front door opened then closed, she returned to the den and plopped back onto the sofa. "Talk about a weird encounter. What do you suppose she really wanted?"

"One fact is certain. She was fishing for information. The real question is why."

"Hopefully we'll find out when Amanda comes home."

Chapter 8

Seven hours after Amanda drifted to sleep, light peeked around the edges of the blinds as her eyes eased open. While basking in heart-warming memories from last night, she swung her legs over the side of the bed. She and Gary had talked and laughed until the wee hours. She closed her eyes while touching her fingertips to her lips. The tender way he gathered her in his arms and kissed her before walking her to her car left no doubt that he was falling in love with her.

Amanda blinked. One glance at her bedside clock hinted her housemates had already left for work. Eager to enjoy a hot cup of coffee without company, she donned a robe and walked out to the hall. Abby's door across the hall stood ajar. After stopping at the bathroom, she continued down the hall, rounding the corner to the den. Surprised to see Abby sitting at the dining room table tapping on her laptop keyboard, she moved closer. "Is today your day off?"

Abby shook her head. "I'll leave as soon as you help me with my wheel-chair."

"Are you ready now?"

Abby's eyes remained focused on her laptop. "Not quite."

"Let me know when you are ready."

"I will."

Amanda ambled to the kitchen and filled her favorite mug. After stirring in sugar and creamer, she returned to the table and sat across from Abby. Was it her imagination, or did she seem unusually tense? "Is everything okay?"

"Actually...I've been waiting for you to wake up." Her eyes met Amanda's. "Something happened last night you need to know about."

"A problem at Hilltop?"

"Not exactly." Abby pushed her laptop aside.

Amanda sat perfectly still, her right hand gripping her coffee mug. "What's going on, Abby?"

"One of our guests showed up a little before eight." She paused. "Her name's Savannah Landry"

"Hold on." Amanda aimed her left palm at Abby, her tone screaming of alarm. "Are you telling me she came here? To our home?"

Abby nodded. "She claimed she wanted to talk to one of the inn's owners."

With each new revealed detail, another cold finger of alarm crept up Amanda's spine. By the time Abby finished explaining, Amanda's eyes burned with the icy edge of controlled fury. "Savannah knew."

Abby stared at her. "What did she know?"

Amanda squeezed her eyes shut, picturing yesterday when Savannah had spotted her and Millie in the driveway. "That I wasn't here."

"I don't understand. How would she know?"

Amanda's eyes popped open. "The truck wasn't in the carport."

Abby snapped her fingers. "I knew she couldn't be trusted when Dusty's conduct toward her changed. What I don't understand is why she's been spying on you."

"All you need to know is that last night Savannah Landry crossed the line."

Abby's brows pinched then released. "What are you going to do?"

"Put an end to whatever con she's trying to pull...after I help you."

Abby closed her laptop. "I'm ready to leave."

"Give me five minutes to dress." After scurrying to her room to change clothes, Amanda followed Abby out to her car. After loading her wheelchair into the trunk and waiting for her to back down the driveway, she returned to the kitchen and grabbed the inn key. Her pulse pounded in her ears while she rushed out to the carport and across the side yard. Halfway to the inn's front porch, she controlled her anger enough to slow her pace. Somehow she had to find a way to handle the situation without causing a scene.

With her patience stretched to the limit, Amanda climbed onto the porch, unlocked the door, and stepped into the foyer. Voices drifted from the dining room. The mouthwatering scent of cinnamon and vanilla sweetened the air. She slipped past the living room then rushed through the den and into the kitchen.

Millie turned toward her. "You look angrier than a kitty that was outsmarted by a mouse. What's going on?"

"Did Savannah show up for breakfast?"

"A few minutes ago."

Amanda prepared a cup of coffee before climbing onto a stool. "Last night she stepped way over the line."

Millie shot a quick glance at Bernie then faced Amanda. "What did she do?"

Amanda repeated every detail Abby had shared.

Millie's eyes narrowed. "That woman is obviously trying to pull some sort of con."

"Which is why I need to confront her without upsetting any of our other guests."

Bernie climbed onto the stool beside Amanda. "We need to come up with a foolproof plan."

"I have an idea." Millie explained. "Are you game?"

Amanda released a heavy sigh. "I can't believe we've allowed Savannah Landry to reduce us to characters in a twisted game of cat and mouse."

Millie drummed her fingers on the island. "Is that a yes or a no?"

"A reluctant yes, with one added detail." Amanda jabbed her finger toward the kitchen counter. "Your gun stays in that drawer."

Millie scoffed. "I don't need my pistol to defend us against a wannabe con artist."

"As long as we understand each other."

Time seemed to pass at a snail's pace while they waited for everyone to finish breakfast and leave the dining room. Shortly after eleven, Millie confirmed that the guests scheduled to check out had left Hilltop.

Bernie walked in from the den. "Savannah's car is the only one still parked outside."

Amanda slid off her stool. "Time to put our plan into action." She headed up the back staircase with Millie following close behind. They stopped ten feet from the Dogwood Suite. Amanda leaned close to Millie. "Stay far enough away so you won't be spotted, but close enough to hear in the event I need a witness."

Millie scoffed. "Have you forgotten that I came up with this plan?"

"No. However, I'm adding one important detail. If the conversation takes an unexpected turn, I'll close the door signaling you to walk away."

Millie stared at her wide-eyed.

"Trust me, I know what I'm doing."

"Doesn't matter what you do." Millie waggled her finger. "I'm not leaving until you walk out of that room."

"Suit yourself. Just stay out of sight." Amanda turned away from Millie, squared her shoulders, and knocked. The door eased open. She locked eyes with the suspect. "We need to talk." Savannah hesitated a moment before walking away. Amanda stepped inside, leaving the door ajar.

Savannah strode to the front window, her back turned toward Amanda. "Abby and Sierra told you about last night, didn't they?"

"Did you honestly expect them to keep your little visit a secret from me?"

She shrugged. "Truth is, I knew they'd tell you."

Amanda moved closer. "Then why did you show up when you knew I wasn't home?"

"I wanted to learn a little more about you." Her voice was soft, bordering on apologetic.

"Why?" Escalating anger narrowed Amanda's eyes. "So you can pull some sort of elaborate con?"

Savannah remained silent for a long moment. "I need to show you something." She turned away from the window. Avoiding eye contact she moved across the room and opened the top dresser drawer.

Amanda recoiled, her lips parted in a silent gasp the moment Savannah pulled out an item she had convinced herself couldn't possibly exist.

Clutching the leather-bound book to her chest, Savannah faced Amanda. "This is one of Mom's journals from before I was born."

Amanda willed her feet to carry her across the room. She pushed the door closed. Her eyes heavy with unshed tears, she stepped away from the door and dropped onto a chair.

Savannah held the journal out to her. "I've marked four pages for you to read."

Reluctantly, Amanda peeled back the cover and flipped to the first bookmarked page. Fighting the sudden urge to flee, she forced her eyes to focus on the words written years ago.

Today when I noticed Preston Smith sitting at the bar, I nearly collapsed. Of all the guys I knew in high school, he's the last one I expected to show up in a sleazy strip joint. Yet there he was, watching me strip down to my G-string. After escaping backstage to dress, I headed out front to fill my secondary role as cocktail waitress. I did my best to ignore him, until he caught my eye. I was surprised when he remembered my name.

When the crowd thinned, I found the courage to sit beside him. Even though he wore a wedding ring, I was drawn to his handsome good looks and gentle manner. We talked and drank for hours. When I learned he needed a place to sleep, I invited him to my apartment. I was surprised but pleased when he accepted.

Amanda's brows furrowed sharply, confusion warring with disbelief when she flipped to the second bookmark.

Yesterday was the twenty-sixth day Preston had spent the night on my couch. As usual, he left my apartment before I woke up. That night, like every other, he had returned by the time I came home from work. Somehow he seemed different, more vulnerable. After we shared a bottle of wine, for the first time I succeeded in luring him into my bed. Day twenty-seven, when I returned from work, he wasn't there. That's the moment my heart broke. I knew he had gone home to his wife.

Amanda squeezed her eyes shut, reality crushing her. Her soulmate had come back to her after breaking their vows and sleeping with another woman. A stripper. She forced her eyelids to lift. Her hand trembled as she turned to the next bookmarked page.

Today, I discovered pregnancy tests don't lie. I believed Preston needed to know my baby was his, so I found out where he lives. I drove there and parked across the street from a sweet little shotgun house. Before I could summon the courage to confront him, he walked out to the porch with his very pregnant wife. Part of me wanted to rush over and tell her the man she'd married had cheated on her. When I realized Preston had seen me, I drove away, hoping he would reach out to me before the end of the day. He didn't.

A flicker of hope burned steady when Amanda's eyes shifted from Jacqueline's writing to Savannah, facing the window. If she walked out now, she could live the rest of her life believing Jacqueline Landry had never told Preston about the baby. Maybe she had only guessed he was the father. After all, as a stripper she'd likely slept with dozens of other men. Deep down she knew she couldn't leave with unanswered questions hanging over her head. Amanda forced her focus to return to the journal. Her hand began trembling again when she turned to the last bookmarked page.

At first I was angry that Preston insisted on a paternity test. But then, why wouldn't he? After all, he'd slept with a French Quarter stripper. When I showed him the results, his eyes remained glued to the document when he mumbled a barely audible apology. At that moment I knew he didn't deserve to have his life ruined by one night of passion. Although it broke my heart, I told him I didn't want him to be part of my baby's life.

Amanda closed the journal and lifted off the chair. The suffocating anguish of betrayal gripped her chest.

Savannah turned toward her. "After Preston paid for all of Mom's medical expenses, she never wrote another word about him."

Amanda held up the journal. "Considering my husband was never part of your life, what did you hope to accomplish by coming here and showing me this?"

Savannah's lips parted then snapped closed as if searching to come up with an acceptable answer and yet failing.

Amanda's emotions teetered between confusion and devastating heartache as she hurled the journal onto the chair. She spun away from her husband's illegitimate daughter and rushed out to the hall.

Millie followed her to the top of the front staircase. "What didn't you want me to hear?"

She turned toward Millie, her expression twisted in torment. Tears erupted and slid down her cheeks. "The truth."

Millie's eyes met hers. In a moment of unspoken understanding, she reached for Amanda's hand. "I'm so sorry."

Amanda swiped her fingers across her cheeks. "I'll fill you in later."

"Whenever you're ready to talk, I'll be ready to listen."

Amanda pulled her hand away then headed down to the first floor and out to the front porch. How could the sun shine so brightly when her world had come crashing down around her? Driven by a sudden urge, Amanda stepped up her pace.

After racing through the ranch house to her bedroom, she grabbed her phone and typed a text. When finished, her fingers hovered over the screen. Maybe she should suffer the pain alone. Except, Millie already knew and Abby suspected something wasn't right. Before she could back out, she pressed send. Then waited.

Wendy responded first, followed by Erica.

Chapter 9

After following Erica's car up the ranch house driveway, Wendy climbed out and caught up with her in the carport. "Do you have any idea why Amanda called us to an emergency meeting?"

"I don't have a clue." Erica stepped onto the pavement. "Unless she has updated news about Savannah Landry." She closed her door. "Where are your little ones?"

Wendy pocketed her cell phone. "Chris's mom came by an hour ago to hug on her grandbabies."

"Perfect timing."

"No kidding." Wendy followed Erica through the kitchen to the den where Amanda sat on a club chair, staring at ceramic logs in the unlit gas fireplace. Dusty stretched out on the floor beside her. "Are you expecting Millie, or is it just the three of us?"

"Millie's not one of our Victory Sorority sisters." Amanda's tone made it clear today's meeting had nothing to do with business.

"Which means this is personal." Erica settled on the other club chair while Wendy dropped onto the sofa. "What's going on?"

Amanda crossed one leg over the other. "I've spent the last hour racking my brain, trying to figure out how Preston pulled it off."

Wendy laid her keys on the end table. "This is about Jacqueline Landry, isn't it?"

"Preston and I poured every penny into refurbishing our little shotgun house before our baby was born. That year, we didn't even buy each other Christmas presents. Yet somehow he came up with enough money to pay her medical expenses."

Erica's brow pinched. "Are you saying Savannah told you the truth about Preston being her father?"

"He took his secret to the grave." Amanda pumped her foot. "Leaving me to discover his infidelity from a dead stripper's journal."

"Hold on." Wendy's eyes locked on Amanda. "How do you know the journal was legit?"

"Facts don't lie." Amanda's foot stilled. "People do."

Erica's brows raised. "What facts?"

"Preston spent twenty-six days living with Jacqueline in her apartment." Amanda's voice changed, suddenly heavy with grief. "The exact number he was gone from our house."

Wendy's heart ached for the woman who had become more like a mother than a sorority sister or a business partner. At the same time, she identified with Savannah Landry. After all, they had both been conceived as the result of men who cheated on women they loved. One on his fiancée, the other on his pregnant wife. "Maybe Preston was too ashamed to admit he'd been unfaithful."

"Or he loved you so much, he wanted to spare you the heartache." Erica's voice came across as soft and reassuring.

"If he had confessed, I would have forgiven him. But now...after all these years believing we had an almost perfect marriage... I have to tell Morgan that her father, whom she adored, had an illegitimate daughter with a French Quarter stripper. The truth will break her heart." Amanda paused for a long moment. "Maybe it's best if I keep this between us."

Erica stole a quick glance at Wendy then faced Amanda. "You can't risk Morgan finding out by accident."

Wendy nodded. "I agree with Erica."

Amanda heaved a heavy sigh. "I know you're right. It's just so unfair."

Footsteps followed the kitchen door closing. Millie rushed in. She stopped beside the sofa and eyed Wendy and Erica, then faced Amanda. "They both know, don't they?"

Amanda released a heavy sigh. "I told them everything."

"Then it's okay to give you this." Millie pulled a folded sheet of paper from her pocket while moving beside Amanda. She held it out to her. "It's from Savannah."

Amanda stared at Millie for a moment then looked away. "Preston's love child needs to go back to New Orleans and leave me alone." She folded her arms tight across her chest, the hard edge of anger returning to her voice.

"Trust me." Millie gently laid the paper on Amanda's lap. "You really need to read this."

Amanda glared up at Millie. "You already did, didn't you?"

"As Awesam's chief information officer, it was my duty." Millie walked away from Amanda then settled on the sofa beside Wendy.

Amanda lifted the paper off her lap. "I can't bear to look at it." She stretched her arm toward Erica. "You read it."

Erica gripped the paper, her eyes locked on Amanda. "Out loud?"

Amanda shot her an incredulous look. "How else will I know what she wrote?"

"I just wanted to make sure."

Wendy fidgeted. Watching Erica unfold the note triggered memories of the day Chris read the letter to her from Gunter Benson. The man she thought was her husband declared how much he loved her despite also being illegally married to Amanda and Erica. She fingered her wedding ring. Discovering she carried a criminal's child in her womb had devastated her, until she fell in love with Chris, and he adopted her child as his son.

Erica gripped Savannah's note with both hands. "Are you ready?"

"Not even close." Amanda crossed one leg over the other. "Go ahead anyway."

"Okay, here goes." Erica's eyes shifted to the note.

Dear Amanda,

You asked me what I hoped to accomplish by coming to Blue Ridge and showing you my mother's journal. Given you had lost a husband and I lost the father I never knew, I had hoped we could become family or at least friends. Now I realize that all I managed to do was cause you unimaginable pain. For that, I am truly sorry.

I had also hoped that moving to a different town would give me a fresh start, away from the painful memories of losing my mother.

Amanda gripped her chair's arms. "I can't believe she expects to move here and become a constant reminder of Preston's infidelity, much less develop some sort of relationship."

"Believe me, you need to listen to the rest of her letter." Millie's tone was gentle yet firm.

Amanda's jaw clenched. "All right."

Erica paused a moment before continuing.

Even though it isn't safe for me to go back to New Orleans, I don't want to stay in Blue Ridge unless you give me your approval. I've extended my stay at Hilltop Inn for another week. Although I won't contact you, I'm hoping you'll reach out to me and give me a chance to prove I'm worthy of being your stepdaughter.

Sincerely,

Savannah

Erica folded the letter before laying it on the end table beside her chair. “At least she seems sincere.”

“Yeah, well.” Amanda’s foot pumped. “So did Gunter Benson before we discovered he was a criminal. What I want to know is the real reason she claims she can’t return to New Orleans.”

Wendy tilted her head. “She most likely wants to avoid painful reminders of her mother’s murder.”

Erica’s focus shifted from Wendy to Amanda. “That theory sounds logical.”

“Didn’t you two listen to what Savannah wrote?” Millie’s tone was laced with scorn as she popped off the sofa. “I need your laptop, Amanda.”

“Why?”

Millie gawked at her as if she’d asked a ridiculous question. “To find out why Savannah claims it isn’t safe for her to go back to New Orleans.”

“Forget it.” Amanda rolled her eyes. “We’re not your mystery club cronies.”

“If you want, I’ll go home and research on my own.”

“I think Millie should stay.” Erica tapped her fingers on Savannah’s note. “The four of us should at least try to find out what’s going on.”

Amanda’s focus shifted to Wendy. “Do you want to go along with this foolishness?”

“How else will we uncover the truth?”

“I’m obviously outnumbered.” Amanda heaved a heavy sigh while uncrossing her legs. She pushed off her chair then pointed toward Erica. “Take my laptop from our office to our table. Wendy, come into the kitchen with me.”

“To do what?”

“Grab reinforcements.”

Wendy followed her. “Cookies?”

"Millie-style investigation calls for something more substantial than sweets." Amanda removed a bottle of white wine and a package of sliced cheddar from the fridge. "Can you join us or do you want lemonade?"

Wendy glanced at her watch. "I won't feed Cindy for a few more hours. An ounce or two is okay."

After twisting the cap off the wine, Amanda pulled a box of crackers and plates from the cabinet. By the time she and Wendy carried food, drink, and glasses to the table, Millie had her laptop turned on. Amanda poured the wine, pushing the last glass to the mystery club's creator. "Let me know if you find anything worth mentioning." She carried her glass to the den sofa.

Ignoring Amanda, Millie tapped the keyboard.

Erica glanced at Wendy then followed Amanda to the sofa.

"You might as well go join your partners, Wendy." Millie's focus remained glued on the screen. "I'm perfectly capable of investigating without any of you looking over my shoulder."

"No doubt." Wendy ambled to the den, settling on one end of the sofa with Amanda between her and Erica. "You know, in a way you and Savannah are both innocent victims in this drama."

"Innocent or not, one fact is certain." Amanda swirled her wine. "I'm finished trusting men."

"That's the same attitude I had when the three of us moved here." Erica propped her feet on the coffee table. "Until I met Brad and realized he's one of the good guys."

Wendy kicked off her shoes, tucking her right foot under her knee. She faced Amanda. "Lucky for you, Gary's also a good guy."

"Easy for you to say." Amanda's tone screamed of anger. "You married a bachelor, and Erica's new husband was a widower. Gary's wife left him—"

"After she cheated on him."

Amanda glared at Wendy. "Maybe she strayed because she discovered he'd had a secret affair."

Wendy raised a brow. "In a town as small as Blue Ridge, don't you think someone would've known if he'd cheated on his wife?"

"More than twenty years passed before I learned about Preston's infidelity." Amanda's words came in a hoarse whisper. "I will never allow another man to break my heart."

"I hope one day you'll change your mind and learn to trust again." Wendy touched Amanda's arm. "Even if you don't, Erica and I will always be here for you."

Amanda tapped her glass to Wendy's then to Erica's. "Our Awesam family and Hilltop Inn are all I need to lead a full life."

Understanding that Amanda needed time to sort through her emotions, Wendy swallowed a sip of wine along with the comment sitting on the tip of her tongue. She remained quiet along with her Victory Sorority sisters, each lost in their own thoughts. Their silence was disrupted only by Millie tapping the keyboard. Wendy leaned back, while her mind drifted to the day she first met Amanda and Erica at Blue Ridge Inn; before their lives were turned upside down.

"There it is." Millie carried the laptop and her wine to the sofa. After setting her glass on the coffee table, she wedged her body between Erica and Amanda. "The reason why Savannah might be afraid to return to New Orleans."

Wendy stared at the headline. "Jacqueline Landry's Killer Still Missing."

"There's more." Millie scrolled down the page, pointing to a paragraph. "Police believe the suspect had a personal grievance against the victim."

Erica stared at Millie. "Are you thinking Savannah is afraid the man who killed her mother will come after her?"

Millie nodded. "In my opinion, that seems like the most logical explanation."

"Unless..." Amanda pressed her lips tight, hinting that second thoughts prevented her from finishing the sentence.

Wendy leaned forward, craning her neck to catch Amanda's eye. "You're not thinking Savannah staying at Hilltop is putting our guests in danger, are you?"

"I wasn't." Amanda stared at Wendy. "Now I'm not so sure."

"Based on the rest of this news story, the suspect is a low-life thug who belongs to a local street gang." Millie logged off the internet. "Which means he's not likely to have the brains or the resources to track Savannah hundreds of miles away. Besides, we keep the inn locked, and I always have my pistol close by. In case you're wondering, I'm a doggone good shot."

Millie set the laptop on the coffee table then picked up her wineglass. "Time for the second most important question of the day." She nudged Amanda's arm. "How are you going to respond to Savannah's note?"

Amanda swallowed a sip of wine. "With deliberate indifference."

Wendy stretched her arm across the back of the sofa. "If I were you, I'd consider taking a different approach."

Amanda frowned. "What are you suggesting?"

"If you want Savannah to go away, write her a note explaining why you two will never have a relationship."

Erica leaned forward. "I don't think that's a good idea, Wendy."

"Why not?"

"Because Amanda not reaching out makes it clear she's rejecting her."

"Not necessarily." Millie took a sip of wine. "Savannah already extended her stay at Hilltop. What makes you think she won't check into another hotel and wait Amanda out?"

"Good point." Wendy tapped her finger to her chin. "Especially if she's terrified to go back home."

Erica swirled her wine. "I still say it's best for Amanda to ignore the letter."

"You know." Millie eyed Wendy, then Erica. "The four of us could invite Savannah over and tell her to get lost."

Wendy tilted her head. "Don't you think that's a little too insensitive?"

"Enough already." Amanda scooted to the edge of the cushion. "Look, I appreciate your suggestions, but unless something happens to change my mind, I intend to ignore Savannah's request."

"You do what you have to do." Millie lifted off the sofa. "Just know that I intend to keep a close eye on Savannah Landry while our mystery club continues to delve into her background."

Chapter 10

Twenty minutes before Brad's son, Jimmy, and his girlfriend, Ashley, were scheduled to arrive, Erica slid the lasagna into the oven and set the timer. After moving a bottle from the built-in wine rack to the granite top island, she ambled to the perfectly set dining room table placed between the kitchen and seating area. Pleased with her sense of style, she fingered one of the crystal candle holders, wedding gifts from Amanda. Her mind drifted to Savannah's revelation. Had the truth doomed the woman she loved as if they were sisters to remain an unmarried widow for the rest of her life?

Responding to Abby's ringtone, Erica pulled her phone off the island. "Hey. Are you still at the crisis center?"

"For another hour. Do you have any idea what's going on with Amanda and one of Hilltop Inn's guests?"

Grateful Amanda had given her permission to bring Abby and Brad into the loop, Erica climbed onto a stool. "Are you referring to Savannah Landry?"

"Yeah. She showed up at our front door yesterday, looking for Amanda."

"Actually, I do know." Erica relayed everything Amanda had shared. "Needless to say, she's devastated."

"Finding out after all these years that her husband cheated on her must be devastating. Has Amanda told her daughter?"

"She's driving to Atlanta tomorrow to break the news."

"Morgan adores her father. When she hears he has a secret daughter...the news will break her heart."

"Amanda and Morgan both need a lot of prayer and support." The garage door rose. "Brad's home from work."

"I'll let you go. Tell Dad hi for me."

Erica smiled, pleased her daughter had decided to call Brad dad. Especially since her biological father was a wife-beating police officer. "We'll talk later. Love you."

"Love you, too, Mom."

Erica headed straight to the stairs to welcome her groom home.

Brad climbed up from the lower level, as always looking movie-star handsome. He pulled his bride into his arms. "I don't know which smells more delicious, you or whatever Italian dish you're cooking."

Erica sniffed the lingering scent of his aftershave. "A long day at work and you still smell sexy."

"Good thing being a high school principal requires more brains than brawn." Brad kissed then released her. "How'd your day go?"

"A lot different than I'd expected."

"Sounds intriguing."

"I'm not sure that's the most appropriate description." Erica settled on a kitchen island stool. "Amanda called Wendy and me to an emergency meeting."

Brad climbed onto the stool beside her. "Problems at Hilltop?"

"Not exactly." Erica relayed every detail she knew about the Savannah Landry saga. "Amanda's emotions ran the gamut from anger to gut-wrenching heartache. What worries Wendy and me the most is her comment about never again trusting another man."

Brad brushed a strand of dark hair away from Erica's cheek. "As I recall, it took a long time for you to trust your heart to me." His voice was soft, rich with understanding.

"True. Except I never really loved either man I married. Jack because he was abusive, and Brian aka Gunter because at some level I didn't trust him. It was different for Amanda. She was deeply in love with Preston and only beginning to fall in love with Gary." Erica paused. "How much do you know about his ex-wife's affair?"

"According to Jan and Lauren, it was quite the scandal."

Erica tilted her head at Brad's mention of his deceased wife and her best friend. "Are you saying you weren't tuned into the rumor mill?"

"Not as much as the gals."

"I suppose that sort of gossip rouses women's curiosity more than men's."

"Believe me, there's always more than enough drama going on with my students and faculty to keep me busy."

"I can only imagine." Erica propped her elbow on the island's granite top, resting her chin on her knuckles. "How well do you know Gary?"

"Well enough to think he most likely didn't do anything to drive his wife into another man's arms."

"What do you mean by most likely?"

"Nothing, other than it's impossible to know what happens behind closed doors. Even in a town as small as Blue Ridge."

"According to Amanda, Chris's dad and Gary are close friends."

"Which speaks well of Gary's character."

"The three of us moved to Blue Ridge to rebuild our lives." Erica lifted her chin off her knuckles and her elbow off the island. "I don't want Amanda to miss out on the love Wendy and I found."

"Knowing you two, you'll find a way to change Amanda's mind."

"I'm not so sure." Erica released a heavy sigh. "Amanda is fiercely independent and stubborn. With Preston's betrayal, she's guarding her heart like Fort Knox."

Brad grinned. "Include Millie in your rescue crew, and you'll have more than a fighting chance to break through."

"Maybe you're right. Especially since Millie is even more stubborn than Amanda. Plus, there's the who's-going-to-land-a-guy first challenge. Although I'm not sure that competition still holds any appeal for Amanda."

"I'd still bet on you, Wendy, and Millie winning the battle."

"For Amanda's sake...and Gary's...I hope you're right."

The doorbell rang, prompting Brad to slide off his stool. "Our guests have arrived." He headed to the foyer, returning with the tall young man who was unmistakenly his son, and his stunning brunette girlfriend.

Erica embraced Ashley, then Jimmy, knowing full well that his first question would be about her daughter. "We're delighted you're joining us."

"Thanks for the invite." Jimmy brushed his fingers through his hair. "What's the latest with Abby?"

Erica's heart ached for the young man. After all these months, he still struggled with guilt over the accident that had put her daughter in a wheelchair. Even after the trial proved a bush obstructing the view of a newly installed stop sign prevented him from braking in time, he still blamed himself. "Her therapy is going well."

"We're confident Abby will take her first steps before long," added Brad.

"Absolutely." Hoping her upbeat tone masked the smidgen of remaining doubt, Erica escorted their guests to the sectional sofa facing the stone fireplace stretching up to the paneled ceiling. "Have you two moved from your apartment into your childhood home?"

Jimmy propped his ankle across his knee. "We will next week when our six-month lease ends."

Ashley, who had moved to Blue Ridge following the accident and taken a teaching job at the high school, looped her arm around her boyfriend's elbow. "It will be nice moving into a fully furnished house. Although Jimmy's parents' style is a bit different from ours."

Brad pulled the cork from a bottle of Sangiovese. "Anything you want to do to make the house your home is fine with me." He ambled over, handing one glass to Ashley and the other to his son. "Italian wine to accompany an Italian dinner." After carrying two more glasses from the kitchen area, he sat beside Erica on the sofa section catercorner to their guests. "How's everything going at your fire station?"

Jimmy shrugged. "Nothing out of the ordinary."

A smile lit Ashley's face. "He's too modest to tell you he's a hero."

"Saving a mutt from a burning shed hardly qualifies as heroism."

Ashley nudged Jimmy's ribs. "According to the dog's grateful owners, my boyfriend warrants a medal. Anyway, I'm proud of my fearless firefighter."

Jimmy fingered his loafer, his modesty on full display. "Saving people and pets is part of the job. The real hero is Ashley and Dad dealing with teenagers every day."

As the conversation shifted to Ashley and Brad's jobs, Erica couldn't help but wonder if her stepson and his girlfriend had come any closer to discussing marriage. Even though Brad wasn't thrilled with them living together, he reluctantly accepted their decision while hoping they would eventually change their minds. After all, they were adults with their own ideas of morality.

As the conversation shifted to high school activities, Erica swirled her wine. She and Brad were worried that Ashley would one day leave his son much the way she had before the accident and break his heart all over again. She dismissed the thought while pulling a deep breath into her lungs then slowly released the air. After all, dealing with one family member's shattered heart at a time was more than enough.

Chapter 11

Memories of the day she, Erica, and Wendy sold nearly all of their jewelry came rushing back when Amanda stared at two gold wedding rings resting on white satin in a small ring box. She touched the tiny diamond embedded in her band. If she'd known about Preston's infidelity, would she have kept the rings or sold them with the rest of her jewelry? If he had confessed the day he returned home or after he learned he'd fathered a child, she would have found it in her heart to forgive him. But now...how many other dark secrets had Preston taken to his grave? She snapped the box shut and dropped it back into the drawer.

Amanda unplugged her phone and entered Morgan's address into Waze, then lifted her purse off the bed. She headed to the kitchen and grabbed the truck keys. Halfway out the back door, she halted. With all the drama, she'd forgotten about tonight's date. After climbing into the truck, she typed a text to Gary. "Sorry to cancel dinner. On my way to Atlanta to visit my daughter. We'll talk later." She paused for a moment then pressed send and secured her phone in the holder.

After backing out of the carport, Amanda pressed the brake pedal then scanned Hilltop's parking pad. Savannah's car was nowhere in sight. She hoped Preston's love child had changed her mind about staying in town and checked out early. With that thought, she continued backing down to the street.

During the two hour drive south, Amanda rehearsed multiple ways to break the news to her daughter. Should she ease into the conversation or blurt it out? By the time she pulled into Morgan's driveway, tension gripped her neck and shoulder muscles tighter than a stretched rubber band. She pulled her phone off the holder and read Gary's response. "Hope all's okay. Call when you return."

Amanda dropped her phone and keys in her purse while eyeing the stately two-story brick house. She hadn't anticipated bearing bad news while visiting Morgan and Kevin's new home for the first time, but here she was. After whispering a silent prayer for courage, she headed to the porch and pressed the bell.

Morgan pulled the door open. "Wow, you look as fabulous as ever."

Grateful her daughter's auburn hair and green eyes favored her more than Preston, Amanda forced a smile while walking into the foyer. "As do you."

After they embraced, Amanda glanced at the empty dining room on the left side of the foyer before eyeing the office on the right. "I hope you didn't have to take the day off."

"After returning from another week out of town, I'm working from home." Morgan linked arms with Amanda while escorting her to the combination kitchen and family room. "With only three rooms furnished, our home isn't ready for an official tour. However, we have a new cappuccino machine, if you'd like a cup."

"I'd love to have one." Amanda set her purse on the granite kitchen counter. "After a trip to your powder room."

Morgan pointed to the left. "Down there."

"Thanks." Amanda headed down the hall. She stepped into the room and closed the door. Gripping the sink, she caught her image in the mirror. At least makeup helped mask evidence of a sleepless night. After washing her hands, Amanda returned to the kitchen and accepted a cup of cappuccino from her daughter. She tasted. "Delicious."

"As good as Starbucks, and we didn't have to wait in a long line." Morgan led the way to the sofa facing a fireplace with a marble façade and a flat screen television over the mantel.

Amanda sat on one end, her daughter on the other, a cushion between them. The words she needed to relay stuck in her throat. She swallowed another sip of coffee. "How's everything else going with your job?"

Morgan ran her finger around her coffee cup rim. "I'm staying plenty busy."

Amanda studied her daughter's profile. "Are you still enjoying the work?"

"Not as much as I thought I would. Especially considering how often I have to travel out of town to meet with clients. Dealing with air travel is challenging at best. My flight home has been cancelled twice this month." She paused to take a sip of her drink. "Turns out the consulting firm I'm working for is more of a churn-and-burn than employee-friendly company. Rumors are flying about Kevin's company facing financial struggles, which makes his future with them questionable."

"How's he handling the uncertainty?"

"You know Kevin. He's always the optimist, but I can tell he's worried." Morgan laid her cup on the end table then tucked her ankle under her knee while turning to face Amanda. "I want to hear about everything going on in Blue Ridge. Especially if you and Gary are officially a couple."

The tension gripping Amanda's muscles intensified, forcing her to break eye contact.

"Uh-oh. Based on your expression, I'm guessing there's been a hiccup in your relationship."

She couldn't stall any longer. "There's something I need to tell you."

"About Gary?"

Amanda's eyes met her daughter's. "About a guest who checked into Hilltop a few days ago." She paused, searching for the right words. "Her name's Savannah Landry. She lives in New Orleans."

"Is she someone you knew back home?"

"No." Amanda set her cup on the coffee table. "Your father knew her mother." Her voice carried the weight of gut-wrenching pain while the truth about Savannah Landry's parents rolled off her tongue.

Morgan's expression transformed from curiosity to confusion to anger. "Don't you know that Daddy would never cheat on you?" Turning away from Amanda, she untucked her ankle. Her fingers curled into fists. "That woman's outrageous claims, the diary, and her mother's death add up to one big lie."

Amanda's heart ached for her child. "I didn't believe her either, honey." Her voice rasped, raw with emotion. "Until I saw the proof with my own eyes."

Morgan sank deeper into the sofa, her shoulders curled forward. She stared straight ahead, clearly attempting to process everything she'd heard. "Did my father know he had another daughter?"

Amanda flinched, her lips pressed tight. If she lied and Morgan heard the truth from someone else...she'd risk betraying her trust. "He knew." She faced her daughter, hoping her next comment was true. "After taking financial responsibility for the delivery, he never had contact with Jacqueline Landry again."

"Gunter Benson had three secret families." Morgan's tone screamed of gut-wrenching pain. "How do you know Daddy didn't have two?"

Her daughter's question ripped a hole in Amanda's heart. "After Savannah was born, her mother never wrote about him again."

Tears erupted and tracked down Morgan's cheeks while she lifted off the sofa and raced through the kitchen to the hall.

Fighting the urge to follow her daughter, Amanda lifted Morgan and Kevin's wedding photo from the end table. They were a happy couple, deeply devoted to each other. She pressed the picture to her chest, praying Preston's dark secret wouldn't cause her daughter to distrust the man she'd married.

Morgan returned, carrying a handful of tissues. She plopped onto the sofa, her eyes reddened. "Thank you for trusting me with the truth, Mom."

For her daughter's sake, she had to defend Preston. She returned the photo to the end table. "Your father was a good man—"

"Who cheated on you when you were pregnant with me, then lied about the affair."

"Omission isn't exactly a lie."

"In a lot of ways, it's worse." Morgan's tears returned. "How could he not trust you enough to confess the truth?"

"Shame is a powerful emotion. Especially if your father was afraid of losing me." Amanda reached across the cushion to place her hand on her daughter's arm. "He especially didn't want to risk losing you."

Morgan fingered her engagement ring. "Savannah's father is dead. What does she want from you?"

Amanda blinked. "A relationship?"

Morgan turned toward Amanda, her brows pinched. "Is that an answer or a question?"

She brushed her fingers through her hair. "Savannah claims we're her only family."

"No!" Her daughter's eyes blazed with uncontrolled fury. "My father obviously didn't want an illegitimate child from a one-night stand with a

French Quarter stripper to be part of our family, and neither do I." She bolted off the sofa and raced out the French doors to the back patio.

Her daughter's harsh tone sent a shiver rippling through Amanda. Controlling her emotions as best she could, she followed Morgan. Sunlight filtered through the array of colorful autumn leaves clinging to the branches in the heavily wooded lot. She settled on a wooden bench beside her daughter. "Since that day Savannah revealed her identity, I've experienced a number of conflicting emotions."

Morgan gawked at her. "You're not considering accepting that woman's request, are you?"

Had she been too quick to dismiss Savannah's desire for a relationship? "You know, Wendy was also conceived during a one-night stand. Which I suppose makes both women innocent victims."

"Wendy's situation is totally different from Dad's illegitimate child."

"How do you figure?"

Morgan plucked a twig off the concrete. "When Gunter married Wendy and Erica after he'd already illegally married you, he made them both part of our family."

"I suppose in a way that makes sense."

Morgan pinched a dead leaf off the twig. "Does Savannah favor Dad?"

Amanda shook her head. "I didn't notice any resemblance."

"Which means she's more her mother's daughter than Dad's." Morgan crumpled the leaf, letting the pieces slip through her fingers. "One more reason she'll never be part of our family."

Amanda fell silent, tuning into a symphony of chirping birds and rustling leaves. Had revealing the truth been a huge mistake? "Your father loved you with all his heart, honey."

"I know he did." Morgan snapped the twig in two. "Given enough time, I'll recover from the shock and forgive him."

Amanda closed her eyes, hoping one day memories of Preston's happy family of three would overcome the pain holding her heart hostage.

Chapter 12

Wendy's stepmother's ringtone awakened her from a much needed afternoon nap. Grateful for the nearly hour-long rest, she lifted her phone off the coffee table. "Hey."

"Did I call at a good time?"

"Your grandbabies are napping, so your timing is perfect." Wendy swung her legs over the side of the sofa and leaned back. "Anything new going on in your neck of the woods?"

"A little holiday planning. My in-laws always make a big production out of Thanksgiving. To prevent my boys from having to answer uncomfortable questions and hearing snide comments, I'm taking them to Atlanta to celebrate with my friend's family. Needless to say, Tyler is thrilled about spending time with their daughter."

"You know Atlanta is only two hours from Blue Ridge."

"Which is why I want to visit you Friday before we drive home Sunday."

"We'd love to see you. If my brothers don't mind sleeping on the pullout sofa in our playroom, you're welcome to stay with us."

"Sounds good. My friend has tickets to the Georgia Aquarium, so I hope you don't mind us arriving after dark?"

"Not a problem."

"Good. Now I want to hear all the latest about my grandbabies."

Wendy shared fun details until the baby monitor, plus Duke bounding in from his self-appointed guard duty, announced Cindy had awakened from her nap. "Speaking of your granddaughter, she's letting me know she's ready for her afternoon feeding."

"I'll let you go. Text me the latest pictures of Cindy and her big brother."

"Will do." After ending the call, Wendy set her phone on the coffee table then patted Duke's head prompting an enthusiastic tail wag. "With you around, we don't need a monitor." She headed to the hall separating her children's bedrooms. Ryan toddled out of his room, rubbing his eyes. Wendy stooped down and kissed his cheek. "Mimi Donna and Uncles Tyler and Carter are coming to visit you soon."

Duke nudged between mother and son to lick her little guy's face. Following a full-belly laugh, Ryan fingered his cheek. "Doggie bath tickles."

Wendy giggled. "From your number one canine pal." She entered the nursery and switched on the crystal chandelier illuminating the light blue ceiling accentuated by fluffy white clouds. After lifting Cindy from her crib and carrying her to the great room sofa, she spent the following hour mothering her babies.

At half past five, the garage door raised, sending Duke scrambling to the kitchen to greet the man of the house. Ryan followed close behind. Chris walked in and set a bag from a local restaurant on the counter. Wendy's heart overflowed with love when her little guy's daddy bent down to scoop his son into his arms.

"How's the smartest little boy on the planet?"

Ryan stroked Chris's cheek. "Daddy's home."

"My favorite place." Chris shifted Ryan to his left hip before wrapping his arm around Wendy. "I brought us takeout from one of your favorite Italian restaurants."

"Spaghetti with lobster?"

"Plus a Caesar salad and traditional spaghetti for our little guy."

"A meal worthy of a special dessert." Wendy leaned close, whispering. "After our babies are down for the night."

Chris winked. "That's a dessert well worth waiting for." After releasing Wendy, he carried Ryan from the kitchen then gazed at his sleeping daughter. "Your little sister is as beautiful as your mommy."

Ryan pointed. "Baby Cindy night night."

Wendy ambled over, marveling at their son's rapidly expanding dialogue. She patted Ryan's cheek. "Before long, you'll speak in full sentences and sound as smart as your daddy."

Chris grinned. "At which point I might recruit him to act as second chair in an upcoming trial." He carried Ryan to his booster seat between him and Wendy.

She poured red wine for Chris, and a glass of nonalcoholic wine for herself while he carried their meal to the table. After they settled across from each other, Ryan pressed his palms together while Chris blessed their meal. Following their son's amen, Wendy swirled noodles around her fork while breathing in the succulent aroma. "Who would believe lobster and spaghetti are such a delicious combination?"

"A creative chef, for sure." Chris dug his fork into his salad. "How'd your day go?"

"I talked to Donna." She relayed her stepmother's travel plans.

"Maybe the holiday spirit will inspire your father to drop his lawsuit."

"That would require a heart." Wendy stabbed a lobster chunk. "Which Douglas Hewitt is sorely lacking."

During the remainder of dinner, they continued catching up on the day's events. When finished, Chris settled on the sofa, kicked off his shoes, and propped his feet on the coffee table. Carrying a book from his toy basket, Ryan climbed onto his daddy's lap. "Read me book."

Wendy sat beside Chris with Duke sprawled at her feet. She leaned back and closed her eyes. Nearly two years ago, she'd checked into the Blue Ridge Inn, expecting her husband and the father of her unborn child, who she'd known as Kurt Peterson, to join her. Discovering his real name was Gunter Benson brought Chris into her life, proving God often turned the most heartbreaking situations into blessings.

Wendy's eyes popped open at the sound of her stepfather's ringtone. She grabbed the phone off the coffee table and swiped her finger across the screen. "Hey, Brent."

"Is Chris home?"

"He's right here beside me."

"Do you two have time to talk?"

"We do." Wendy activated the speaker. "What's on your mind?"

Brent released an audible sigh. "I'm at my wits' end with Zach."

Wendy inhaled deeply, then exhaled slowly to steady herself for troubling news about her stepbrother. "What's going on?"

"After playing sick and refusing to go to school for weeks, he finally relented. Then two days after returning to class, he and two other guys were suspended for starting a fight. Last night he announced he wants to drop out of school and get a job. His behavior was challenging enough before his mother died...now the only person he seems to respond to is you, Chris."

"Only because we connected over a video game. Would you like me to call him more often?"

"I'm afraid my son needs a lot more interaction than daily phone conversations."

Anticipating the real reason for the call, Wendy exchanged a knowing glance with Chris. "What are you suggesting, Brent?"

"You worked wonders with Kayla when she spent time with you and Chris." Brent paused. "I know it's asking a lot with your new baby, but would you consider letting Zach stay with you for a while? I understand if you need time to talk it over before answering."

Chris wrapped his arm around his son. "Wendy and I will discuss your idea tonight."

"Fair enough, and I'll understand if you turn me down."

Wendy's mind raced with questions. "How are my sisters holding up?"

"Thanks to Kayla, she and Riley are adjusting to their new reality."

"Did Kayla mention you guys coming to Blue Ridge for the holidays?"

"She did. Thanksgiving won't work. Maybe Christmas."

"Hilltop is closed Christmas Eve and Christmas day. Y'all are welcome to stay as our guests."

"I'll try to make that work. My band's break is over, so I need to head back to the stage."

"Chris and I will give you our answer tomorrow." After ending the call, Wendy set her phone on the coffee table and sunk back onto the sofa. "What do you suppose is going on with Zach?"

"He's a thirteen-year-old kid dealing with his mother's death and his last year in middle school."

"He obviously connected with you."

"Only because I showed interest in gaming. Disciplining Zach full-time would be a whole different ballgame."

While Ryan climbed off his daddy's lap and toddled to his toy basket, Wendy looped her arm around Chris's elbow. "A couple of months after I moved into my third foster home, a new boy showed up. We were both thirteen years old. Everyone called him TJ. His mother had died from a drug overdose, and his father was behind bars. I was the only person in the house he would talk to."

"Let me guess. This is your way of telling me you're considering Brent's request."

"Zach's my little brother."

"Half-brother." Chris's eyes met hers. "Do you remember what happened while Kayla stayed with us?"

"If you mean the marijuana incident, yeah, I remember."

"We have no idea what sort of trouble Zach's gotten himself into."

Wendy lifted her knee onto the sofa and turned her shoulders toward Chris. "Are you suggesting we shouldn't take him in?"

"I'm saying we need to consider all the pros and cons before committing."

"From a lawyer's perspective?"

"Parenting a troubled teenager would be far more complicated than taking an afternoon stroll down Main Street."

Wendy's thoughts drifted back to the foster home. "Not that I'm bragging, but me befriending TJ is the only reason he eventually talked to our foster mother."

Chris shot Wendy a knowing look. "You've already made up your mind, haven't you?"

"I'm leaning in that direction, but only if you approve."

He stroked her cheek. "I'll let you know after that dessert you promised."

Wendy trailed her finger along his chest while flashing a smile and summoning her best Southern accent. "Well now, it seems I need to make tonight's dessert extra special."

Chapter 13

Millie sat on a stool at Hilltop's kitchen island reviewing the inn's front door camera footage. "There it is." She tapped her iPad. "Third day in a row Savannah left right after breakfast. What do you suppose she's up to?"

Bernie closed the dishwasher and pressed the start button. "Considering Blue Ridge is a popular tourist town, she's most likely taking in the sights."

"If she heads out after breakfast again tomorrow, we should follow her."

Millie raised a brow. "And have one of our guests accuse us of stalking?"

"You're right. Following a suspect undetected requires special training. I'll ask Gordon to track her."

Bernie climbed onto the stool beside Millie. "Has Amanda changed her mind about communicating with Savannah?"

"I'll find out." Millie grabbed her phone and typed a text. A minute later Amanda responded. Millie aimed her phone toward Bernie. "There's your answer. A definitive no."

"Which means in a few more days, Savannah will leave Blue Ridge for good."

Millie pushed her phone aside. "What's your point?"

"In my opinion, spying on her is an unnecessary waste of time and energy."

"Don't you know that good detectives don't stop gathering intel until the threat is officially gone?"

Bernie rolled her eyes. "You're a chief information officer and a mystery club leader, not some hotshot gumshoe."

"That's a strange name for an investigator, don't you think? What do you suppose it means?"

"Changing the subject won't change the facts."

"You have your opinion; I have mine." Millie slid off her stool and moved toward the door.

"Where are you going?"

"To talk to Amanda."

"At least try not to give her a hard time."

Millie turned toward Bernie, her brows arched. "Meaning what?"

"You're my best friend and one of the smartest women I know, but sometimes you irritate the dickens out of people. Especially Amanda."

Millie scowled. "Don't you have a couple of suites to prepare for today's arrivals?"

"Look." Bernie climbed off her stool. "I'm just saying Amanda needs a friend, not a buttinsky."

"I'm watching out for her, not butting in." Millie spun away from Bernie and dashed out of the kitchen. She rushed out the French doors to the backyard patio. Halfway across the driveway she slowed her pace when the middle-aged couple staying in the Azalea Suite stepped onto the driveway. "Are you folks heading off for a fun day of sightseeing?"

"We are." The woman smiled. "Beginning with Mercier Orchards."

"Good choice." Millie continued on to the side yard, glancing back at the empty parking spaces. Maybe Bernie had been right about Savannah playing tourist. If she'd been out trying to stir up trouble in a town as small as Blue Ridge, at least one of the mystery club members would have heard.

She hastened through the carport. Surprised to find the kitchen door locked, she headed to the front porch and rang the bell. Twice. The door swung open. "You're worried about Savannah barging in, aren't you?" Millie stepped inside.

Amanda shrugged. "Locking up our house is the new normal."

"In that case I need to start carrying the key you gave me when I lived here for all those months after the fire."

"Better yet, here's a novel idea." Amanda closed then locked the door. "You could ring the bell like every other person who doesn't live here." Her tone mocked.

Resisting the urge to respond with a cutting remark, Millie moved closer. "Seems as if you need a hug."

Amanda stared at her. "Don't be ridiculous." She brushed past, rolling her eyes.

Millie followed her into the den.

"If you're here to hound me about our ridiculous who's-going-to-land-a-man-first bet, forget it." Amanda dropped onto a club chair, her arms clutched tight across her body in a defensive mode. "Because I'm conceding defeat."

Millie sat in the other club chair, her eyes fixed on Amanda. "You can't let the past define your future."

Amanda hitched one leg over the other. "I don't recall asking for your advice."

"All I'm saying is I don't want you to make the same mistake I made."

Amanda pumped her foot. "Are you referring to that affair you had with a married man decades ago?"

"Clinging to the belief that he would leave his wife and marry me nearly destroyed my marriage. Worse, my stubbornness turned Rupert into a cranky old curmudgeon."

"Which proves my point."

"Meaning what?"

Amanda's foot stilled. "Gary's too good a guy to end up burdened with a woman who can no longer trust her heart to any man."

"You realize if Savannah hadn't checked into Hilltop, you'd never have known about Preston's indiscretion."

"The fact is, she did check in, and now I know the man I loved with all my heart slept with another woman when I was six-months pregnant." Amanda uncrossed her arms. "Worse..." Her tone thinned, as if frayed by the effort to speak. "He didn't trust me enough to admit he had fathered another child."

"Which raises an important question." Millie locked eyes with Amanda. "If Preston had confessed that day he came back home, would you have forgiven him?"

"I thought I would, but now I'm not so sure."

Millie scooted to the edge of her chair. "To keep your family together for your daughter's sake?"

She remained silent for a long moment. "When you put it that way, yes, I eventually would have forgiven him."

"Then why not forgive him now?"

"My decision to remain single isn't about forgiveness. It's about never allowing another man to break my heart."

Millie's lips parted.

"Please." Amanda aimed her palm at Millie. "No more. My mind's made up." She broke eye contact. "If you don't mind, I want to be left alone."

Millie studied the gloom clouding Amanda's expression. "You're not thinking of doing anything destructive, are you?"

Amanda shot her an agitated look. "Don't be ridiculous. I'm taking control of my life, not planning to end it."

"Don't take offense. I'm simply making sure your head's clear."

"All you need to know is that after Savannah leaves Blue Ridge, I'll put her out of my mind and move on with my life." Amanda lifted off her chair. "With one important change. As an independent woman, I will never allow another man to warm my bed. So, go do whatever you need to do and stop worrying about me." She spun away then rushed from the den, disappearing around the corner.

Millie waited to hear the door close before walking out of the ranch house. A plan took root while she scurried across Hilltop Inn's front lawn to the sidewalk leading to her porch. She rushed inside and yanked her phone from her pocket. After sending the text, she dropped onto her recliner to wait for responses. Hopefully everyone would understand that saving Amanda from becoming a lonely old woman called for a serious intervention.

How could Millie even entertain the idea that she would do anything drastic? Amanda leaned back against her bedroom door. Choosing to never allow another man into her heart wasn't the end of the world. After all, considering she and Gunter were never legally married, she had lived as a single woman for more than a decade.

Amanda ambled to her dresser and grabbed her phone then dropped onto the chair beside the window. Time to stop stalling. She read the text Gary had sent an hour ago. "Dinner tonight?" Should she accept and end their relationship tonight or wait a while longer before facing him? Better to wait until she had full control of her emotions. She tapped her phone's keyboard. "Tonight's not good. Raincheck?" Amanda's finger hovered over the screen. Would such a vague response trigger a phone call?

She erased the message and typed a new one. "I've come down with a massive headache. Rain check okay?" Amanda wavered for a moment before pressing send. Thirty seconds later her phone pinged an incoming text. "Anything I can do to help?"

Stop being such a good guy. "No thanks. Just need lots of rest. Okay if I call as soon as I feel better?"

A minute passed then another. Amanda fidgeted. Why had she ended the text with a question? Her eyes drifted to the wooded front lawn. If she had summoned the courage to accept his invitation tonight, she wouldn't have been forced to lie. Six more minutes passed.

Another ping. "I'll wait to hear from you."

Hoping he believed her explanation, she responded with a thumbs-up emoji then tossed her phone on her bed. The little white lie released a pain in the back of her throat. If she had resisted falling in love with Gary, she wouldn't be in this mess. Now she had to figure out how to end what was fast becoming a serious relationship without shattering Gary's heart.

Chapter 14

Disappointed that only three other mystery club members had agreed to attend the last-minute meeting, Millie set a plate of brownies on her living room coffee table then settled on her recliner. The smaller of her two cats sprang onto her lap, inviting a back stroke. "What do you think, Mittens? Will it be easier for four instead of six people to agree on a plan?" The kitty responded by licking her paw, until the doorbell sent her bounding to the floor and slithering under the coffee table. "One fraidy-cat..." Millie pushed off her recliner while nodding toward Whiskers keeping watch on the windowsill. "...and one that fancies himself a guard kitty."

Millie headed to the foyer and pulled the door open.

Bernie stepped in from the cold night air. "Is this meeting about Savannah, or has another unsuspecting Hilltop guest become a person of interest?"

Millie scoffed. "Which guest might that be?"

"How would I know what goes on inside your noggin when I'm not around?"

"The same brilliant thoughts I have when you are around."

Millie turned toward Susan stepping onto the porch and nodding toward the driveway. "Gordon just pulled up in his fancy three-wheeled motorcycle." She crossed the threshold and sniffed. "Do I smell brownies?"

"With walnuts, fresh out of the oven."

"Must be something important going on."

Millie shot Susan a questioning look. "Why else would I call an emergency meeting?"

"I don't know." Susan grinned. "Maybe as a ruse to invite Gordon over?"

Millie propped her hand on her hip. "Believe me, if I wanted to spend time alone with a man, I wouldn't need a couple of old ladies to chaperone."

Bernie nudged Susan's arm. "Seems our friend has forgotten she's older than us." They peeled out of their jackets while heading to the living room sofa.

Millie rolled her eyes before turning to greet Gordon. "Seems as if it's too cold to be riding in a vehicle without a top."

He stepped inside carrying his laptop. "Not for a hot-blooded ex-cop."

"Are you bragging?"

Gordon grinned. "Just stating the facts. What's this impromptu meeting all about?"

"A serious situation has come up that needs our attention."

"Has another suspicious guest roused your investigative bravado?"

"What is it with you and Bernie?" Millie turned away from him and headed straight to her recliner.

Gordon followed. "Evening, ladies."

Susan peered up at him. "Considering you've brought your laptop, I assume Millie's clued you in."

"Incorrect assumption." After setting his laptop on the coffee table, he peeled out of his leather jacket and sat in a chair across from the recliner. "I'm obviously not the only one who doesn't have a clue about what's going on."

With her feet planted firmly on the floor, Millie faced Susan while explaining what happened at the mystery club meeting she and Eileen missed. "What we didn't reveal was that Savannah alleges her mother had an affair with Preston Smith when Amanda was six months pregnant. Worse, she claims he's her biological father. The five of us left that night mistakenly believing Savannah had pegged Amanda for some sort of elaborate con."

Gordon propped an ankle over his knee. "Are you telling us her claim is legit?"

Millie nodded. "As proven by Jacqueline Landry's journal entries."

"Talk about a shocker." Susan's eyes met Millie's. "I imagine Amanda is heartbroken."

"So much so that she's vowed never to trust her heart to another man, which is why I called this emergency meeting." Millie's focus shifted from Susan, to Bernie, then to Gordon. "The four of us need to devise a foolproof plan to save Amanda's relationship with Gary Redding."

Gordon fingered his sneaker. "If you've added romance counseling to our mystery club agenda, you can count me out."

Millie's eyes remained focused on him. "Think of this as a type of intervention."

"Interventions are meant to rescue addicts, not strong-willed women who are perfectly capable of making their own decisions."

Susan reached for a brownie. "You're right about Amanda being stubborn, Gordon. She's also a woman whose heart has been shattered. Which means she's making her decision based on emotion rather than logic."

Bernie nodded. "Something women tend to do when they're most vulnerable." She turned toward Millie. "What do you have in mind?"

"Nothing yet. Which is why we need some serious brainstorming." Millie aimed her finger toward Gordon. "Are you in or are you out?"

Gordon chuckled. “I’ll stick around if for no other reason than to find out what sort of scheme you three come up with.”

“Suit yourself.” Millie angled toward the sofa. “Seems to me we have two options. The first is to meet with Amanda and help her understand that she’s making an irrational decision.”

“You can’t be serious.” Bernie raised a brow. “Amanda’s almost as stubborn as you are. What makes you think she’d listen to any of us?”

Susan swallowed a bite of brownie. “Assuming Bernie’s right, what’s option number two?”

“We arrange some sort of surprise meeting between her and Gary.”

Gordon guffawed. “You’re talking about the president of a bank and the president of a company. They’re both too smart to fall for such shenanigans.”

Millie tapped her foot on the floor. “All of a sudden you want to be part of our team?”

“Only when common sense from a male perspective is called for.”

Millie’s foot stilled. “Let’s say you’re right.” She turned her attention back toward the ladies. “If a one-on-one won’t work, what about planning an event where they’re both invited?”

Bernie snapped her fingers. “Now we’re getting somewhere.”

Susan tapped her knuckle to her chin. “My son and daughter-in-law could invite them both to join the family for Thanksgiving dinner.”

Millie shook her head. “That won’t work. Amanda’s spending the holiday in Atlanta with her daughter and son-in-law. We’ve already celebrated Wendy’s birthday, so that’s out.”

“Whatever we do has to seem natural and not in the least bit contrived.” Bernie plucked a brownie off the plate and took a bite.

Susan fingered her wedding rings. “Back before my sweet husband passed on to his eternal home, every few years we hosted New Year’s Eve parties at our house. I could plan another party to recreate the scene from one of my favorite movies."

Bernie's head tilted. "You're talking about *When Harry met Sally,* aren't you?"

Susan nodded. "I cry every time I watch Harry running through the streets of New York to tell Sally he wants to spend the rest of his life with her."

Bernie pressed her hand to her chest. "It's such a sweet love story."

Millie rolled her eyes. "This is real life, not a movie. Besides, New Year's is too far away. We need to do something much sooner."

"You're right about the timing." Bernie faced Susan. "Although your idea is perfect for a second when-Gary-meets-Amanda event."

"I agree. Now for a first event." Susan tapped her finger to her chin. "My son's birthday is the Friday after Thanksgiving. Linda and I will throw him a surprise party. There's no way either of our targets will stay away."

Millie snapped her fingers. "Perfect."

Susan nodded. "We'll begin planning tomorrow."

Bernie crossed her legs. "Now that we have that settled, I have a bit of good news. Savannah's reservation ends in a couple of days, which will give Amanda a little time to settle down before Keith's birthday."

Gordon reached for a brownie. "Now that you have a reconciliation plan in place and our suspect is leaving Blue Ridge, I assume our investigation into her mother's murder is closed."

Millie pursed her lips. It was possible Preston's illegitimate daughter would change her mind about leaving Amanda alone. "We have to continue investigating."

Gordon swallowed a bite. "To what end?"

"To protect Amanda if Savannah still wants something from her."

"Protect her from what?"

"Whatever's going on in New Orleans. You know that town is notorious for crime." Millie crossed her arms, tapping her biceps with mock impatience. "What if the mob put out a hit on her?"

Gordon arched a brow. "Why would a gangster waste a bullet on a blackjack dealer without a criminal record?"

Millie huffed. "In case you've forgotten, she earned a living as a stripper before she worked in that casino. I can only imagine what sort of low-life men she attracted."

A sly grin tugged at the corners of Gordon's mouth while he planted both feet on the floor and placed his laptop on his thighs. "To humor you, I'll continue digging into the notorious Jacqueline Landry."

"You'll thank me when we solve this case."

Bernie's head tilted. "To think that a year ago I had been a lonely widow for six months." Her eyes focused on Millie. "I applied for the job at Hilltop because I needed something to do. Little did I know that I was on the verge of transitioning from a life of homemaking to the fascinating world of crime investigation."

"One fact is certain." Gordon looked up from his screen, his eyes dancing with mischief. "Anyone who partners with Mildred Cunningham is in for one wild ride."

Millie flipped her hair back. "Bless your little old pea pickin' heart, Officer. You actually believe you have this old gal all figured out."

Gordon burst into laughter. "Figured out? Maybe. Although one fact is undeniable. Next time you call an emergency meeting, I'm bringing my helmet in. Because partnering with you is as unpredictable as riding on a roller coaster blindfolded."

Susan grinned and nudged Bernie's arm. "I believe you and I are playing the roles of extras in this romantic comedy starring a couple of septuagenarians."

Bernie nodded. "Definitely."

"What do you think, Millie?" Gordon's eyes continued to glint with mischief. "Should we pay the extras or charge admission to our performances?"

Delighting in the playful banter, she laced her fingers and tapped her thumbs. "We should keep the entertainment free unless our performance turns into a box office hit. If that happens we'll pay them the going rate for extras."

"There's a deal I can go along with."

Chapter 15

Wendy turned in a slow circle while checking every detail in their guest room. The pale blue walls, Scandinavian-style furniture, and overstuffed club chair created a cozy environment. Not exactly a cool room for a thirteen-year-old boy. At least the television anchored to the wall opposite the bed and the ensuite bathroom would have some appeal. Had agreeing to welcome Zach into their home been a big mistake? Would he be more or less difficult to deal with than some of the teenaged boys she had known growing up in foster homes? She moved to the French doors leading to the patio beneath the deck. Erica and Amanda had doubts when they took Sierra in and everything turned out okay.

"Let me guess." Chris walked in. "You're questioning whether or not we made the right decision."

"Maybe a little." Wendy turned away from the doors and ran her fingers along the smooth comforter. "We have no idea how Zach will react to tough love."

"Most likely a toss-up between indifference and defiance." He wrapped his arm around her shoulders. "If all goes as planned, he'll experience a major attitude adjustment and be ready to go home the day after Christmas."

"What if our plan doesn't work out?"

"We'll double down on our strategy until he comes around." Responding to the doorbell, Chris released her and rushed out of the room.

Grateful their babies were still napping, Wendy followed him up to the main level.

Duke stood at the door, his tail tucked ready to protect his family. Chris patted his head. "Everything's okay. Sit." The dog responded. His tail slapped the floor signaling he understood the intruder was safe.

Wendy breathed deeply to slow her pulse while Chris headed to the door and greeted Brent with a handshake. "Please come in."

"I can only stay for a couple of minutes." Brent handed a book bag to Chris then stepped aside and motioned to his son. "I have to head back to Nashville to interview a prospective bass player for my band."

With a duffel slung over his shoulder, Zach stepped across the threshold. The thrust of his chin hinted of defiance more than indifference.

Chris set the book bag down then clasped his hand on the young man's shoulder. "Welcome to our home." In response to Zach inching away from his grasp, Chris pulled his hand off his shoulder while turning toward Wendy. "Will you pour our guest a glass of lemonade while I talk to Brent?"

"Glad to." When Chris stepped outside, Wendy summoned her best smile. "We're looking forward to spending time with you."

Avoiding eye contact, Zach snarled. "I hate lemonade."

So much for a pleasant beginning. "How about a glass of orange juice?"

"Don't you have any soft drinks?"

"Just ginger ale."

Zach glanced around. "Never tried the stuff."

Struggling to control her emotions, Wendy swept her arm toward the sofa. "You're welcome to have a seat while I pour a glass for you to try."

Zach trudged past Wendy. After dropping his duffel on the floor, he pulled his phone from his pocket and plopped onto the sofa.

A fist-sized knot took up residence in Wendy's belly. How long before they regretted bringing him into their home? One day? A week? After pouring a glass of ginger ale, she carried it from the kitchen and set it on the end table beside Zach.

His eyes remained laser focused on his phone while his thumbs tapped the keypad.

Unsure how to react to her brother's rude behavior, Wendy settled on a chair, keeping a close eye on him.

When Chris returned, he glanced at Wendy then sat on the coffee table facing their guest. "We need to talk."

Zach continued thumbing his phone.

"Put your phone down." Chris's tone came across as firm. "Now, Zach."

After a long moment, he set his phone on the cushion beside him and folded his arms across his chest.

"Here's the thing." Chris leaned forward, his forearms planted on his knees. "Follow our rules and we'll all get along fine."

"What rules?"

"First and foremost, treat your sister with respect at all times. Show up for dinner on time without your phone. Do your own laundry and keep your room clean. Lights out at ten every night except Saturday."

"Whatever." His tone mocked.

"'Whatever' isn't a commitment."

Zach scowled. "I'll follow your rules."

"All right. Now we understand each other." Chris lifted his arms off his knees and straightened his back. "Before we show you to your room, you need to make an important decision."

Zach's eyes narrowed. "About what?"

"How to spend your time while you're here. You have two choices. Go to school or go to work and study during your lunch hour."

For the first time since he'd arrived, Zach made eye contact with Chris. "What sort of work?"

"Construction."

Zach uncrossed his arms. "Will I get paid?"

"Minimum wage, which will go toward room and board."

Zach's brows arched. "You mean I gotta pay to stay here?"

"If you choose to work, yes."

"No way I'm going to school with a bunch of small-town losers."

"All right, then. Five days a week, you'll work from seven to eleven and from three to five. In between those hours you'll study assignments we give you. Every Saturday, we'll test you on what you've learned."

Zach glared at Chris, his chin thrust forward. "Why do I have to study and take tests if I'm not going to school?"

"Because you're too young to drop out officially. Are we on the same page?"

Zach shrugged. "I guess."

"I'll take your response as a yes." Chris stood. "Come on, I'll take you to your room."

Zach grabbed his phone and lifted off the sofa. After slinging his duffel over his shoulder, he followed Chris down the stairs.

Grateful Abby's boyfriend had agreed to take Zach on, Wendy returned to the kitchen, plucked her phone off the counter, and texted Tommy. "Zach's taking the job. Chris will bring him to your office at seven tomorrow morning." She pocketed her phone then poured herself a glass of ginger ale and settled on the sofa. Relieved she wouldn't be forced to parent her brother while Chris was working, Wendy propped her feet on the coffee table and sipped her drink.

Five minutes passed before Chris returned. He sat beside Wendy and sank into the sofa. "I searched Zach's duffel and book bag. Nothing illegal."

"At least he knows we won't tolerate destructive or illegal behavior." Wendy set her drink on the end table beside the still full glass she'd poured for Zach. "How did Brent react when you explained our strategy?"

"He's on board."

"Good to know." Wendy pulled her pinging phone from her pocket. "Tommy responded to my text with a thumbs-up. Thankfully his family is going along with our plan."

"The Bennetts are good people."

"Yeah, they are. Are you going back to your office?"

Chris shook his head. "Following suggestions from Zach's teachers back in Nashville, we need to create his study assignments for the next six weeks, plus tests." Ryan toddled in from the hallway and climbed onto his lap. "After I spend time with our son."

By five minutes to six, they'd finished their task, tended to their infant, and prepared dinner. Wendy plated the spaghetti while Chris lifted Ryan onto his booster seat. "Do you suppose Zach will come up on time?"

"I made him set two alarms. One to wake up and one for dinner. Unless he's escaped, I expect him to show up any minute."

Moments after their dog raced to the top of the stairs, Zach emerged. He patted Duke's head. "I'm allergic to cats but not to dogs."

"Good to know." Chris pulled out the chair across from Ryan. "This is your seat."

Zach dropped onto the chair.

Wendy carried plates to the table she had already set with salad and bread. "I hope you like spaghetti."

He shrugged. "Guess so."

Ignoring the curt response, Chris seated Wendy, then himself. The moment Zach grabbed his fork, Chris touched his arm. "In our home, we bless our food before we eat."

Zach laid his hand on the table with his fingers still wrapped around his fork while Ryan pressed his palms together and eyed his uncle. His nephew's amen following Chris's blessing solicited a momentary hint of a grin. After clearing his throat, Zach curled spaghetti around his fork and took a bite, slurping a long noodle through his pursed lips.

Chris dug his fork into his salad. "Tommy Bennett will be your work supervisor. He's not much older than you."

Zach swallowed. "How come he's not in school?"

"He graduated last year and chose to work in his family's construction company instead of going to college. When his dad retires, he'll take over the business."

"Lucky kid."

Wendy exchanged a glance with Chris then turned toward Zach. "Have you settled into your room?"

"I guess." He shoveled another forkful of spaghetti into his mouth while continuing to avoid eye contact.

Remembering how awkward she had felt every time she moved into a new foster home, Wendy understood the need to give Zach time to adjust. "Let us know if you need anything to make you more comfortable."

"Maybe buy me some soft drinks. Coke's my favorite."

Quashing the urge to resist his request, Wendy nodded. "After you pass your first test."

"Whatever," Zach mumbled.

Chris gripped their guest's arm. "I suggest you rephrase your response." While his voice was low, his tone was undeniably firm.

Zach hesitated as if trying to decide how to respond. "Thank you."

"That's better." Chris released his arm.

Wendy's eyes shifted from Chris to Zach. How long would it take for her brother to trust them enough to come clean about what was going on inside his head?

Chapter 16

After parking on the street, Erica made her way up the driveway to the sidewalk fronting Hilltop. Inky, the black cat that had claimed the inn's front porch as its private domain, looked up from the railing and meowed before returning to licking its paw.

Erica unlocked the door and walked into the foyer the same time a couple descended the stairs. "Good afternoon. I hope you're enjoying your stay with us."

"Even more than we expected." The woman's head tilted. "Are you one of the owners?"

"I am."

"Last night my husband and I read the story about you ladies transforming this old place into a luxury inn. What you accomplished is amazing."

"Thank you. The project was a work of love." *And survival.* "I hope you have a fun afternoon and evening planned."

"We're going into town to shop, then have dinner at Southern Charm."

Her husband chuckled. "My wife is eager to support the local economy."

"Don't let him kid you. He enjoys shopping almost as much as I do."

Erica smiled. "Make sure you stop by the Owl's Nest and say hello to Jennifer. She's the owner."

"We will." He held the door for his wife then followed her out to the porch.

Erica opened the guest book before entering the living room and heading straight to the bookstand displaying Hilltop Inn's scrapbook detailing the renovation. She lifted the cover then leafed through the array of before photos. The broken front window. Blistered sheetrock. Water-damaged floors. The ceiling collapsing in the upstairs turret room. Pictures of her, Amanda, and Wendy working tirelessly to transform the run-down mansion into a luxury inn released a warm sensation. Her eyes drifted up to Hilltop Inn's first holiday dessert-competition plaque awarded to Millie. Without her, the English country garden wouldn't exist.

The front doorbell chimed, sending Erica rushing to greet the new arrivals. After checking them in, giving them the spiel about Hilltop, and escorting them upstairs to the Azalea Suite overlooking the backyard, she returned to the living room. A half hour later after following the same routine with the second couple checking in, Erica closed the guest book.

The bell chimed again. Expecting to greet guests who had forgotten their key, she pulled the door open. Her hand froze on the handle at the sight of Sierra's mother.

The woman with shoulder-length dark hair and an overweight body squeezed into tight pants and an oversized pink sweatshirt jabbed her thumb toward the ranch house. "Ain't nobody home at your house."

"Your daughter's at work." No way she'd allow that woman into the inn. Erica stepped out, pulling the door closed behind her. "Can I help you with something?"

"You can let me in the house so's I can visit my grandson when Sierra comes home."

"All right." Knowing full well Theo wasn't the primary reason she'd traveled all the way from Chattanooga, Erica led the woman away from the inn. The moment they stepped into the ranch house, Dusty sniffed the woman then sneezed.

"What's with your dog?"

"Must be allergies." *To cheap perfume.* Clearing her throat to quash a giggle, Erica led the way to the den. "Would you like a glass of water?"

"You got any of that lemonade like you had last time I was here?"

"I'll check."

Erica hastened to the kitchen and opened the fridge. "Sorry, no lemonade."

"Bet you don't got no soft drinks, neither."

"Just water and orange juice."

"I'll take the juice."

Erica pulled her phone from her pocket and texted Sierra about her mother's arrival, then filled a glass and carried it to the den. After placing the drink on a coffee table coaster, she settled on a club chair. "Other than visiting your grandson, what brings you to Blue Ridge?"

Ms. Wellington grabbed the glass. "I got personal business to discuss with Sierra." She took a long sip then set the glass back on the coaster. "You still live here?"

Erica shook her head.

The back door opened followed by footsteps. Amanda walked into the den. After exchanging a glance with Erica, she stopped beside the sofa. Her eyes flicked to their guest. "We weren't expecting you."

"Didn't know I needed an appointment to visit my daughter and grandson."

"You don't." Amanda ambled to the other club chair. "What's happening in your neck of the woods?"

Ms. Wellington's eyes narrowed. "Why you wanna know?"

Amanda crossed one leg over the other. "The last time you showed up, you wanted to take Sierra back to Chattanooga."

"I ain't got the same idea this time."

"Good, because she's thriving here in Blue Ridge."

"Same thing she told me." Ms. Wellington fidgeted. "How long before she comes home?"

Amanda glanced at her watch. "I expect her any time now."

Ms. Wellington glanced around the room, her eyes skimming past Erica and Amanda. "I hear Sierra's bought herself a car."

Amanda nodded. "She has."

"That's more than I got."

Erica stared at her. Was she looking for a handout from her daughter? "Sierra needed a car to drive to work."

"Are you sayin' I don't need wheels 'cause I ain't got a job?"

Erica's shoulders tightened. "That's not what I meant."

"If you were, I reckon you'd be tellin' the truth."

Responding to the back door creaking open, Dusty padded to the kitchen. Sierra walked in with Theo propped on her hip. "I wasn't expecting you."

Her mother peered up at her. "You look all fancy."

"I'm a professional woman now." Sierra skirted the coffee table then sat on the sofa and propped Theo on the cushion between them. "How are my sisters and brother doing?"

"Same as usual." Her mother touched the skin between Theo's nose and upper lip. "His scar ain't so noticeable anymore."

Sierra pulled her knee onto the cushion, facing her mother. "Are you here to visit, or is something on your mind?"

Her mother angled her shoulders toward Sierra. "You need to know that after Jay was hauled off to jail, Dereck went and got himself a job working the night shift at a local factory." She paused. "If any one of my kid's fathers had stuck around, I might have married him."

Erica exchanged a knowing glance with Amanda. They both understood that if Sierra hadn't fled home when she discovered she was pregnant, she'd likely be following the same destructive path her mother had chosen.

Sierra pulled Theo closer to her. "What are you trying to tell me?"

"Dereck wants to do right by you and his boy."

Sierra's brows raised. "Does he know you're here?"

"Maybe. I dunno."

"Either he does or doesn't know."

Her mother hesitated for a moment. "I borrowed his truck, so yeah, he knows."

"Look." Sierra lifted her child onto her lap. "I'm glad Dereck is trying to turn his life around, and maybe from time to time he can visit Theo, but I don't need or want him to be part of our lives."

Her mother's eyes narrowed. "Are you gonna stay single the rest of your life?"

"Maybe I will; maybe I won't." Sierra's voice was laced with confidence. "What matters is me raising my son to be a good man and a productive citizen. When Theo needs male influence, I'll ask Tommy or Brad or Chris to help out."

"You think you have everything all figured out, don't you?" Her mother's tone mocked.

"I don't think, Mom. I know."

Erica resisted the urge to applaud. *Good for you, Sierra.*

Ms. Wellington stared at her daughter, as if seeing her for the first time. "Truth is, I'm proud of you gettin' a good job instead of going on welfare. So's Dereck."

"Even though I wish him the best and hope he turns his life around, he'll never be the kind of man I want in my son's life."

"Dereck would be a lot different if he didn't have Jay as a big brother." Her mother hoisted her girth off the sofa. "I've gotta get the truck back so he can go to work."

Erica stood. Would she ask for gas money like last time? "I'll walk you out."

"Don't bother. I know the way." She pointed her finger at her daughter. "Don't be so quick to reject Dereck. The least you can do is give him a chance to prove himself." Ms. Wellington faced Erica and Amanda. "You ladies have lots more influence over my daughter than me. So I'm countin' on you to do what's right." She spun around and headed to the foyer then out to the front porch.

Amanda moved to the sofa and slid her arm around Sierra's shoulders. "Erica and I are proud of you standing your ground."

"Mom's right about Jay being a bad influence on Dereck. That doesn't change the fact that he's not good enough for me or for Theo."

"One day you'll meet an upstanding young man who's worthy of the woman you've become."

"Thank you both for believing in me."

Erica smiled. After arguing against Sierra moving into their home, Amanda had come to treat her more like a daughter than a housemate. Hopefully, she'd find it in her heart to forgive Preston and fall in love with Gary.

Chapter 17

Millie spritzed her favorite perfume behind her ears then stood in front of her closet mirror. For the second time in as far back as she could remember, she'd bought a new outfit—dark form-fitting pants and a thigh-length red tunic. Not bad for an old lady going to dinner with a sexy old man. The mental image triggered a giggle. No one younger than seventy would consider either of them sexy. So much for the younger generation having a clue about old folks. Responding to the front door chime, she grabbed her coat and headed straight to the foyer. Summoning her best smile, Millie swung the door open and faced Savannah Landry. Her smile vanished. "What are you doing here?"

Savannah, wearing a sweatshirt and jeans, folded her arms tight across her chest. "I don't have anyone else to talk to."

"You're mistaken if you think I'm your friend." Millie eyed Gordon's car pulling up the driveway. "My investigative partner has arrived."

Savannah turned toward the new arrival, shivering. "Mr. Davenport seemed like a nice man."

"Don't for a minute misjudge his good manners. He's a tough former detective who doesn't take nonsense from anyone."

"Maybe he's the person I need to talk to."

Gordon climbed out of his car then headed up the sidewalk and stepped onto the porch. "Is there a problem here?"

Her investigative curiosity on overdrive, Millie's eyes remained focused on Savannah. "Ms. Landry wants to talk."

"I suggest we invite her in and find out what's on her mind."

"We'll give you ten minutes." Millie stepped aside then pointed toward the living room sofa. "Sit over there."

Savannah stepped inside. She lowered her arms to her sides while peering into the living room then made her way to the sofa.

Gordon motioned Millie out to the porch. He leaned close. "Any idea what she wants?"

"I don't have a clue. Should we play good cop, bad cop?"

He grinned. "You can't help yourself, can you?"

Millie huffed. "Now you're acting like Amanda, responding to my question with a question instead of an answer."

"Good detectives listen before interrogating. Considering I'm the only legitimate officer, I'll take the lead with our newest suspect."

"All right, but if we discover she's up to something nefarious, I'll play the bad cop."

He leaned closer. "You're the best smelling bad cop I've ever partnered with."

Sensing her cheeks were seconds from turning pink, Millie stepped back inside. She hung her coat on a hook then strode straight to her recliner.

Gordon followed, settling in the chair across from Millie. He angled toward Savannah. "What's on your mind?"

Her eyes flicked from Gordon, to Millie, then back to Gordon. "I um...know Marcel, the guy who killed my mother."

Millie gawked at her. Resisting the urge to fire the first question, she pressed her lips tight and shifted her focus to Gordon.

"How do you know him?"

Savannah shrugged. "We were kind of dating."

"What do you mean by kind of?"

"We hung out for a couple of months. When I met Marcel, he seemed like a nice enough guy. Only a couple of his tattoos looked scary." Savannah picked at a cuticle. "Even though I told him about Mom working at the casino, I didn't tell her about him."

Gordon glanced at Millie, then back at Savannah. "Because you didn't think she'd understand?"

"Mom wasn't exactly a fan of tats. Besides I wanted to wait until I knew where our relationship was going. I had no idea Marcel was in one of New Orlean's most violent gangs."

Millie could no longer resist sitting on the sideline. "Is he the reason you're afraid to go back home?"

"Sort of, but not exactly."

"Then why exactly?"

Savannah fidgeted. "I think I know where he's hiding."

Gordon leaned forward, his elbows on his knees, his fingers laced. "Are you afraid if you go back and tell the police, they'll believe you were involved?"

Savannah tucked her chin toward her chest. "I kind of was."

Millie eyed her with suspicion. "Meaning what?"

"The night before Mom was killed, Marcel took me to a bar to meet his friends. That's when I realized he wasn't the nice person he pretended to be. The guy who acted like the gang leader told me he'd found someone to take care of the dealer who had him arrested and kicked out of the casino." Tears welled in Savannah's eyes. "If I'd known he was talking about my mother, I would have warned her."

"Want to know what I think?" Millie scooted to the edge of her recliner. "The gang leader ordered the hit on your mother. Part of his vengeance might have been to let you know and at the same time scare you into silence."

"I want the police to catch Marcel and put him behind bars." Savannah swiped her fingers across her cheeks. "If I go back home and tell them what I know, his gang will come after me."

Gordon unlaced his fingers. "Do you trust me to pass what you know on to the New Orleans police department without involving you?"

Savannah's brows pinched. "How can you do that?"

"The year before I retired, I helped a hotshot detective catch a killer who had fled from New Orleans. He still owes me a favor."

Millie's eyes shifted from Gordon to Savannah. "You can trust Detective Davenport."

Savannah gave a quick nod. "Okay."

"All right, then. Time to get to work." Gordon removed his phone from his pocket. After tapping the screen, he laid it down and eyed Millie. "I need paper and a pen."

"I'm on it." She obliged then returned to her recliner. Eager to watch a real-life detective in action, she leaned back to take in the show. To her surprise and delight, Gordon came across more like a caring grandfather than a tough cop. Probably because Savannah was also a victim of gang violence if her story was true.

When Gordon finished questioning Savannah, he laid the paper and pen on the coffee table. "You have given me everything I need. Tomorrow morning I'll make the necessary contacts and put the New Orleans police department on Marcel's trail. In the meantime, you can return to the inn knowing you're helping to bring justice for your mother."

Savannah sniffled. "Thank you for helping me."

"You're welcome."

Millie lifted off her recliner. "It's cold outside. Do you need a coat or some sort of wrap?"

"No thanks." Savannah rose. "It's a short walk."

"Do you have your key?"

She patted her jeans pocket. "I remembered. Maybe I'll drive into town and find someplace to eat." Savannah headed toward the foyer, then stopped and faced Millie. "Even if I don't want you to, I know you'll probably tell Amanda about me and Marcel."

Millie couldn't help but notice the pain in Savannah's eyes. "You don't want me to tell her, do you?"

Savannah hesitated. "I don't want to give her any more reasons not to like me."

"I understand. Which is why everything you shared tonight will stay between you, me, and Detective Davenport."

"Thank you." Savannah embraced her for a brief moment before dashing out the door.

Millie returned to the living room.

Gordon stood, leaning against the back of his chair, grinning. "You're an old softy after all."

"You're one to talk. You treated Savannah the same way you would treat a granddaughter." Millie crossed her arms. "Why are you waiting until tomorrow to call your friend?"

"Because tonight I have a dinner date with a beautiful and interesting woman."

Millie tilted her head. No one had ever called her beautiful. Maybe Bernie had been right about using subtle flirtation to prove she had at least one romantic bone in her body. She already had the sexy perfume down. Why not try another one of her suggestions? She batted her eyelashes. "Such flattery."

Gordon chuckled. "Are you flirting with me, or is something in your eye?"

Millie huffed. "Some detective you are."

"You know, if you had batted your lashes like that back in high school, I might have taken you instead of the cheerleader to the prom."

"If you hadn't been so sure of yourself, maybe I would have accepted."

"At least after all these years, we're making up for lost time." Gordon slid his arm around her shoulders. "Proving it's never too late for a couple of senior citizens to find a little romance."

Millie elbowed his ribs. "Now who's flirting?"

"Guilty as charged, detective." After escorting her to the foyer, he lifted her coat off the hook and held it out for her. "Now what do you say we head to town before we miss our updated reservation?"

Millie slid her arms into the sleeves. "If I'd known a little romance came with detective work, I'd have started a mystery club a long time ago."

"Good thing you waited until I moved back to town." Gordon eased the door open. "Or some other old guy might have found you as intriguing as I have."

Millie's chest puffed. If their plan to save Amanda and Gary's relationship worked, their competition on who would reel in a man first might end in a draw.

The morning after her late-night date, Millie hummed while preparing frittatas for their guests.

Bernie folded fresh berries into a bowl of yogurt. "Does your cheerful mood mean you and Gordon enjoyed an especially fun evening, or are you going through a late-life personality change?"

As much as she was itching to tell someone about Savannah's revelation, Millie vowed to honor her promise. "Can't I hum without rousing suspicion?"

"During all these months we've worked together, you've never been this cheerful."

Ignoring Bernie as best she could, Millie slid the frittatas into the oven and set the timer. "We have three new guests arriving today."

"You can't fool me by changing the subject. I know something's going on."

Millie rolled her eyes. "You're not going to give up, are you?"

"I've learned to be as stubborn as you are."

"If you must know—" Millie moved closer. "You were wrong about me not having a romantic bone in my body."

"Oh my gosh." Bernie's eyes widened. "Did Gordon spend the night at your house?"

"What? No." She paused. "Although we carried on as if we were a couple of teenagers."

"Meaning what?"

A sly grin tugged at the corners of Millie's mouth. "I'll leave that for you to figure out."

Chapter 18

After escorting Ryan into the ranch house kitchen and setting a diaper bag and her laptop on the kitchen counter, Wendy returned to her car and released Cindy's carrier from the back seat. She looped her arm around the handle while heading back inside to prepare for Awesam's board meeting.

Ryan plopped a book onto Amanda's lap then climbed onto the sofa beside her. "Read me book, Nana."

"Of course, sweet boy." She slid her arm around her honorary grandson.

Moments after Wendy set the carrier on the sofa, Dusty sat on her haunches and laid her head across the infant's body.

Ryan giggled. "Doggie loves baby Cindy."

"Dusty loves everyone." Wendy settled between her babies while Amanda pulled back the book's cover. After she finished reading, Ryan climbed down and headed straight to the toy basket.

Amanda turned toward Wendy. "I'm in the mood for hot chocolate. How about you?"

"Sounds delish."

"Sit tight and I'll bring you a cup."

"Thanks." Wendy kicked off her shoes, then leaned back and propped her feet on the coffee table. Amazing how she and a woman who had been married to the same man had become as close as a mother and daughter. Life had a funny way of working out.

Amanda returned and handed over a mug before sitting beside Wendy. "How's everything going with Zach?"

"When he's home he barely says a word to either one of us. Every night after dinner he heads to his room and stays there until morning. We're convinced he's reacting to Chris taking on the role of disciplinarian instead of his gaming buddy. Hopefully at some point, he'll trust us enough to let us help him deal with the turmoil going on inside his head."

"With Chris's patience and your experience as a foster kid, he couldn't be in better hands."

Wendy sipped her hot chocolate. "Brent left instructions for us to give Zach the letter from his mother the day before Thanksgiving. Why he picked that date is a mystery, especially since Cynthia left instructions to give Kayla and Riley their letters on their birthdays."

"Brent must have a good reason."

"Maybe Zach's sour mood convinced Brent he needed to read his mother's letter sooner rather than later."

The back door opened. "I brought oatmeal raisin cookies to celebrate." Millie set her iPad and a plate on the dining room table beside four water bottles then strode to a club chair.

Wendy set her mug on the coffee table while breathing in cinnamon and vanilla scents. "What are we celebrating?"

"Savannah Landry checked out an hour ago."

"Did she say anything before she left?"

Millie hesitated, her eyes moving from Wendy to Amanda. "I didn't see her after breakfast."

Wendy studied Millie's blank expression. What was she not telling them? "I suppose we can conclude that Savannah isn't trying to con anyone." Her focus drifted to Amanda's downcast eyes and lowered chin. Did she regret refusing to accept a relationship with Preston's daughter? Wendy reached across Cindy's carrier and touched Amanda's arm. "Are you okay?"

She lifted her chin. "How can I be okay knowing my husband had an affair with a French Quarter stripper." She blinked. "Sorry, Wendy, I don't mean to snap at you."

"No need to apologize. At least with Savannah gone, you can move on."

"Wendy's right." Millie abandoned her chair then headed straight to the table. She returned and held the cookie plate in front of Amanda. "Time for a sugar rush."

"Typical chef's approach to solving life's problems." Amanda rolled her eyes while reaching for a cookie.

"Sweet treats beat the dickens out of legal or illegal drugs." Millie eyed Wendy. "Do you mind if I treat Ryan to a cookie?"

"Of course not, but only one."

Millie ambled toward her honorary great grandson, then leaned down and handed him a cookie. "Baked with love by Grammy Millie."

Ryan tilted his head back and looked up at her, grinning. "Grammy cookie."

Millie pressed her hand to her chest. "What a smart boy you are."

Dusty sprawled beside Ryan, ready to scarf up whatever crumbs he dropped while Millie carried the plate back to the table.

Wendy glanced at her watch. "Erica should arrive any minute now. We might as well take our places." She retrieved her laptop from the kitchen. Moments after settling at the dining room table, she turned toward Awesam's CEO walking in from the carport. "Perfect timing."

Erica set down her laptop and pulled out a chair across from Wendy while Dusty padded over to greet her.

Amanda joined them. "Hot chocolate, anyone?"

"Water's fine." Erica reached for a bottle.

"I'll take a hot drink." Millie settled between Wendy and Erica.

Amanda headed to the kitchen, returning moments later with a mug for Millie. "Why don't we kick off our meeting with a financial update."

"Not yet." Erica twisted the cap off her water bottle.

Amanda turned toward her. "What's on your mind?"

Erica took a sip then leaned back. "The wife of one of our high school teachers manages an apartment complex. Brad overheard him talking in the teacher's lounge about a new tenant." She paused, her eyes focused on Amanda. "Savannah Landry signed a lease for a furnished apartment yesterday."

Amanda's features contorted. "Are you kidding me?"

"I'm afraid not."

"What about me ignoring her didn't she understand?" Amanda's tone screamed of anger.

Millie wrapped her fingers around her mug. "Maybe she feels safe here."

Amanda glared at Millie. "Meaning what?"

"Would you return to the city where your mother was killed?"

"Probably not." Amanda drummed her fingers. "But I for doggone sure wouldn't move to a town where I wasn't wanted."

Wendy turned toward Millie. "Do you know something the three of us don't know?"

Millie huffed. "Why would you ask me that question?"

Wendy shrugged. "Call it a hunch."

"Hunches are worthless unless based on facts."

"Hold on." Amanda crossed her arms on the table, her eyes focused on Millie. "You do know something, don't you?"

"Have you forgotten that Jacqueline Landry's killer is still on the loose?"

"What's your point?" Amanda's eyes narrowed. "Savannah could escape to any town in the entire country."

"Except for one fact." Erica reached for her water. "She isn't a total stranger here."

Amanda scoffed. "Worse than a stranger, she's an unwelcome outsider."

"I don't know." Wendy reached for a cookie. "I kind of feel sorry for her."

"As would anyone who has a heart." Amanda scooted her chair away from the table. "Having empathy doesn't change the facts."

Millie pushed her mug aside. "You're going to confront her, aren't you?"

"If she understands she doesn't belong here, she might change her mind about staying."

"I suggest you take Erica with you to function as peacemaker when you come across as irrational."

Amanda glared at Millie. "You should know by now that I'm never irrational."

"All right then, insensitive. Erica can also serve as a witness to anything that might happen."

Amanda rolled her eyes. "You've obviously let your mystery club muddle your brain."

"Actually—" Erica capped her water bottle. "I agree with Millie."

"I suppose you're both right. As Awesam's president I'm postponing our board meeting until next week." Amanda lifted off her chair then headed straight to the kitchen with Erica following close behind.

The moment they walked out to the carport, Wendy turned toward Millie. "Okay. Time for you to fess up."

"About what?"

"Why you insisted Erica tag along instead of you."

Millie sighed. "If I showed up with Amanda, Savannah would think I had broken my promise."

Wendy arched a brow. "What promise?"

Millie hesitated as if mentally debating the best way to explain. "I suppose technically Savannah doesn't want Amanda to know." Her eyes met Wendy's. "I need to tell you something, mostly because you're married to a lawyer. You have to promise that no one other than you and Chris will hear."

"What's going on, Millie?"

"Not until you promise."

"You have my word."

She leaned closer to Wendy. "Last night, Savannah showed up at my house the same time as Gordon."

Her jaw dropped while she listened to Savannah's story about her mother's killer. When Millie finished, Wendy drew in a deep breath. "She has a good reason to stay far away from New Orleans. Even after her mother's killer is captured, she'll remain a potential target of gang violence. Maybe if Amanda knew, she'd have a little compassion."

"I agree, but I can't go back on my word. Savannah will tell Amanda what's going on if and when she wants her to know."

Wendy sank against the back of her chair. "Every day it seems the Landry saga becomes a little more complicated."

"One fact is as clear as glass." Millie reached for her mug. "The saga isn't going away any time soon."

By the time Amanda turned into the apartment complex driveway to search for Savannah's car, heart-pounding tension gripped her shoulder and neck muscles. "There it is." She pulled into an empty parking spot.

Erica turned toward her. "Are you sure you want to do this?"

Amanda eyed the end unit. "I don't have a choice." She climbed out before Erica had a chance to respond. Halfway to the door, she slowed her pace. Maybe she should wait a few more days. No. Better to face Savannah before she had a chance to become too settled in. Breathing deeply to slow her pulse, Amanda stepped onto the porch and knocked.

Erica stood beside her.

They waited.

Amanda knocked again.

The door swung inward following the third knock. Savannah's eyes shifted to Erica then back to Amanda. "What are you doing here?"

"We need to talk."

Amanda slid her keys into her pocket. "Are you going to invite us in, or do you want the neighbors to hear what I have to say?"

Savannah delayed a moment longer then led them to a well-worn sofa in the sparsely furnished living area. "How'd you know I was here?"

Amanda sat beside Erica while keeping a close eye on Savannah. "Word travels fast in small towns."

"So it seems." Savannah lowered onto a straight-backed chair on the other side of the scratched coffee table. "What do you want to talk about?"

Amanda's back stiffened. "You need to know that renting this apartment won't change my mind about refusing to form any sort of relationship with you."

A flicker of pain clouded Savannah's eyes, gone in an instant yet unmistakable. "I already have two job interviews scheduled."

Amanda glared at her. "What sort of jobs?"

"I'm trained as a hair stylist."

Conflicting thoughts played havoc with Amanda's emotions. Savannah had every right to live and work in Blue Ridge, and she didn't seem to want anything tangible from her. On the other hand, why would she choose to stay in the town where she was flat-out rejected? *Unless she's clinging to the hope that one day I'll experience a change of heart.*

"I understand why you don't want me in your life. I suppose I'd feel the same way if someone I loved had cheated on me. It's just...I don't have any place else to go. I promise I won't bother you." Savannah's gaze dropped to her lap. "If we accidentally run into each other, I'll pretend I don't know you."

Amanda remained silent for a long moment, teetering between standing firm and showing a modicum of empathy. Better not to give her false hope. "I believe we understand each other." She stood. "We'll show ourselves out." Avoiding eye contact, she hastened to the door then straight to the truck.

Erica followed close behind and climbed onto the passenger seat. "For a moment you had second thoughts about rejecting her, didn't you?"

"Until common sense kicked in." Amanda cranked the engine then backed out of the parking space. Savannah refusing to leave solidified one important fact. She could no longer avoid talking to Gary.

Chapter 19

The morning after confronting Savannah, Amanda's mind raced with conflicting questions about her pending task. Should she talk to Gary in public or in private? If the situation was reversed, where would she want him to end their relationship? Definitely away from prying eyes. But where? His condo would summon uncomfortable memories of their romantic evening. Inviting him to her home would likely confuse him. Only one location made sense. Amanda slipped her arms into a lightweight jacket then grabbed her purse. She headed out to the carport and climbed into the truck.

Ten minutes later, she turned onto the bank parking lot. If she had to wait long, would she wimp out? With only three other cars parked, maybe he could see her right away. A woman walked out and headed straight to her car. Best to go in now before more customers showed up. Amanda climbed out, dropped her keys into her purse, and walked inside.

A middle-aged woman approached her. "How can I help you?"

"I'd like to talk to Mr. Redding."

"Who may I tell him is calling?"

"Amanda Smith."

"Wait here. I'll find out if he's available."

Sweat popping out on the back of Amanda's neck forced her to peel out of her jacket. A gentleman walked away from a teller then smiled at her while brushing past. Had he recognized her, or was he being friendly?

The woman returned. "Mr. Redding will see you now." She escorted Amanda to a private office.

Her heart pounded against her ribs as she stepped into the tastefully appointed room.

"What a nice surprise." Gary rounded his desk. He kissed her cheek then motioned toward one of two chairs facing his desk. "Is this a personal or business visit?"

Was she moments away from making a huge mistake? No. She had to go through with her plan. Amanda draped her coat across the back of the chair then took a seat. "Personal."

He closed his door then settled beside her. "What's on your mind?"

Amanda glanced around his office. Pale blue walls. Sheer curtains drawn across the window facing the parking lot. A landscape painting on the side wall. She couldn't allow his charm to break her resolve. "Something happened you need to know about." She folded her hands on her lap. For five agonizing minutes, Amanda avoided eye contact while relaying every detail from the moment she'd first laid eyes on Savannah until showing up at her apartment yesterday. By the time she finished, the sweat on the back of her neck had dripped down her back.

Gary reached across the space between them and placed his hand on her arm. "I can imagine how devastated you must feel."

Amanda flinched. How could she explain her trust in men had been shattered?

He withdrew his hand. "What aren't you telling me?"

She stared blindly across his desk. "I've trusted three men in my life. The first was my father, who abandoned me and my mother, forcing her to work two jobs to put food on our table. The second was Preston Smith, who fathered another child while I was pregnant with our daughter. Paul Sullivan aka Gunter Benson was the third. He stole everything from me and Morgan." She swallowed hard. The words she needed to express stuck in her throat.

Silence enveloped them when Gary slowly lifted off his chair and moved to the other side of his desk. He remained standing, facing the window. "Now you're afraid you can't trust me or any other man."

Amanda's lips trembled as she lost the battle to hold back the tears threatening to erupt. "My heart has been shattered too many times."

"After my wife cheated on me, I didn't believe I could ever trust another woman. Until I fell in love with you." He turned toward her then dropped onto his executive chair and folded his arms on his desk. Their eyes met. "While I understand how you're feeling, I don't want to lose you."

"I can't—"

"Please, let me finish." A flicker of hope burned in his eyes. "While I wait for your heart to heal, I want us to remain friends."

Amanda blinked. "After everything that has happened, I don't believe my heart will ever heal." Her voice rang in her own ears. It carried the heavy weight of a woman who had endured more than she could bear.

His eyes dimmed for a brief moment. "If that happens I'll settle for your friendship."

Could she deny her feelings for him enough to remain his friend? Fearing she was moments from losing total control of her emotions, Amanda lifted off her chair. She extended her hand toward him as if they were business partners who had just closed a deal. "I appreciate your understanding."

He stood, his hands enfolding hers. "You're a strong woman, Amanda. I'm confident in time you'll learn to trust again."

For a brief moment her resolve began to slip away until an image of Preston in bed with another woman crept into her mind. "I'll be in touch." She pulled her hand away then grabbed her coat and walked out of his office.

The woman who had greeted her smiled. "Have a wonderful day, Ms. Smith."

Afraid to utter a word, Amanda nodded while easing toward the exit. She hastened to her truck, backed out of the parking spot, and headed straight to a car dealership. The time had come to ditch the last physical reminder of her former life.

Three hours after leaving the bank, Amanda drove her newly purchased, late-model SUV into the ranch house carport. She walked inside to find Millie sitting at the dining room table. "What are you doing here?" She couldn't keep the snark out of her voice.

"Waiting for you."

"Why?"

"We haven't talked since you left our meeting yesterday to confront Savannah."

Amanda tossed her purse onto the table. "Are you playing the role of detective, or are you just plain nosy?"

"Neither." Millie waggled her finger at Amanda. "I'm your friend and business partner, which is why I care when you march off madder than an old wet goat."

Amanda rolled her eyes as she dropped onto a chair across from Millie. "What would I do without you irritating the dickens out of me?"

"I'm glad to oblige." Millie leaned forward. "About Savannah."

"Let's just say we came to an understanding. She stays out of my way, and I stay out of hers."

Millie eyed her for a long moment. “Where have you been for the past three and a half hours?”

“Have you been spying on me?”

“Don’t get your britches in a wad. You drove off the same moment I took food to the porch for Inky.”

No way she’d tell Millie about meeting Gary. “For your information, I went car shopping.”

“Good for you. It’s about time you traded in Gunter’s old truck. What’d you buy?”

“I’ll show you.” Amanda pulled her phone from her purse then headed to the kitchen.

Millie followed her out to the carport. “Good choice. Is it new?”

“Two years old. Low mileage.”

“Did you negotiate a good deal?”

“What do you think?”

Millie ran her fingers along the shiny white fender. “You threatened to walk out three times before the salesperson relented.”

“Good guess but only twice.”

“Well now.” Millie shot Amanda a quick glance. “With a new car and a new man in your life, you have everything you need to move on.”

Refusing to take the bait, Amanda handed Millie her phone. “Take a picture so I can show Morgan.”

Millie snapped pictures then returned the phone to Amanda. “Are Morgan and Kevin coming up for a visit any time soon?”

“No. If you don’t mind, I need time alone to talk to my daughter.”

“I can take a hint. Don’t forget tomorrow’s Bernie’s day off, so I’ll expect you at the inn at seven.”

Amanda flicked her hand over her shoulder as Millie headed to the back door. “I’ll be there.” Relieved to be alone, she stepped into the kitchen and pulled a water bottle from the fridge then headed to the den. She settled on the sofa with Dusty sprawled on the floor at her feet. Hoping she'd catch Morgan at a good time, she pressed her number.

Her daughter answered after the third ring. "Hey, Mom."

"Are you home?"

"I'm in Chicago meeting with a client."

"Do you have time to talk?"

"Everyone's taking a break, so I have five minutes. Anything new happening in Blue Ridge since we last talked?"

"I traded the truck for a nearly new SUV. I'm texting a picture now."

"Good choice. Even better, there's nothing left to remind us of Gunter."

One more difficult conversation she couldn't delay. "There's something else."

"About Gary?"

"Not directly." Amanda's eyes drifted to the unlit fireplace. "Savannah rented an apartment in town."

Morgan gasped. "Are you kidding me?"

Amanda relayed most of her conversation with Savannah the day she and Erica showed up at her apartment. "She knows I don't want a relationship with her."

"Knowing is a lot different than believing."

Amanda's brows pinched. "Meaning what?"

"Let me put it this way. If I were Savannah, I'd stay in town hoping one day you'd change your mind and welcome me into your family."

"Doesn't matter what Savannah might or might not hope. I'll never change my mind."

"All I'm saying is you need to be prepared if she doesn't stay out of your way." Morgan paused. "My clients are returning. We'll talk more later." She ended the call.

Desperate to ease a mounting tension headache, Amanda pressed her fingers to her temples. If Morgan was right, how long before Savannah gave up and moved away? Six months? A year? Or never?

Chapter 20

After pulling on a light blue sweater and releasing her long blonde hair down her back, Wendy inserted gold dangling earrings to complete her outfit. "If Zach agrees to play pool with you and your dad, maybe he'll begin to break down the wall of silence he's been hiding behind."

Chris wrapped his arms around her waist. "Hanging out with the two of us before dinner should make him feel like one of the guys."

"How could he resist two men who have as much fun as you and Keith?"

"I have a question for you. Why are two lawyers more charming than one?"

Wendy tilted her head. "Is that an honest question or one of your lawyer jokes?"

"A little of both."

"Okay, I'll bite." Wendy laced her fingers behind his neck, her chin tilted up. "Why are two lawyers more charming than one?"

"Because they have twice the appeal."

Wendy laughed while playfully rolling her eyes. "Two years ago I wouldn't have caught the double meaning." Reacting to Ryan toddling into their bedroom, she unlaced her fingers. "We have company."

Chris released her then gathered his son in his arms. "We're going to visit Grandma and Grandpa."

Wendy lifted Cindy secured in her carrier off the bed then followed the guys into the den. She approached Zach slouched on the sofa. "You'll enjoy meeting Chris's parents."

"I guess."

Relieved he hadn't said 'whatever,' Wendy waited for Zach to lift off the sofa before following Chris and Ryan to the kitchen then out to the garage. Zach slid onto the third row in Wendy's SUV with his phone in hand while she and Chris secured their babies safely in the middle seat.

During the short drive, Wendy leaned back and closed her eyes. Her thoughts drifted to the day she first met with Armstrong Law Firm's private investigator and asked him to search for her mother. Little did she know how much hung in the balance when she discovered he had succeeded. The months that followed played in her mind like a television drama. Discovering her mother was seriously ill. Developing a relationship with her half-siblings. The day her mother succumbed to her illness.

"We're here."

Wendy's eyes popped open.

Chris parked in the driveway leading to the stone-and-brick house overlooking downtown Blue Ridge. White holiday lights accented the eaves and roofline, and a Christmas wreath adorned the front door.

"Your mom's already decked out for the holidays."

"Most years she's all decorated for Christmas by the first week in November." Chris climbed out and lifted Cindy's carrier while Wendy opened the other passenger door to release Ryan from his car seat. Zach shoved his phone in his pocket before following them across the sidewalk.

Linda, dressed in a red sweater and black pants, responded seconds after Chris rang the bell. "There's my adorable grandson." She lifted Ryan into her arms while smiling at Zach. "This handsome young man must be your uncle. Welcome to our home."

"Thanks." Zach's tone lacked even the slightest hint of enthusiasm.

"Keith's down stairs waiting for you guys to join him."

Chris handed Cindy's carrier to Wendy then nudged Zach's arm. "Are you ready for a spirited game of pool?"

"Dunno." He shrugged. "I've never played."

"Now's the perfect time for you to learn."

Linda kissed Ryan's cheek before returning him to Chris's arms.

While the guys made their way down to the terrace level, Wendy followed Linda into the massive but cozy combination kitchen and family room. A ten-foot tall, elaborately decorated Christmas tree anchored the corner beside the floor-to-ceiling stone fireplace adorned with ribbon-laced garland. "Gorgeous tree."

"Thanks. There are two more. One in the dining room, the other downstairs." Moments after Wendy set the carrier on the L-shaped sectional sofa, Linda lifted her granddaughter into her arms. "Nothing smells as sweet as a new baby."

"Speaking of scents." Wendy sniffed the tomato, garlic, and cheese aromas. "You're serving an Italian-style dish tonight, aren't you?"

Linda nodded while gently rocking her granddaughter. "Based on experience, I know teenaged boys like lasagna. Are you making any progress with Zach?"

"Not really. When he's home, he mostly ignores us."

"Under normal circumstances adolescent boys are complicated. When Chris was Zach's age, he was fiercely independent." She relayed humorous stories of his shenanigans until he left for college. "If Keith hadn't suffered a heart attack, Chris wouldn't have returned to Blue Ridge after graduating from law school. Falling in love with you made returning to his hometown a blessing beyond anything he could have imagined."

A sensation akin to a warm spring breeze flowed over Wendy. "I was attracted to your son the first day we met in Blue Ridge Inn's dining room. I tried to ignore my feelings for him because I was pregnant with a con man's child. Fortunately, my heart overruled my head."

"For good reason. You and Chris are meant to spend the rest of your lives together." Linda paused for a long moment. "Speaking of heart overriding one's head, when did you last talk to Amanda?"

"A couple of days ago." Wendy's eyes met Linda's. "You know about Savannah Landry, don't you?"

She nodded. "Gary filled us in. He's heartbroken over the possibility of losing Amanda." Linda returned her sleeping granddaughter to the carrier. "Which is why we all have to ensure Gary and Amanda both show up for Susan's second party."

Wendy raised a brow. "What party?"

Linda stared wide-eyed as if she couldn't believe Wendy didn't have a clue. "After Keith's surprise birthday party, Millie and her mystery club members are planning to invite Gary and Amanda to a New Year's Eve party at Susan's house. They're hoping to recreate the ending of the film *When Harry Met Sally*."

"I've never seen that movie."

"It's one of my favorites. After the two characters spent years drifting in and out of each other's lives, they finally admitted they were in love on New Year's Eve."

"Believe me, it will take more than two staged events to heal Amanda's shattered heart. Perhaps the best we can hope for is both nights will serve as starting points to her healing process."

"Especially since she and Gary are perfect for each other." They continued chatting about family until the oven timer buzzed. "That's my signal. Will you let the guys know dinner's ready?"

“Glad to.” Wendy headed downstairs to the high-ceiling paneled room with French doors leading out to a patio beneath the deck. Chris sat on the floor with Ryan on his lap beside the second tree featuring a train circling the village underneath.

Zach drew back the cue stick then tapped a ball sending it straight into a side pocket.

“Well done.” Keith clasped his hand on the boy’s shoulder. “You’re a natural.”

Was it her imagination, or was there the slightest hint of a smile on Zach’s face? “Are you guys ready to come up for dinner?”

Chris pushed off the floor. “Your brother is on his way to becoming a bona fide pool champion.”

A grin tugged at Wendy’s lips. Was it possible a game of pool with two amazing men marked the beginning of Zach’s wall of resistance breaking down? “Good for you, Zach.”

He shrugged. “No big deal.”

The guys followed Wendy upstairs then into the dining room where a tree decorated in a gold and white motif stood in front of the window. While enjoying dinner, Wendy kept a close eye on Zach. Although he never made eye contact, he followed Chris’s no-cell-phone-at-the-table rule and responded to questions with two word answers. During the ride home, he remained silent in the third row seat. After arriving and carrying their babies to their rooms, Wendy and Chris joined each other in the great room.

Zach stood with his hand on the stair railing. “Ryan and Cindy are lucky to have nice grandparents who live close by. Mom’s mother died before I was born. Dad’s mother visited us one time before she died. His father lives somewhere on the West Coast. They haven’t spoken in years.”

"I'm confident my parents would love to adopt you as their honorary grandson." Chris moved beside him. "Especially since you've proven yourself a worthy pool opponent."

"Whatever." Zach turned away then headed down to the terrace level, ending his longest conversation since the day he'd arrived.

Chris wrapped his arm around Wendy's waist while they headed toward their room. "Seems we've come one tiny step closer to breaking through your brother's barrier."

"I hope you're right."

Chapter 21

Balancing on stepladders, Millie and Bernie hung the 'Hilltop Inn's Holiday Dessert Competition' banner across the dining room entrance. "Last year I competed and won. This year I'm the head judge."

Bernie climbed down. "I don't recall any of us judges selecting you as our leader."

Millie scoffed as she stepped off her ladder. "Why wouldn't I lead? After all, the competition is my brainchild—"

"Created to make you an award-winning chef."

"Are you taking contrarian lessons from Amanda?"

"No need to." Bernie folded her ladder. "I study the master antagonist every morning."

"Either you're an excellent student, or I'm a brilliant teacher." Millie stepped back, eyeing the banner. "Eleven people have entered this year's competition, including Gladys Zander."

"The rich lady who discovered Crystal Bullock had been falsely convicted of murder by District Attorney Richard Watson?"

Millie nodded. "Her discovery helped Keith Armstrong defeat the bum. I know I shouldn't have favorites, but I hope Gladys wins."

"She will if she enters the best dessert."

A woman who had checked in the day before meandered into the living room. "Are Hilltop's guests welcome to attend the competition?"

"Absolutely." Millie folded her stepstool and leaned it against the wall. "I won last year."

"I know." The woman gestured toward the plaque on the wall above the inn's scrapbook. "Amanda pointed out your award when we checked in. This morning's breakfast proved you deserve the accolade."

Millie's chest puffed. "We all strive to give our guests first-class experiences."

"Thus far, everyone has accomplished the goal." The woman turned toward her husband descending the stairs. "We're going to town, but we'll return in time for the competition."

After the couple walked out, Millie headed to the kitchen and lifted the lid off the pedestal plate holding her chocolate peppermint cake.

Bernie followed her. "Don't you think displaying your creation is a bit pretentious?"

"I've earned bragging rights." Millie carried the cake to the dining room to display it in the center of the sideboard beside a tent card identifying it as last year's winner. A half hour later, a chime sent her rushing to open the front door. "You're the first judge to arrive."

Susan stepped into the foyer. "It doesn't seem possible an entire year has already flown by."

"At our age we need to slow time down, not speed it up."

Jody, the Sweet Shoppe chef who had judged last year, climbed onto the porch. "I'm glad you invited me back." She aimed her thumb over her shoulder. "A man on a three-wheeled motorcycle pulled in behind me."

"That's Gordon." Millie stepped aside. "He's our only male judge."

Susan grinned. "He's also a member of our mystery club."

"Is that some sort of book club?"

"As Millie would say, the word book isn't in the name, although we read books when we're not investigating and solving crimes. We're the group version of Jessica Fletcher."

Jody's eyes widened. "Does she live in Blue Ridge?"

Susan shook her head. "Jessica's the main character in the old television show *Murder, She Wrote.*"

"Oh."

Gordon ambled onto the porch and stepped inside. "This is the first time anyone invited me to judge a cooking contest."

"Three of us are professionals, and Susan's a master amateur. We need you to balance the team as an impartial citizen who enjoys good desserts." Millie looped her arm around his elbow while leading the way to the kitchen. "Amanda's on her way over to greet our contestants and guests. We'll sequester ourselves, so we won't know who brings which entry."

Gordon chuckled. "Sounds as if you're gathering the jurors to debate a defendant's guilt or innocence."

"We're protecting ourselves from being accused of rigging the competition."

Susan choked. "You mean like last year?"

Millie glanced over her shoulder. "Even if we hadn't predetermined the winner, you know my entry would have won." She released Gordon's arm and stepped into the kitchen.

Bernie sat on one of the island stools. "I had planned to submit an entry until you recruited me to participate as a judge."

"For good reason." Millie climbed onto the stool beside Bernie. "How would it look if another Hilltop chef won?"

"At least you're willing to admit I'm talented enough to win."

"Only because I've been sharing my secrets with you for the past year."

"One fact is undeniable." Susan nudged Millie's arm. "No one could ever accuse you of suffering from a lack of self-confidence."

Gordon moved across the island from Millie. "Seems everyone has your number."

"Careful, detective, or you might be forced to attract another woman to ride in your fancy tricycle."

Jody, the Sweet Shoppe chef who was young enough to be every other judge's granddaughter, leaned against the counter, smiling. "I'm beginning to understand what your mystery club is really all about."

Millie caught Jody's eye. "What do you think you know?"

"You enjoy getting together to have a good time and tease each other."

Bernie laughed. "There is that."

While they continued chatting, voices began drifting in from the living room. By the time forty minutes had passed, it had become obvious a crowd had gathered.

Amanda walked in from the dining room. "Are our esteemed judges ready to select this year's winner?"

"Ready and able." Millie handed each judge a clipboard, a pen, and a ballot.

"All right then, it's showtime." Amanda led the way into the dining room then moved to the parted pocket doors. "Welcome to Hilltop, everyone." She paused until the guests quieted and turned toward her. "On behalf of Hilltop's partners, I welcome you to our second annual holiday dessert competition. This year we have eleven talented competitors who brought what promises to be mouthwatering entries. After the winner is announced, we'll share these desserts with all of you, including last year's winner baked by our own Chef Millie." After explaining the process, Amanda faced the judges. "Are you ready?"

"We are." Millie lifted a bottle of water off the sideboard then moved to the front of the table. Five small plates with single bites had been staged in front of each entry. She tasted the first, checked boxes on her ballot, then took a sip of water and moved to the next dessert. After following the same pattern and sampling every entry, the judges returned to the kitchen.

Amanda followed them.

Susan pulled her ballot off the clipboard and laid it on the island. "Although every dessert was exceptional, one clearly stood out."

Jody laid her ballot on top of Susan's. "In my opinion two are worthy of a win."

"They were all delicious." Gordon handed over his ballot. "I don't know how much I helped."

While Bernie gathered the ballots and typed the responses onto a spreadsheet, the other judges debated which candidate would end up the winner.

"I have the results." Bernie turned her laptop around. "It's close, but our winner is number eight."

Amanda unfolded a sheet of paper. "Entered by Gladys Zander."

Susan applauded. "Millie and I both hoped she'd win."

"So did I." Amanda lifted the plaque off the counter then led the way to the competitors. Conversation stopped when she stepped into the living room. "Choosing this year's winner proved a difficult task for our distinguished judges, as you all will realize when you taste the entries. However, one dessert has emerged as the winner." She paused. "The red velvet, white chocolate cheesecake lovingly baked by Gladys Zander."

Applause erupted as Gladys stepped forward, her palm pressed to her chest. "I'm surprised and deeply honored."

"A well-deserved honor." Amanda handed her the plaque. "We'll deliver an engraved nameplate to you in a few days. Now ladies and gentlemen, we invite you to enjoy all of our amazing entries."

While the guests and contestants headed into the dining room, Gordon leaned close to Millie. "You need to come with me."

"Where are we going?"

"Outside." He pressed his hand to her back while they made their way through the kitchen and den to the backyard.

"Are we sneaking out back to neck?"

"A good idea, but no." They strode to one of the wrought-iron benches facing the five-foot-tall, three-tier bronze fountain. "My New Orleans connection called this morning. Jacqueline Landry's killer has been arrested. I've already informed Savannah."

"How'd she take the news?"

"Best I could tell, with a mixture of relief and apprehension."

Millie eyed rivulets of water splashing from the third tier into the pool. "If Amanda understood what's going on, she might be inclined to cut Savannah some slack."

"You're not thinking of telling her, are you?"

"As much as I want to, I won't break my promise to Savannah."

"Despite your contrariness, you have a good heart."

"If that's your idea of flattery, you seriously need a refresher course."

Gordon chuckled. "Hanging out with you is such a wild ride, I might have to buy a season pass."

Millie patted his knee. "I might get a hankering to give you one."

"If you do—" He slid his arm around her shoulders. "I'll take you up on that offer."

The unspoken promise of romance warmed her heart. It suddenly dawned on her she'd been waiting years to experience what she felt at the moment. "Considering the press is covering our event, we should go back inside before our disappearance raises all sorts of rumors." She lifted off the bench. "After all, Hilltop's famous chef caught in a senior-citizen scandal might not be good for business."

Gordon joined her. "On the other hand, a well-planned scandal could attract old folks looking for one last adventure."

Millie looped her arm around his elbow while they headed toward the patio. "When did you add marketing expert to your list of skills?"

"Ten seconds ago."

"You'll need more experience before testing your theory."

"In marketing or romance?"

"I think I'll keep you guessing."

"Careful, Millie." He leaned close. "Folks might believe we're two old fogies looking for a little late-in-life romance."

She playfully batted her eyelashes. "Bless your heart, detective. You actually believe I would fall for you."

"Every time you say, 'bless your heart,' I start checking for incoming trouble."

"A top-notch detective who expected trouble wouldn't hesitate to frisk the suspect."

Gordon burst out laughing. "Is your comment a concealed invitation or a bold dare?"

"I'll let you figure that out."

Chapter 22

After igniting the gas fireplace, Wendy balanced her laptop on her legs then logged onto her online management course. Two more months and she'd earn a two-year college degree and qualify as an educated woman—not to mention the newly required skills she would use to help grow Awesam's profits. Maybe they could create a second bed-and-breakfast.

Responding to her stepmother's ringtone, Wendy swiped her finger across her phone. "Hey."

"Do you have time to talk?"

"I do." Wendy set her laptop on the cushion beside her. "Before you tell me what's on your mind, there's been a slight change of plans. My Nashville brother is staying with us until Christmas—"

"If visiting you the night after Thanksgiving is too much—"

"Not at all. Because Zach is camped out in our guest room, I've reserved two Hilltop rooms for the three of you—compliments of Awesam."

"I appreciate you accommodating us."

"The family that reserved the entire inn to celebrate the holiday will check out that morning and only three other guests are checking in. So we'll have plenty of space. Now, what's on your mind?"

"You know I'm working part-time at a bookstore to stay busy."

"Yeah." Wendy pictured Donna greeting shoppers and helping them find specific titles. "How's the job going?"

"Fine. Except for the unwelcome intruders who barged in this morning."

"Oh my gosh, were you robbed?"

"Worse. I was humiliated." Donna's tone hinted of disgust. "My husband's father and brother showed up at the store pretending to look for a book. Even though I was suspicious, I offered to help. Big mistake."

"What did they do?"

"Those two bullies urged me to drop my petition for divorce to protect the family's business reputation."

"I can't believe they confronted you where you work."

"They were counting on me not to make a scene, which I didn't, mostly out of respect for my friend who owns the store. Although I did tell them in no uncertain terms that my marriage with Douglas had been over long before I filed. I also made it clear that no matter how much they pressured me, nothing would change my mind about the divorce."

"How did they react?"

"The way you'd expect wealthy men who don't want to lose one shred of influence would react."

"Did they threaten you?"

"My father-in-law suggested that I might not want to risk losing custody of my sons. Meaning Douglas is stooping to playing dirty."

Wendy propped her feet on the coffee table. "You're not considering buckling under, are you?"

"There's no way I'll ever go back to being the dutiful wife while pretending my husband will come to his senses and stop chasing women."

"In that case I hope you have a good divorce attorney."

A sigh resonated. "Based on her reputation, she's good enough to fight the Hewitt dynasty."

"Maybe she's the real reason the Hewitt men cornered you."

"Same thing I'm thinking. Enough talk about my divorce drama. What's happening in your life?"

Wendy relayed details about Zach moving into their guest room.

"As the mother of two boys, I'm impressed with your willingness to take on a troubled teenager."

"Up to this point, his behavior has only been annoying. If all goes well, he'll return to Nashville with his family the day after Christmas." Duke bolted off the floor at the sound of the garage door. "Chris is home a couple of hours earlier than I expected." Wendy rose to her feet. "Which means something unexpected might have happened."

"I'll let you go. Tell Chris hi, and give my grandbabies a hug for me."

"I will. We're looking forward to seeing you and your boys." Wendy ended the call then set her phone on the coffee table and rushed to the kitchen.

The back door swung inward. Zach marched inside, his expression loaded with attitude.

Chris followed close behind, his jaw clenched. He gripped Zach's arm, steering him to his chair at their dining room table. "Your pretrial hearing begins now." His voice was firm but edged with anger.

Wendy's back stiffened. "Pretrial hearing for what offense?"

Duke, his tail tucked, sat on his haunches between Zach and Wendy.

Chris lowered onto the chair to Zach's right. "Fifteen minutes ago I bailed Zach out of jail for shoplifting."

Wendy's mouth fell open. "What did he steal?"

"An e-cigarette."

"Are you serious?" Wendy eyed Zach's scowl as she dropped onto the seat across from Chris. "How? Why?"

"During his study time, your brother snuck away from the worksite and hightailed a quarter mile to the smoke shop. He didn't count on one of the legitimate customers being an off-duty sheriff."

Shocked, Wendy pressed her hand to her chest. "Did you vape in Nashville?"

"With my friends. Not at home."

Anger narrowed her gaze. "Yet you broke the law so you could continue vaping in our home?"

"I've been smoking out back." Zach folded his arms across his chest. "I don't know what the big deal is. I only took one."

Chris leaned forward, his eyes laser focused on Zach. "Based on the sheriff's observation, this wasn't your first attempt at shoplifting."

"Kids I know steal stuff all the time."

"Are you telling us the kids you hang with consider breaking the law acceptable behavior?"

"If vapes and other stuff weren't illegal for kids to buy, we wouldn't have to shoplift." Zach's tone carried a heavy measure of defiance. "Besides, stores have insurance."

Chris's pupils seemed to sharpen. "You're facing two serious issues, young man. Beginning with your blatant disrespect for the law. Given this is your first offense in our state, the district attorney won't press for jail time."

Zach's eyes widened, hinting reality had suddenly struck home.

"However, beginning now, the following rules of probation will apply." Chris's eyes remained locked on Zach while he held out his hand, palm up. "Give me your cell phone."

"Why?"

"Because your actions come with consequences."

Zach hesitated.

"Now." Chris's voice remained calm while projecting the undeniable tone of authority.

Zach relented and slapped his phone on Chris's hand.

"I'll return it to you when your probation ends."

"Are you serious?"

"You bet I am." Chris pocketed the phone. "Beginning tomorrow and every day for the foreseeable future, I'll pick you up from your worksite at eleven and take you to my office. You'll study under my staff's supervision until time to return to work. When you're home, if you attempt to sneak out of the guest room, you'll trigger an alarm which will automatically extend your probation period."

Zach dropped his arms to his sides while his shoulders slumped under the weight of his sentence. "How long is the probation?"

"Until Christmas Eve, unless we grant you leniency for good behavior. Now, for problem number two." Chris unfolded his arms. "Do you have any idea what's in an e-cigarette?"

Zach shrugged. "Mostly water?"

"Wrong. I'll tell you what's been in every drop you've inhaled into your lungs." Chris rattled off a list of complex ingredients. "The reason vaping is illegal for minors goes beyond the danger of addiction. The toxic mix of chemicals damages vital organs and stunts brain development. When you turn twenty-one, you'll be free to abuse your body. Until then you'll submit to periodic drug tests to ensure you're not breaking the law. In case you're wondering, your father is fully on board with our decisions."

Zach's brows shot up. "Why did you tell him?"

"Because he cares about you—"

"Yeah, right." Zach's tone mocked. "He cares more about his stupid band and Gilmore's Bar more than us kids."

Wendy's breath caught. Had her brother just revealed a key reason for his destructive behavior?

Chris inched closer to Zach. "You need to tell your dad how you feel."

"What's the point?"

"He can't respond to something he doesn't know."

Zach smirked. "Like he cares."

Chris remained silent for a long moment. "Why do you think he sent you to stay with us?"

"So he'd have one less kid to deal with."

"You're wrong, Zach. Your father loves you. He's hurting as much as you are."

Wendy swallowed the lump in her throat before reaching across the table to touch Zach's arm. "I understand your reluctance to talk to your dad. Instead of calling him, you could express how you feel in a letter."

Chris nodded. "Excellent idea. You have twenty-four hours to decide whether to call or to write."

Zach eased his arm out from under Wendy's hand, his eyes downcast. "I'm sorry I caused all this trouble."

"Chris and I accept your apology."

"Can I go to my room now?"

Wendy's eyes met Chris's. "What do you think, Counselor?"

"I believe we've come to an understanding, which means the pretrial hearing is concluded."

Zach stood. After taking two steps, he halted. "Without a phone, how will I know what time to wake up and come up for dinner?"

"Good question. Set the alarm clock in your room to wake you. One of us will call down to you five minutes before dinner."

Wendy's eyes followed Zach while he lumbered to the stairs then down to the terrace level. "Anger at Brent isn't the only issue driving my brother's behavior."

"One fact is certain. He's hanging with the wrong crowd." Chris strode to the kitchen, returning with a beer.

"How are you going to manage chauffeuring him to and from his job in the middle of the day."

Chris twisted the cap off the bottle. "I'll ask our receptionist to fill in when I'm not available."

"You'll need to pay Rosalie a sizable bonus for going above and beyond. Especially since she'll be saddled with supervising Zach when you and Regina are out of the office."

"I know." Chris swallowed a sip. "She raised two boys, which guarantees she won't take any nonsense from Zach."

An unexpected twinge of doubt pricked Wendy's conscience. "I hope we weren't too hard on him."

Chris reached for her hand. "As difficult as it is to dish out, tough love is exactly what he needs."

The doubt evaporated the moment Wendy's eyes met his. "If every young boy had a father as wise as you, there would be a lot less crime."

He squeezed her hand. "I promise I'll never put my job ahead of my family."

Wendy's smile burst forth the moment Ryan toddled in and headed straight to his daddy. One fact became undeniably clear. God would never give her and Chris more than they could handle.

Wendy awakened before dawn and tiptoed into the great room to avoid waking Chris. Surprised to find Zach sitting in the dark with his feet propped on the coffee table, she switched on the side table lamp and sat beside him. “Good morning. How long have you been awake?”

“Couple of hours.” He paused. “I wrote a letter to Dad.”

“Good for you.” She sat beside him.

“Will you read it...you know...to make sure it doesn’t sound stupid?”

“I’d be happy to.”

Zach hesitated a moment before handing her a sheet of paper.

Wendy gripped the letter in both hands while silently reading her brother’s words.

Dear Dad,

Every time I complained about you being gone all the time, Mom said you worked hard so our family would have everything we needed for a good life. She never understood that I needed you, not what your money could buy. Maybe if I’d told you that I believe you care more about your band and Gilmore’s Bar than you do about us kids, you’d have spent more time at home. I’m telling you now because Chris thinks you should know how I feel. No matter how you react to this letter, I’ll try to be a better son.

Love,

Zach

Wendy pressed her hand to her heart. “It’s perfect.”

“You really think it’s okay?”

“Way more than okay. You wrote this from your heart.”

Chris ambled in, yawning. “You two are up early.” He hiked his hip on the sofa arm beside Wendy.

“You need to read this.” Wendy handed him the letter the moment the automatic coffee maker switched on.

After reading the letter, Chris pushed off the sofa arm and sat on the coffee table in front of Zach. “I’m proud of you for taking the first step toward healing the divide between you and your dad.”

“How do you think he’ll react?”

“With humility and understanding.”

Chapter 23

The Monday before Thanksgiving, Amanda responded to Morgan's ringtone while making her way from Hilltop's kitchen to the inn's front porch. "Hey, honey. I'm looking forward to spending Thanksgiving in Atlanta with you."

"That's why I'm calling. Kevin and I want to celebrate the holiday in Blue Ridge."

Amanda swallowed hard as she lowered onto one of the rocking chairs. "Why the sudden change of plans?"

"I've given this a lot of thought during the past few days." Morgan paused as if debating how to break the news. "Truth is...I want to meet Savannah."

Amanda recoiled sharply, her lips parted in a silent gasp.

"I know this comes as a surprise, Mom."

More like a lightning bolt. "We've agreed she'll never be part of our family, so why subject yourself to the heartache?"

"Here's the thing. Even though I'll never understand Dad's infidelity, I can't deny that Savannah is my sister."

Amanda's body froze. Did Morgan feel sorry for Savannah, or was her desire to meet her driven by curiosity? Heat flushed through her body. What if the unthinkable happened...and they bonded? "Whatever happens between you two, you can count me out." Amanda winced, shocked by the anger in her voice. "I'm sorry, honey. I have no right to take my anger out on you."

"You don't need to apologize, Mom. If Kevin had a child with another woman, I don't know if I could forgive him." A long moment of silence. "Anyway, we're going to meet for coffee."

A gust of wind sent a shiver through Amanda while a cascade of autumn leaves detached and swirled onto the front lawn. If Jacqueline Landry had wanted Preston to be in her child's life, wouldn't Morgan and Savannah already know each other? She drew in a deep breath. "I suppose I'd be more surprised if you didn't want to satisfy your curiosity. Savannah is, after all, your father's other daughter."

"I knew you'd understand. I'll drive up the day before, and Kevin will come up Thanksgiving morning with a complete dinner, so you'll still be our guest. Sierra's welcome to join us. I have a Zoom call with a client in a few minutes, we'll talk more in a few days."

The moment the call ended, Amanda closed her eyes and dug deep into her memory bank. Why couldn't she remember the reason Preston left home all those years ago?

The front door opened followed by approaching footsteps. Amanda's eyes popped open.

Millie strode over. "What's with the long face? Did someone just call with bad news?"

"More disappointing than bad. Morgan and Kevin are coming here for Thanksgiving."

"Interesting." Millie settled on the rocker beside Amanda, her curiosity obviously on overdrive. "She wants to meet Savannah, doesn't she?"

Feigning astonishment, Amanda raised a brow. "What gave you that ridiculous idea?"

"Human nature. Plus, your exaggerated reaction confirms my suspicion."

"You might as well lower your antenna, detective." Amanda eyed the text pinging her phone while lifting off her chair. "A friend is inviting me to lunch."

"Tell Gary hi for me."

Resisting a cutting remark, Amanda turned away from Millie and headed to the stairs. She hadn't communicated with Gary since showing up at his office to end their romantic relationship. Should she meet him for lunch or come up with an excuse to decline? She slowed her pace. One of her responsibilities as Awesam's president was protecting the company's reputation, and his text made it clear he was inviting her as a friend. Besides, if she accepted his invitation, wouldn't she confirm that their relationship fell squarely in the friendship category? Before she could back out, she responded to the text.

Thirty minutes after making the decision, Amanda pulled into a parking spot a block from Southern Charm Restaurant. Hoping she hadn't made a big mistake, she climbed out and dashed across the street. Her pulse accelerated when she spotted Gary waiting for her on the restaurant's front porch. She extended her hand as if meeting her banker to close a business deal. "Mr. Redding."

Taking her cue, Gary shook her hand. "Ms. Smith."

The hostess seemed to eye them with suspicion before escorting them to a corner booth.

Gary settled across from Amanda. "Anything new happening at Hilltop?"

Her posture remained poised while her fingers laced tightly on her lap. Afraid to make eye contact, she focused on Gary's tie. "Millie will prepare

Thanksgiving for a family staying at the inn. It's interesting how her idea to offer private dinners to guests has been such a financial success."

"You and your partners are smart businesswomen."

"We've learned a lot since moving to Blue Ridge." Amanda's eyes skimmed to the waitress approaching their table.

After the young woman delivered menus and the restaurant's signature bread, she took their drink orders. When she left, Gary slathered apple butter on his biscuit and took a bite. "Are you spending Thanksgiving with your daughter?"

"Morgan and Kevin are bringing dinner here." Had he noticed her reluctance to make eye contact? "What about you?"

"Linda and Keith invited me to join their family."

How would a friend respond? With kindness, that's how. Amanda unlaced her fingers while peering around the restaurant. "I'm glad you're not spending the holiday alone."

"Last year, my nosy neighbor, Lila, invited me to join her and a woman she thought I should meet. I respectfully declined."

"Maybe next time you should accept, if there is a next time."

Silence settled like a barrier between them. A moment passed. "Lila gave up trying to set me up after she met you."

The waitress returned with their drinks. "Are you ready to order?"

Amanda fidgeted while stealing a quick glance at Gary.

He shook his head, his eyes remaining on Amanda. "We need a few more minutes."

Desperate for a moment to pull her thoughts together, Amanda attempted to focus on her menu. Had her comment about accepting his neighbor's next invitation been too brash? Sensing he was still staring at her, Amanda looked up from her menu. "What?"

"Do you know what you want?"

She blinked. His tone, the way his eyes fixed on hers...was he talking about lunch or something else?

"It isn't a trick question."

Struggling to prevent the heat warming her neck from migrating to her cheeks, Amanda cleared her throat. "The B.L.T."

"Good choice." After signaling their waitress and ordering the same, Gary polished off a second biscuit. "Britany, the woman who cuts my hair, hired Savannah to work in her salon."

Startled, Amanda met his eyes for a second. *Chris Armstrong's former girlfriend*? "Didn't you tell me you weren't tuned in to local gossip?"

"Would you rather I hadn't told you?"

Amanda shrugged. "Doesn't matter one way or the other." Had her tone contradicted her words? Time to change the subject. "Won't be long before Keith begins his new position as our district attorney."

"A few more weeks. You and I ran one heck of a campaign, especially for two political rookies."

"Four if you count Keith and Linda."

"It helps when your opponent is one corrupt politician." Gary reached for his iced tea. "If the opportunity ever presents itself, I'd manage another campaign. What about you?"

"Depends on the candidate and the office." After she and Gary had spent months helping Keith win the election, why did idle conversation suddenly feel so awkward? Because as much as she didn't want to admit the truth, sitting this close to Gary still stirred her emotions. Was he experiencing the same sensation? "Morgan wants to meet her half-sister." Amanda flinched, shocked she'd rerouted the conversation back to Savannah. Maybe the need to speak her mind superseded common sense.

"How are you taking the news?"

"I'm not happy with her decision." Amanda wrapped her fingers around her water glass. "I hope once my daughter's curiosity is satisfied, she won't want to see Savannah again."

"There's always a possibility they'll hit it off."

"Because they happen to share the same DNA as the man who cheated on me?" Amanda's tone screamed of anger. "Sorry. That's the second time today I've taken my anger out on someone I...count as a friend."

"Any time you need to yell at someone, I'm your guy." The hint of a smile warmed his face. "That is, if you don't swing at me with a powerful left hook. My reputation as a tough-guy banker would be toast if folks found out I'd been beaten up by a woman, even if she was a redhead."

Gary's lighthearted banter eased the tension gripping Amanda's muscles. "I promise no left hooks."

"In that case, I'll consider it safe to meet you for lunch from time to time."

Her eyes met his. "As friends, right?"

He hesitated, his focus remaining locked on her. "As friends." His tone belied his words.

When Amanda opened her mouth to respond, words failed to form.

Gary reached across the table and touched her arm. "Unless one day you find the courage to trust me with your heart."

Her lips trembled while she struggled to hold back the cry forming in her throat. "Friendship is all my heart will allow."

His eyes seemed to search her face, as if hoping to find even a small crack in her resolve. "As long as you don't shut me out, I'll accept our relationship on whatever terms make you comfortable."

For a brief moment, the tenderness in his tone compelled her to question her decision...until images of the three men who had betrayed her returned with a vengeance. "I value your friendship too much to shut you out." Her eyes remained locked on his. "As long as you understand that my emotional wounds are too deep to heal."

"For your sake, I hope one day those wounds will fade. If they do, I'll still be here...as your friend."

For a brief moment, Amanda gazed deep into his eyes. Was it possible time would heal what betrayal had broken?

Chapter 24

Two hours before it was time for her to head home, the Crisis Center buzzer sent Abby wheeling down the hall to the front entrance. She pressed the intercom. "Can I help you?"

"It's Deputy Gibson. We have a situation."

Recognizing his voice, Abby released the lock.

The door eased toward her. The officer stepped inside with an oversized duffel swung over his shoulder. One hand gripped a teenaged girl's arm; the other held a young child's hand. The teenager's scowl made it clear she hadn't come voluntarily. "Their mother is hospitalized with a skull fracture, and the man who hurt her is jailed for domestic violence and firing on a law enforcement officer."

The older girl wrenched her arm away from the deputy. "No way I'll let you or anyone else take my sister away from me and put her in the foster system."

"Separating you two isn't our intention." The deputy set the duffel on the floor. "Bringing you here to keep you safe is our duty."

"Officer Gibson is right about this being a safe place." Confident she could manage the situation, Abby nodded at the deputy, signaling for him to leave. After he walked out, she peered up at the older sister. "My name's Abby. What's yours?"

The teenager pressed her lips tight while eyeing her with more than a little suspicion.

Recognizing she needed to earn the girl's trust, Abby motioned toward the center's comfort dog heading straight to the younger sister. "Meet Lucky, our canine welcoming committee of one."

The child bent down and wrapped her arms around the golden retriever's neck. "Our dog ran away after Daddy threw him out to the backyard."

"Lucky loves living here. He won't run away." Abby turned her attention back to the older sister. "I suppose I could call you big sister and little sister. Although that might be confusing for the other folks staying with us. If I shortened the names to initials, everyone would call you B.S."

The teenager's features softened for a brief moment, the hint of a grin tugging at her lips. "My name's Autumn. My sister is Summer. If we had a kid brother, our mother probably would have named him Winter." Her tone mocked.

Summer thumped her sister's arm. "I like my name."

"I like both of your names." Abby's eyes remained focused on Autumn. "If you and Summer come with me, I'll help you settle in."

Autumn lifted the duffel off the floor. "Don't count on us staying around for more than a couple of days."

"This isn't prison. You're free to leave whenever you choose." Confident they would follow her, Abby spun her wheelchair around and headed down the hall. She stopped beside her office. "Please come into my home away from home."

Summer glanced up at her sister as if asking for permission. Responding to her nod, she hastened to the loveseat. Lucky followed and planted his hindquarter on the floor beside her. His tail slapped the floor as he plopped his head on her lap.

Autumn ambled in, sat beside her sister, and placed the duffel at her feet. "Now what? You grill us about our lousy family life?"

Abby wheeled close. "First I want to know more about you two, starting with how old you are."

"I'm a few months short of eighteen and capable of taking care of me and Summer without anyone butting in."

Abby nodded. "I can tell you're a responsible young woman." She turned her attention to Summer. "How old are you?"

"I'm seven and a half."

"When I was about your age, my mom and I ran away from home because my father wouldn't stop hitting her. We stayed in a nice place like this for a while."

The young girl's eyes widened. "Did you ever go back home?"

Abby shook her head. "We moved to a new town. Now Mom's married to a wonderful man who loves her and never hits her."

Autumn folded her arms tight across her chest. "No matter how many times that man beat her up, Mom refused to kick him out or press charges. She even begged me not to turn him in, saying it was her fault he couldn't control his temper. Today when he knocked her unconscious, I called 911."

"You made the right decision. Is he your biological father?"

"The creep is our mother's live-in scumbag boyfriend. Our real father's serving a life sentence for murder." Autumn's tone screamed of anger. "Proof Mom has lousy taste in men. What she does with her life doesn't much matter anymore. In a few months when I turn eighteen, the state will consider me an adult. That's when I'll need a tough female lawyer to help me fight for custody of my sister so we can move somewhere far away."

"Summer is blessed to have a big sister who looks out for her." Abby's voice hinted of heartfelt understanding.

Autumn looped her arm around her sister's elbow. "She deserves a better life than we've had up to this point."

"You both do." Abby inched her chair closer to the sisters. "If you're willing to stay here until you turn eighteen, I promise to put you in touch with an attorney who can help you."

Autumn cocked her head to the side. "How do I know I can trust you to keep your word?"

"If I were in your shoes, I'd ask the same question. To prove you can count on me, I'll reach out to an attorney before I leave today."

Autumn hesitated, her brows pinched. "Why would you do that for us?"

"Because I can tell you have a good heart."

A long moment passed before Autumn's brows unfurrowed. "You're not much older than me. What made you decide to work in a place like this?"

Abby eyed Tommy's photo on her desk. "I've come to understand that every experience shapes who we are. I suppose all those months my mother and I lived in a crisis center—plus everything that happened after we left—prepared my heart to help families in crisis."

Summer pointed to Abby's legs. "Are you in a wheelchair because you're paralyzed?"

"Good question. An accident damaged my spinal cord but not permanently. Three times a week, I go to therapy to learn how to walk again." Summer's eyes widened while she described the process. When finished, Abby's attention shifted back to her big sister. "Now that you know a lot about me, how about you and Summer agreeing to stay here for a few months?"

Summer stroked Lucky's muzzle. "I don't mind living here."

Autumn scanned the room, seemingly looking for a reason to agree. "Would we have our own room?"

Progress. "Yes, with twin beds, a sitting area, and a private bathroom. Plus we'll make sure you'll both continue to go to school."

Autumn grabbed the duffel. "The only reason I'll agree is because you promise to find me a good lawyer."

"All right then. We have a deal. Come with me, and I'll show you around." She led the way out of her office and down the hall, stopping beside the combination kitchen and dining room. "Everyone who stays here pitches in to prepare meals." She wheeled to the next door. "This classroom is where the children are tutored."

A girl sitting at one of the tables waved. Summer waved back. "They don't go to school?"

Abby shook her head. "They're safe here. You'll like Bonnie. She's the same age as you."

"What if I want to go to school here too?"

"You and your sister can decide what's best." Abby rolled past the door to the newly installed elevator. "Our suites are on the second floor."

Summer stepped inside. "Is this kinda like a hotel?"

"Even better. You won't have to pay to stay here."

Summer pressed the button for the second floor. "Me and Autumn never stayed in a hotel."

"We never went anywhere." Autumn scoffed. "Most months we barely had enough money to buy food and pay the rent."

While the elevator rose, an idea began to take root. Abby made a mental note to contact Sierra. When the doors yawned open, she led the way to the end of the hall. "Welcome to your private suite."

Autumn followed her sister into the room. A chest of drawers separated twin beds adorned with pale blue comforters and sunshine yellow throw pillows. An oversized ottoman separated the dark blue and white striped sofa from the flat screen television atop a second dresser. A desk and chair placed in front of a window completed the arrangement.

Summer stepped into the bathroom. "This is way nicer than our house."

"Bet this fancy room doesn't come with room service." Autumn's tone hinted of humor.

"Not exactly but sort of."

Autumn set the duffel in the closet. "Meaning Summer and I are responsible to keep our room neat and clean?"

"I was right about you being smart. You'll find all the supplies you need under the bathroom sink." Abby wheeled her chair toward the hall. "After you settle in, come back to my office."

"So you can tell us about all the rules you'll make us follow?"

"Know what I think?"

"That I'm gonna end up becoming a giant pain in your backside?"

"Probably. I also believe you and I are destined to become good friends." Abby wheeled out to the hall before Autumn had a chance to respond. The moment she returned to her office, she pulled her phone from her pocket and tapped Wendy's number.

She answered. "Hey, what's up?"

"I have a favor." Abby explained Autumn's request for a lawyer. "I'm thinking the new attorney at Armstrong Law Office would be perfect."

"Regina's coming over for dinner tonight. Chris and I will talk to her and let you know tomorrow."

"Thanks." The moment the call ended, Abby texted Sierra. After reading her response, she settled in to wait for Autumn and Summer to return. The same time they walked into her office, the front door buzzer sounded. "Wait here. There's someone I want you to meet." Abby wheeled down the hall then returned. "Meet my close friend, Sierra. She's living proof that you can overcome your past and create a bright future."

While Sierra told her story, beginning with leaving her baby on the crisis center doorstep, a sensation similar to a first deep breath after letting go of a heavy burden flowed over Abby. She pressed her palms together, confident that God was working behind the scenes to turn Autumn and Summer's tragedy into victory.

Chapter 25

The succulent aroma of chili wafted through the space as the thrum of a car engine drew Wendy to her kitchen window. Armstrong Law's new partner followed Chris's car up the driveway. While Ryan and Duke hastened to the back door, Wendy made her way to the front entrance. She stepped onto the porch, folding her arms across her chest to ward off the cold breeze.

Regina pocketed her keys then strode from her car to the steps. "Thanks for the invite."

"We're delighted you're joining us."

"I never turn down a homecooked meal with good friends."

Wendy led the way inside, closing the door behind them. "We're casual tonight."

"Casual suits me fine." Regina peeled out of her jacket.

Zach, his shoulders sagging from the weight of his book bag, walked into the kitchen from the garage. He sniffed. "Smells like chili."

"With slaw and cornbread. Dinner's served in fifteen minutes."

"No need to call. I'll show up on time." Zach brushed past Wendy without making eye contact with her or Regina.

While he headed toward the stairs, Wendy's focus shifted to the sealed envelope on the end table beside the sofa. Giving Zach the letter from his father would have to wait until after dinner.

Chris stepped inside and set down his briefcase then held Ryan's hand while approaching their guest. "Our little guy is happy to see you."

Regina patted Ryan's head. "Your daddy's mighty proud of you. Maybe you'll grow up to become a fourth-generation Armstrong lawyer."

"Or a successful business owner like his mother. What would you like to drink?"

"Beer if you have any."

"Coming right up." Chris released Ryan's hand then pulled two bottles from the fridge and twisted off the caps. He handed one to Regina, motioned to the stools on the other side of the counter, then followed and sat beside her.

Wendy stood across from her husband and their guest. "Before we settle down at our table, I have a proposal to run by you two."

Chris set down his beer. "Legal or personal?"

"Both. A seventeen-year-old girl and her little sister arrived at the crisis center earlier today." Wendy relayed their story and Autumn's request for a tough female attorney. "Based on everything Chris has told me, I'm convinced you're the perfect person to help her."

A mischievous grin curled Regina's lips. "What do you call a lawyer's pro bono case?"

Wendy mirrored her expression. "A free trial?"

Regina elbowed Chris. "You nailed it when you described your wife as gorgeous and smart."

He winked at Wendy. "I definitely married up."

"Don't let my husband kid you. He's the real brains in our family. Back to the request." Wendy adopted a more serious expression. "Are you willing to take Autumn's case?"

Regina wrapped her fingers around her beer. "During my years as an assistant district attorney, I successfully prosecuted more than a dozen domestic violence cases. Ironic that my next case will be defending a victim."

Wendy tilted her head. "Are you saying you'll take the case?"

"Considering two of my three cases as an Armstrong Law associate have generated zero revenue, I'll need Chris's approval to work for free."

"Which you have." Chris faced Wendy. "If I turned down a request from one of Awesam's partners, I'd have five of the smartest women I know hounding me until I agreed."

"Thank you, darling. Now for my second request." Wendy's attention returned to Regina. "According to Abby, Autumn has a serious problem with trust issues—"

"Meaning I need to meet with my new client ASAP, right?"

Wendy nodded. "Will tomorrow work for you?"

Regina chuckled. "You're as tough as your husband. I'll work her into my schedule tomorrow afternoon. You understand I'll need to wait until her birthday to bring the case to court."

"Of course." Wendy retrieved her phone and texted Autumn. Moments later a ping signaled a return text. She smiled while turning her phone toward Regina. "You can add Autumn as your newest fan."

Regina snapped her fingers. "The count is up to seven. Before long I'll rack up a dozen. Even better, I won't be threatened by crazy people who believed their criminal family members didn't deserve jail sentences. Life as a big-city prosecutor."

Wendy and Chris shared a knowing look. Despite the rarity of capital crimes in their district, there was always a chance a disgruntled relative would hold Keith responsible for doing his job as the new district attorney.

Regina's eyes shifted from Wendy to Chris, then back to Wendy. "Don't worry about your father-in-law's safety. One fact I've already learned about

Blue Ridge; if anyone dared to threaten Keith, an army of citizens would protect him from the crazies. It's one of the reasons I changed sides and moved to a small town."

Chris faced Regina. "How many times were you threatened?"

"Fortunately, only three times in my thirty-year career. Enough legal jargon. This morning I signed a contract for a house with a fenced backyard. When I close, my first mission will be adopting a housebroken pooch."

Chris clicked his beer to Regina's. "Welcome to the community of dog lovers."

"One more big change in my world."

Zach emerged from downstairs. "Fifteen minutes is up."

Wendy nodded. "You're right. How about giving me a hand?"

"Whatever."

Regina shook her finger at him. "Whatever is not a respectful answer, young man."

Zach smirked.

"Neither is that response."

He hesitated, avoiding eye contact with Regina. "Glad to help."

She nodded. "Much better."

Wendy's eyes widened. The woman who'd never had children obviously knew how to handle an obstinate teenager. She pointed to four soup mugs. "Fill those with chili while I take the slaw and cornbread to the table."

During the meal, conversation focused on small-town life, the best dog breeds, and realistic crime-focused television shows. Other than uttering a single sentence touting online gaming, Zach remained silent. After they finished dessert, Regina pointed her finger at him. "You go help Wendy clean up while Chris walks me to my car."

"Yes, ma'am." Zach stood and began gathering dishes.

Stifling a chuckle, Wendy lifted Ryan off his booster seat before assuming kitchen duty. Chris returned to pitch in. When they finished, Zach shoved his hands in his pockets. "Can I go to my room now?"

"Not yet." Wendy's eyes met Zach's. "A letter from your dad arrived in today's mail."

"Did you read it?"

She shook her head. "Opening another person's mail is illegal."

Zach's body stiffened, his jaw clenched. "Where is it?"

"On the table beside the sofa." He wavered before shuffling across the space.

Chris and Wendy followed with Ryan toddling behind them. "Do you want us to leave you alone while you read what your dad wrote?"

Zach stared at the envelope. "I want you to read it to me." He moved to the hearth and stood facing the fireplace with his arms folded across his chest.

Wendy settled on the sofa while Ryan toddled to his toy basket.

Chris plucked the envelope off the end table before sitting beside her. He slid his finger under the flap then removed and unfolded a single sheet of paper. "Are you ready?"

Zach shrugged. "I guess."

"All right then, here goes."

Dear Zach,

After reading your letter twice, I wrote and ripped up four responses. Each one was a little less angry and a little more reflective. Facing the truth doesn't come easy for a man who believed devoting excessive hours to generating income was what a family expected and needed from a father.

During these past few days, I've come to accept the fact that while owning and operating Gilmore's requires a substantial time commitment, performing every night feeds my ego. Especially since I am one of many talented

Nashville singers who aren't quite good enough to become country-music stars.

Your letter shocked me into reality. While I have succeeded as a small-time entertainer and provider, I have failed as a father. Asking for your forgiveness is the first step in making amends. The second is changing my priorities. To that end I will hire a singer to perform in my place every night except Friday and Saturday. Every other night I will be at home with you and your sisters. Tomorrow I will promote my assistant to general manager and delegate more of the business responsibilities to her, which will also free up more of my time.

In closing, I want to thank you for having the courage to tell me how you feel. In time I hope to prove worthy of being your father.

Love,

Dad

Chris folded the letter then slid it back into the envelope and set it on the coffee table. "It took a lot of courage for your father to write that response."

Zach slowly turned to face them while swiping his cheeks, clearly embarrassed by his own dampened eyes. "Can I have my phone back so I can call Dad?"

"Yes." Chris hastened to their bedroom, then returned and handed the phone to Zach. "You need to return it to me tomorrow morning."

"What—" Zach stopped abruptly as if swallowing the word 'ever.' After pocketing his phone, he headed down to the terrace level.

Chris dropped onto the sofa beside Wendy. "It seems healing has begun for the Gilmore family."

"I paid close attention to my brother's body language while you read the letter. The way his shoulders stiffened. More than Brent's absence is bothering him. Maybe it's something he or one of his friends has done."

"Based on Zach's comments, the kids he hangs out with consider stealing acceptable. That's one big problem Brent will have to face head-on when his son returns home."

Chapter 26

Seconds after Amanda eased up her home's driveway, Wendy, bundled in a coat with a fur collar, dashed out and climbed onto the passenger seat. "Wouldn't you know a cold front would move in today of all days." She buckled her seatbelt. "Reminds me of the morning you, Erica, and I first met."

Amanda backed up and turned around. "When you talked us into shopping before all the stores closed."

"With a snow storm heading to Blue Ridge, you needed a proper coat. Instead you bought a hooded sweatshirt."

At the end of the driveway, Amanda turned right. "Because I didn't have the slightest notion I'd end up living anywhere except in New Orleans."

"Same thing I thought about Gulfport." Wendy paused. "That morning Chris met us in the dining room to tell us we were all married to the same man, I had no idea I'd end up marrying him."

"His fate was sealed the moment you began flirting with him."

Wendy huffed. "I did no such thing."

"Yeah, you did." Amanda grinned while glancing at her. "Do you remember what we did the day after Chris read Gunter's letter to us?"

"Are you talking about him treating us to lunch at Harvest on Main?"

"Uh-huh." Amanda turned onto the main road to town. "You asked Chris if he was married. When he said no and wanted to know why you were asking, you said…and I quote 'Because you'd make someone an awesome husband.'"

Wendy giggled. "You obviously mistook Southern charm for flirtation."

"Whether charm or shameless flirtation, you captured his heart."

"Growing up in foster homes, I sometimes dreamed of marrying a prince and living in a big white castle." Wendy ran her fingers along her seatbelt. "Turns out my prince has a law degree and lives in a cozy cabin in the woods."

"Like the family in *Sugar Snow*."

Wendy nodded. "The last gift from Mom before she abandoned me. Now I read the story to my son. Although I still haven't explained why a miniature snowman lives in our freezer."

Amanda chuckled. "The three of us are the only women on the planet who spent a perfectly good afternoon creating a miniature snow family on a front porch railing."

"You and Erica were good sports to go along with my crazy idea."

"We humored you."

Wendy reached across the console and thumped Amanda's arm. "You might as well admit you had almost as much fun as I had turning snow into cute little people."

"Too bad there isn't a Guinness World Record category for the largest miniature snow village."

"We'd definitely win that competition." Wendy paused. "Since I met you two and Chris, I've collected way more happy memories than I did during my first twenty-three years. Little did we know that in a town as small as Blue Ridge, we'd each find the perfect man."

Amanda rolled her eyes. "Clever move, weaseling your way into a conversation about Gary."

"Now that you've brought the subject up—"

"I didn't, so here's the deal. Gary and I have agreed to remain friends. Nothing more." Amanda glanced in her rearview mirror. "And yes, I know he'll also attend Keith's surprise birthday party, so how about we drop the subject."

"Except that event is the reason we're on a shopping mission."

"To buy gifts for your father-in-law, not to discuss the guest list. Understood?"

Wendy zipped her fingers across her lips.

Stifling a chuckle, Amanda turned off the main road and found a parking space on East Main beside the train station. They climbed out and walked across the street. "Any idea what Keith might like?"

"Linda suggested shirts or sweaters." Wendy stopped beside a women's boutique where Amanda had bought the hooded sweatshirt during their first shopping trip. "Every time I walk by here, I remember my humiliation when my credit card was declined. Even though you acted as if you hadn't heard, I knew you had."

"After you'd bragged about what you'd bought the day before, I assumed you'd maxed out your card."

"I had no idea Gunter hadn't paid a dime on the balance for months."

"At least there was a positive result from the incident." Amanda looped her arm around Wendy's elbow. "That day you began recovering from a serious shopping addiction."

"Encouraged by Gunter." Wendy sighed. "Probably because he figured if I spent enough time and energy shopping, I wouldn't question why he spent so much time away from home."

"The mind of a devious con artist."

"Good news is I haven't heard from him since Chris responded to his last letter. Hopefully he finally got the message." They resumed walking until they arrived at a men's clothing store. After browsing, they each chose pullover sweaters. "Not very exciting but practical."

"A fitting gift for our next district attorney." Amanda followed Wendy out to the sidewalk. "Do you have time for lunch?"

"I do. Is Harvest on Main okay with you? Hopefully there won't be a crowd this early."

Amanda hesitated for a brief moment. Suggesting they choose another restaurant would raise unwanted questions. "Works for me." They crossed the street, headed toward the end of the block, and climbed onto the restaurant's lodge-like front porch. Wendy had been right about beating the crowds. They followed the hostess to a table along the wall—the same table where she and Gary had last dined. Forcing the memory aside, Amanda sat across from Wendy and set Keith's gift on the floor.

Their server arrived with menus. "Welcome to Harvest on Main. Have you dined with us before?"

Wendy smiled up at the young woman. "The first time a couple of days after the once-in-a-century blizzard."

"When the entire town closed." Their server took their drink orders then walked away.

Amanda focused on the menu. "Wild gulf shrimp sounds delish."

Wendy nodded. "A little taste of Southern Mississippi."

"Do you ever miss living on the coast?"

"Every once in a while, I miss the sound of the surf and the salty aromas of the sea. Then I remember the hurricanes and mosquitoes."

Amanda chuckled. "Two more reasons why we're glad we moved to North Georgia."

"Definitely." Wendy brows raised, her eyes seemingly fixed on the entrance. She leaned close to the table. "You won't believe who just walked in with Chris's former girlfriend."

Amanda's chest tightened, hoping she was wrong while knowing she was right. The moment she turned her head, Savannah and Britany followed the hostess to a table on the opposite side of the restaurant. Unable to turn away, her eyes remained glued on the new arrivals. Her body froze the moment Savannah lowered onto a chair and turned in her direction. Their eyes met. With a sharp intake of air, Amanda looked away.

Wendy reached across the table and touched her arm. "We can leave if you're uncomfortable staying."

"I'm fine."

"Are you sure?"

At least Savannah had honored her commitment to pretend they didn't know each other. "I have to accept the fact that I'm bound to run into her occasionally." Amanda refocused her attention on the menu. "When I first told Morgan about her father's love child, she wanted nothing to do with her. Now she plans to meet her."

Wendy pushed her menu aside. "Becoming acquainted with siblings I didn't know existed turned out to be a blessing for me and my family."

"Even though I don't approve, I understand Morgan's motivation. The cold hard fact is Preston cheated on me, not on his daughter."

"One day before long—for Morgan's sake—you need to stop pretending you don't know Savannah."

Amanda sneaked a quick glance across the room. Her stepdaughter's chin tilted down, her eyes seemingly focused on her menu. Was she also reeling from the encounter? Amanda turned away. Although difficult to accept, deep down she knew Wendy was right.

Chapter 27

Following a sleepless night after yesterday's silent encounter with Savannah, Amanda carried breakfast dishes from Hilltop's dining room to the kitchen sink and squeezed her eyes closed. The pain lingering in her stepdaughter's expression the moment their eyes met a second time had been raw, almost suffocating and impossible to ignore. Startled by a touch, Amanda spun away from the sink.

"If you want to talk about whatever's bothering you, I'm ready to listen."

Given Millie's fine-tuned observation skills, denying reality would be a big waste of time. Maybe confiding would help ease the guilt weighing her down. "Something happened yesterday when Wendy and I stopped for lunch." She refreshed her coffee then skirted the island and climbed onto a stool.

Millie followed and sat beside her. "You chanced upon Savannah, didn't you?"

Amanda stared at her. "Who told you?"

"You did just now."

Amanda rolled her eyes. "Clever ploy, detective."

"You're an easy target." Millie swiveled toward her. "Now that I've discovered what happened, you might as well spill the rest of the details.

Where did you see her? How did she react? Have you changed your mind about forming a relationship with her?"

"Hold onto your chickens already. One question at a time." Amanda relayed the incident at Harvest on Main. "I can't shake the look I saw in her eyes."

Millie's eyes seemingly clouded with something heavy. She turned her face away from Amanda. "You know that I married Rupert on the rebound from an illicit love affair with a married man."

"At least after you married Rupert, you didn't cheat on him."

"Not physically. My misguided loyalty to a fantasy nearly destroyed our marriage." Millie turned back toward Amanda. "You and Preston's daughter are both struggling to deal with the loss of innocence. Savannah because her mother spent years lying about her father and that he hadn't wanted her in his life."

"She should have settled someplace far away from here to put the past behind her and move on with her life."

"When Rupert learned my heart foolishly belonged to another man, he had every right to end our marriage. Fortunately, he preferred an imperfect relationship over none at all. Perhaps that's the reason Savannah didn't leave Blue Ridge."

"Seeing her walk into the restaurant..." Amanda struggled to hold back the cry rising in her throat.

"She serves as a reminder that Preston was an imperfect man." Millie placed her hand on Amanda's arm. "Forgiving him is the only way you'll overcome your pain and move on with your life."

"If Preston had trusted me with the truth..." Amanda paused for a long moment. "It was easier to forgive Gunter for his deception. Truth was, I married him because I believed he would provide what my daughter and I needed financially. I always thought Morgan failed to warm up to him because she missed her father. Now I understand that even as a child she sensed he wasn't a good man."

"Maybe Savannah needs to hear that her father was a good person."

Millie's comment struck a chord in Amanda's soul. Had her wounded pride compelled her to reject Preston's other daughter? Even though she would never trust her heart to another man, could she accept Savannah as her stepdaughter?

Millie withdrew her hand. "You have a lot to think about."

"Believe it or not, I appreciate your words of wisdom."

"You're the daughter I never had. Besides, I haven't lived this long without learning a thing or two about relationships."

Eager to end the conversation, Amanda glanced at her watch. "Time to cover Bernie's housekeeping duties." She slid off the stool then headed up the back staircase. After retrieving cleaning supplies from the linen closet, she unlocked the Butterfly Suite and stepped inside. Two years ago the ceiling in the upstairs turret room was collapsed, opening a gaping hole to the unfinished third floor. If only mending broken hearts were as easy as repairing damaged rooms.

After preparing the suite for new arrivals, Amanda moved across the hall to the Dogwood Suite. She froze at the door, her hand gripping the doorknob, her eyes squeezed shut. The last time she'd entered the room, Savannah had revealed her mother's journal.

"No need to clean this suite today."

Amanda's eyes popped open at the sound of Millie's voice.

"It isn't reserved until the day after tomorrow when Bernie returns from her two days off."

"Thanks for reminding me." Amanda pulled her hand off the doorknob. "The couple who reserved the Butterfly Suite requested an early check-in. If you don't mind putting the supplies away, I'll wait for them to arrive."

"Glad to help."

Amanda placed her hand on Millie's arm. "Thank you for caring."

"You're welcome." Millie patted her hand the moment the doorbell rang. "Time to turn on your innkeeper charm and go greet our guests."

Remembering the reserving couples' last name, Amanda rushed down the front stairs, summoned her best smile, and opened the door. "Welcome to Hilltop Inn, Mr. and Mrs. Cooper." After delivering her standard spiel and escorting the couple to the Butterfly Suite, Amanda retrieved her coat from the kitchen then exited to the backyard. The bright sun did little to offset the cold air, sending her rushing across the driveway and side yard to the ranch house.

When she entered the kitchen, Dusty greeted her with a tail wag. She patted the dog's head then dropped a teabag in a mug of water, placed it in the microwave, and set the timer. After peeling out of her coat, she carried the hot tea to her bedroom, and settled in the chair beside the window. Dusty followed and sprawled on the floor between her chair and bed. She lifted her book off the end table and opened to the bookmarked page. Halfway through the chapter, she struggled to keep her eyes open. Giving in to exhaustion, she leaned back, closed her eyes, and drifted to sleep.

After what seemed like no more than a few minutes, the doorbell and Dusty's muffled bark awakened her. Amanda glanced at her bedside clock. She had slept for nearly two hours. Struggling to find her bearings, she hastened to the front door and glanced through the peep hole. The young man looked familiar. Amanda blinked. Dereck Hackett, Theo's father. She hesitated a moment then pulled the door open. "Sierra isn't home from work."

He removed his ball cap. "Do you mind if I wait for her inside?"

"Is she expecting you?"

"I don't think so."

"Either she is or she isn't."

His chin tilted down a fraction. "She don't know."

Amanda hesitated. At least he seemed harmless enough. "Are you alone?"

"Yes, ma'am."

"Well, all right then, you might as well come on in."

He stepped across the threshold. "I'm not here to cause no trouble."

Dusty wagged her tail as if confirming the young man's statement.

Amanda closed the door then led the way to the den. "Are you thirsty? Would you like a glass of water or a cup of hot tea?"

"Water's good." Responding to Amanda's gesture, Dereck lowered onto the sofa and set his ball cap on the cushion beside him.

After hastening to the kitchen then returning with a glass of ice water, Amanda settled on a club chair. Her eyes drifted to the Tennessee Titans logo on his sweatshirt. "I assume you're a football fan."

"Yes, ma'am."

Irritated by the word *ma'am*, Amanda crossed one leg over the other. "I prefer you call me Ms. Smith."

"Okay." Dereck fidgeted, his eyes darting around the room.

"You seem as nervous as a mouse in a roomful of kitties."

"I guess 'cause of what happened the last time I was here, when the old lady—"

"You mean Ms. Millie?"

Dereck nodded. "When she sort of threatened me."

Because you impregnated Sierra when she was technically still a minor. "No one's planning to have you arrested..." Amanda clamped her mouth shut to avoid adding 'like your brother.'

Dereck sipped his water then set the glass on a coffee table coaster. "Do you mind if I go to the bathroom?"

He really was nervous. "Around the corner. First door on the right."

"Thanks."

When he walked away, Amanda glanced at her watch. Today was an early-release day, meaning Sierra was due home any minute. She uncrossed then crossed her legs again. What was the real reason Dereck had driven all the way from Chattanooga?

He returned to the sofa, scratching his head. "How's Theo doing?"

Amanda hesitated. Why not respond? After all, he was the child's legal father. "The boy's thriving."

He blinked, perhaps wondering why she hadn't referred to Theo as his son.

Sierra breezed in from the carport with Theo in her arms. She stopped beside the sofa, peering down at Dereck. "Hey."

Astonished that Sierra didn't seem all that surprised to see him, Amanda stood. "I'll give you two some privacy." She eased past them and headed to her room, leaving the door open.

For the better part of an hour, Amanda attempted to read while keeping her ears tuned to any sign of trouble. Seconds after hearing the front door closing, she headed straight to the foyer where Sierra hiked Theo on her left hip while clutching bills in her right hand. "What's going on?"

"Dereck gave me money to help with expenses." She carried her child to his playpen then plopped onto the sofa and set the cash on the coffee table. "He's trying his best to be a good man and help take care of me and Theo."

Unsure how to respond, Amanda took a seat beside her. "With enough time, I suppose anyone can change."

Sierra picked at a fingernail, seemingly avoiding eye contact. "I invited him to celebrate Thanksgiving with us."

Speechless, Amanda's jaw tightened.

Sierra let out a slow breath. "If you want, I'll call him and tell him not to come."

Amanda's shoulders slumped under the weight of her shame. She had no right to deny Theo access to his father. "This is your home too. You're welcome to invite whomever you want."

"Thank you for understanding. Given enough time, everything will work out the way it's supposed to."

Resisting the urge to express skepticism, Amanda forced a smile and patted Sierra's arm. "I suppose you're right."

Chapter 28

The day before Thanksgiving, thoughts played havoc with Amanda's emotions while she read Morgan's text for the fourth time. Her daughter's ETA was only five minutes from now. Desperate to alleviate the emerging tension headache, she swallowed two aspirin then massaged her temples with slow circular motions. Maybe meeting Savannah would satisfy Morgan's curiosity and help her move on. Unless...what if they bonded? Impossible. Morgan would never form a relationship with her. Would she?

Gary's ringtone startled Amanda. She hesitated, torn between accepting and ignoring his call. Considering they'd agreed on remaining friends, there was no reason not to answer. She grabbed her phone and tapped the screen. "Hey. What's going on?"

"I wanted to make sure you're okay."

"Other than a massive headache and bewilderment over Morgan's morbid curiosity, I'm fine." Shocked by her harsh tone, Amanda winced. "Sorry. I don't mean to take my frustration out on you."

"Better on your pal than on your daughter."

"I still don't understand why Morgan changed her mind about meeting Savannah. Especially since Preston betrayed her as much as he did me."

"Do you mind a little advice from your friendly bank president?"

Amanda leaned back against the kitchen counter, imagining Gary sitting behind his desk counseling a client. "Go ahead, Mr. President, and lay your advice on me."

"I suggest you rein in your emotions at least enough to appear neutral."

"What's the point? Morgan already knows how I feel."

"To prevent her from feeling guilty about betraying you."

Amanda pressed her lips tight, willing the flood of emotion to wash away. She had to admit Gary was right. "I appreciate your honesty, and I'll do my best to heed your advice."

"Glad I could help."

The purr of a car engine sent a shiver racing through Amanda's limbs. "She just drove into the carport."

"I'm available any time you need to talk."

"Thank you." Amanda ended the call then laid her phone on the counter. Controlling her emotions as best she could, she breathed deeply then walked out to the carport. While summoning her best smile, she pulled Morgan into an embrace the moment she climbed out of her car. "How was your trip?"

"Uneventful after I escaped Atlanta traffic."

"Welcome to a slower pace." Amanda released her daughter. "Do you need help with luggage?"

"No thanks." Morgan removed a carry-on bag from her trunk then followed Amanda inside. After Dusty greeted her with an enthusiastic tail wag, she strode to the bedroom Erica had occupied before she married Brad.

Amanda remained at the door. "At least now I have a guest room for you and Kevin."

Morgan smiled as she hoisted her bag onto the bed. "Until you take in another stray soul."

Amanda chuckled. "The only strays I'll take in from now on will need to have four paws and bark."

"What? No stray cats?"

"Felines are Millie's thing, not mine."

Morgan unzipped her suitcase. "Speaking of Millie, anything interesting going on at Hilltop?"

"Tomorrow she and Bernie are scheduled to prepare Thanksgiving dinner for a family that reserved every room. Gordon offered to help them serve."

"Hopefully the guests won't do anything to rouse the mystery club members' suspicions."

"We can count on Gordon to keep Millie from overreacting." Amanda paused. Should she ask about her daughter's plans or wait?

As if on cue, Morgan turned toward her. "I'll head to town in a few minutes to meet Savannah for coffee."

Struggling to heed Gary's advice, Amanda forced her expression to remain neutral. "I'll fix us lunch when you return."

"I don't blame you for not approving my decision, Mom. At the same time, I hope you understand I need to talk to her at least one time." Morgan moved closer. "While I'm gone, decide if you want me to tell you about our conversation."

"I'll think about it."

"Through all our heartaches and disappointments, you and I have always leaned on each other. No matter what happens this morning, we always will."

Amanda brushed a lock of hair—more auburn than red—away from Morgan's cheek. "You're an amazing young woman and my most precious blessing."

"I love you, Mom."

"I love you too, honey."

Morgan eased past Amanda leaving her alone to wrestle with her emotions.

Ten minutes after backing down the driveway, Morgan found a parking space beside the downtown park. She waited for a car to pass before climbing out, then hastened across the street and turned toward Mountain Mama's Coffee Lounge. Her pulse seemed to accelerate with each step. Three feet from the door, a dizzy sensation forced her to halt. She breathed deeply, filling her lungs to capacity.

An elderly woman heading in her direction stopped in front of her. "Are you okay, honey?"

Sensing a flush was seconds from creeping across her cheeks, Morgan released the air and forced a smile. "I'm fine, just a little out of breath."

The woman's brows raised. "Are you sure?"

"I'm positive. Besides, I'm meeting someone for coffee."

The woman smiled as if she understood, then she moved on.

Grateful her pulse had slowed to a nearly normal beat, Morgan walked into Mountain Mama's a few minutes before Savannah was due to arrive. After selecting her drink, she settled at a high-top table facing the door. Would she recognize her half-sister? Before Morgan had time to take her first sip, a stunning dark-haired young woman walked in.

After glancing around, she headed straight to Morgan. "You look a lot like your mother, red hair and all. I'm Savannah."

Relieved her mother had been right about her sister not looking anything like their father, she extended her hand. "I'm Morgan."

Savannah accepted, her fingers as cold as ice. "Sorry for the icy grip. I haven't been this far north long enough to adjust to the cold."

"I know what you mean." Morgan released her hand. "After Mom and I left New Orleans, it took me a while to adjust to the temperature change. Do you have time for a cup of coffee?"

"I do. What did you order?"

"Cappuccino."

"Sounds good."

"I'll wait for you." Morgan's eyes followed Savannah while she made her way to the counter. She seemed normal enough, even pleasant. Her mind drifted to the stormy afternoon she came home from school to find her mother curled up on the sofa in their tiny shotgun house. Her eyes were red, her cheeks stained with tears. In that instant she knew something terrible had happened. Morgan pictured the last photo taken of her family of three before a drunk driver stole her daddy from them. How different would her life have turned out if he had survived the accident?

Savannah returned and slid onto the stool across from Morgan. "How much has your mother told you about me?"

"Everything she read in your mother's journal." Morgan's eyes met Savannah's. "What's the real reason you came to Blue Ridge?"

She held Morgan's gaze for a moment before looking away. "Growing up with a single parent seemed normal until I started kindergarten. That's when I learned that other kids had a mother and a father." Her voice was soft, each word sounding as if pulled from somewhere deep within. "When I asked Mom why I didn't have a daddy, she told me he had died and gone to heaven before I was born."

Stunned, Morgan tightened her fingers around her coffee cup.

"When I learned the truth from Mom's journals, I hated her for lying to me all those years. Until my own guilt broke my heart." Savannah's hand trembled when she lifted her cup and took a sip. "Did your mom tell you I had a relationship with the man who killed my mother?"

Morgan's brow lifted. No way she'd admit her mom had failed to share that detail. "Why don't you tell me your version?"

Savannah stared as if she somehow knew the truth. "His name is Marcel." A faraway look clouded her eyes while the story poured out, ending with Gordon's efforts to have the killer arrested. "Now you know why I can never return to New Orleans."

Morgan gave a slight nod while turning away to gather her thoughts. "One thing I don't understand is why you didn't leave Blue Ridge. Especially after Mom made it clear she doesn't want you in her life."

Savannah remained silent for a long moment, her eyes downcast. "I don't blame her for rejecting me. Discovering I existed after all these years must have broken her heart." Her gaze flicked to Amanda. "When Mom died I was left completely alone."

"Don't you have other family?"

"I didn't until I read Mom's journals and discovered I had a stepmother...and a sister. Now I feel like I belong here. As strange as it might seem, just knowing I'm not alone is comforting." Savannah's gaze flicked to Morgan. "Even though you and I have the same father, I understand why a relationship with you and your mother might never happen."

Torn between loyalty to her mother and empathy for her half-sister, Morgan struggled to find the right words. "Blue Ridge is a small town. At some point you're bound to run into Mom."

"When that happens, we'll both pretend we don't know each other." Savannah fell silent for a long moment. "I hope you realize how blessed you were to have had a daddy who loved you so much he wanted to protect you from the truth."

Morgan gripped her cappuccino with both hands. If her father hadn't kept his affair secret, and if her mother had forgiven him, would she and her sister have grown up as family?

"Please tell your mother that I believe my mom kept her journals secret because she wanted to protect all of us from heartache." Savannah slid off her stool and took a step.

"Wait." When she halted and turned back toward their table, Morgan extended an invitation she had thought impossible a half hour earlier.

Savannah's eyes reddened. "You have no idea how much that means to me." She dabbed at her cheeks then made her way to the exit.

Morgan stared at the coffee cup left behind. Maybe she and her mom were meant to discover the truth. Her focus shifted past the window to the park across the street. A young couple about the same age as Wendy and Chris pushed a stroller along the sidewalk. Morgan blinked, encouraged by Wendy's courage to develop a relationship with siblings she hadn't known existed.

Having failed to focus on work, Amanda set her laptop on the cushion beside her and grabbed the remote. She flipped through the channels twice then tossed the remote aside and headed to her bedroom. Maybe reading would help pass the time. She settled on the chair and opened a book. After reading three paragraphs without comprehending a single word, she set her book down, eased to her dresser, and opened the top drawer.

Amanda removed the ring box, then hesitated a moment before lifting the lid. She gripped her wedding ring between her thumb and forefinger, holding it close to read the inscription. *All my love forever.* Her chest tightened. Had she given Preston a reason not to trust her enough to reveal the truth about his infidelity? Had it been her fault he had left and not returned for twenty-six days?

The ring slipped through her fingers and fell onto the floor. She stared at the fallen symbol of Preston's love for a long moment before retrieving it and placing it beside his ring. Maybe leaving the box on top of the dresser would jog her memory.

"Are those your and Daddy's wedding rings?"

Startled, Amanda set the ring box on the dresser then turned toward Morgan. "I didn't hear you come in."

"You were too deep in thought to notice." Morgan leaned against the doorframe. "Have you decided whether or not you want to hear about my visit?"

Amanda hesitated. If she declined, she'd avoid hearing something that might drive a stake deeper into her broken heart. On the other hand, not knowing would send her curiosity into overdrive.

Morgan moved closer. "I've never known you to struggle this much over a decision."

"I have one question before I decide."

"All right."

"Has meeting Savannah changed your mind about accepting her into our family?"

Morgan lifted the ring box off the dresser. "I suppose every daughter believes her daddy is perfect. To find out otherwise shatters unrealistic illusions." She paused. "One fact is undeniable. Savannah is also an innocent victim in this drama."

Amanda stared at her daughter. "You feel sorry for her, don't you?"

Morgan set the open ring box back on the dresser. "One reason she's staying in Blue Ridge is because we're the only family she has left."

Amanda grabbed the ring box and snapped it shut then dropped it into the top drawer. "You and Savannah share the same father, so I understand why you might want a relationship with her. At the same time, I hope you understand why the idea of accepting her into our family is beyond painful."

"I do, but I also believe one day you'll find it in your heart to forgive Dad." Morgan reached for her mother's hand while gazing deep into her eyes. "Which is why I invited Savannah to celebrate Thanksgiving with us."

Stunned, Amanda shifted her weight from one foot to the other. "Did she accept?"

Morgan nodded. "With tears in her eyes."

Amanda hesitated a long moment before withdrawing her hand and turning away. "I'll do my best to make her feel welcome."

Morgan wrapped her arms around Amanda's shoulders. "I know you will."

Chapter 29

Abby hummed one of her favorite tunes while maneuvering her wheelchair from the rehab center to her car.

Following close behind, Anna pulled the driver's door open. "Based on your progress, by this time next year, you'll likely be able to ditch the wheels and the leg braces."

"If you're half the therapist you claim to be, that'll happen well before next November."

"With my skills and your new-found optimism, you might be right."

"You bet I am." Abby slid onto the seat and popped the trunk.

After folding the chair and stashing it in the trunk, Anna propped her arm on the door and leaned down. "I'll see you Monday. In the meantime, Happy Thanksgiving."

Abby smiled at her friend. "Thanks, same to you."

Anna straightened and closed the door.

Using handheld controls, Abby backed onto the street and turned toward home. Tomorrow she would surprise her mom and Brad with her latest accomplishment. She turned the radio to a country music station and hummed along with familiar tunes until she parked in the carport and typed a text.

Morgan rushed out the back door and moved the wheelchair from the trunk to the open passenger door. "How'd therapy go?"

"My best session yet." Abby slid onto her chair then wheeled up the sidewalk and ramp to the front porch. Seconds after Morgan opened the door, Dusty bounded out and plopped her front paws on Abby's lap. "My sixty-pound lapdog." She smiled while pushing Dusty off her lap then wheeled into the foyer and on to the den. "After today's workout, I'm in the mood for something sweet."

Amanda walked in from the kitchen. "Since Tommy isn't here to kiss you, how about a cup of hot chocolate with marshmallows?"

Abby chuckled. "Almost as good as a kiss."

"That depends on who's doing the kissing." Amanda headed back to the kitchen while flicking her hand over her shoulder. "Three hot chocolates coming up."

Abby lifted her body from her chair to the sofa. "I've been dying to hear what happened when you met with Savannah."

"We talked." Morgan moved the wheelchair aside then settled beside Abby while relaying the conversation. "I invited her to celebrate Thanksgiving with us."

Abby's mouth fell open. "Oh my gosh, how did your mom take the news?"

Amanda returned and set two mugs on the coffee table. "Before or after I picked my jaw up off the floor?"

"After."

"I suppose I wasn't all that surprised." Still gripping the third mug, Amanda settled on a club chair. "Although if someone had told me a week ago we'd celebrate Thanksgiving with Dereck and Savannah, I would have questioned their sanity. At least tomorrow will be the most unusual Thanksgiving I've ever experienced."

"When I come home from Mom and Brad's tomorrow night, one of you will have to share every little detail."

"I'll give you the full scoop." Morgan propped her feet on the coffee table. "Mom's likely to end up speechless."

"That's a distinct possibility. Oh, I almost forgot." Amanda set her mug on the end table then pulled an envelope from her jeans pocket and carried it to Abby. "This came in the mail today."

"More junk?"

"I don't think so." Amanda returned to her chair.

Roused by curiosity, Abby gripped the envelope in both hands while staring at the handwritten name and address. Her focus shifted to the upper left-hand corner. She blinked then squeezed her eyes shut hoping she had misread the return address. A moment passed before she dared open her eyes. Her pulse accelerated. She hadn't been mistaken. "This was sent from Baltimore."

Morgan raised a brow. "Isn't that where you and your mom lived before you moved to Asheville?"

Abby nodded. Had someone written to share bad news about her father? Or worse. She pressed her hand to her chest while struggling to catch her breath. Was it possible the letter was from him? If his former fiancée hadn't reserved a room for the two of them at Hilltop Inn last year, he wouldn't have any idea where she lived.

Morgan reached across the cushion and touched Abby's arm. "Do you want me to open it for you?"

Abby shook her head then struggled to steady her trembling hand while sliding her finger under the flap. After hesitating a moment, she removed and unfolded a sheet of paper. Her eyes drifted to the scrawled signature confirming her fear. "It's from Jack."

Amanda stared wide-eyed. "Jack, as in your father?"

Abby nodded as the letter slipped from her fingers.

Morgan scooted closer and lifted the letter off Abby's lap. "I'll read it to you if you'd like me to."

"I don't know." Abby drew in a deep breath and slowly released the air. What if Jack had written to share bad news? "I need to know what's going on, so yeah."

"All right." Gripping the letter in both hands, Morgan lowered her feet to the floor. "Here goes."

"*Dear Abby,*

I imagine your first reaction to receiving a letter from me is shock, and the second is anger. I can't blame you for either, considering how I mistreated your mother."

Abby's jaw tightened. "Classic denial. Describing beating Mom with his fists as anything other than criminal abuse."

"Do you want me to continue?"

"You might as well."

"*I can't go back and undo the damage, and I don't ever expect Erica to forgive me. Which brings me to the reason I'm writing this letter. That day I walked out of Hilltop Inn without my fiancée, I shattered my car's driver's side window with my fist and broke two fingers. That's when I began to understand the damage I was capable of inflicting.*"

Abby scoffed. "Mom's bruises and cuts weren't a clue? Something is seriously wrong with him."

"As with any man who beats a woman," added Amanda.

Morgan tapped her finger on the letter. "There's more."

Abby's shoulders slumped. "Keep reading."

"*After I returned to Baltimore, I began drinking even more than before I left. Everything came crashing down the day I staggered from a bar, climbed into my police cruiser, ran a red light, and sideswiped another car.*

Fortunately, I was the only person seriously injured. The chief suspended me and ordered me to go to rehab or lose my job and my pension. I checked in the next day and have been here and sober for six weeks.

I know your mother is married."

Morgan looked up. "How does he know?"

Amanda crossed one leg over the other. "Police officers have access to all sorts of information."

"Good point." Morgan continued reading.

"I wish her all the best. The reason I'm writing to you is because I realize how much I've missed not having you in my life. If you can find it in your heart to visit me here in rehab, I'll do my best to make amends. If I don't hear back from you, I'll understand and will never bother you again.

That's all I have to say.

Your father,

Jack Smith."

"Talk about a shocker." Morgan folded the letter then placed it back on Abby's lap.

Abby's brows furrowed, absolute confusion warring with disbelief. "I don't know if my father has experienced a transformation, or if he's trying to pull a Gunter-style con on me."

Amanda rose, walked across the room, and lowered onto the sofa arm beside Abby. "You have an important decision to make."

"I don't even know if I should tell Mom about this letter."

"When I first learned about Savannah, I considered not telling Morgan. Until I realized that hearing the news from someone else would put a strain on our relationship."

"Mom's right." Morgan touched Abby's arm. "You'll find the right time to show the letter to Erica. Then you'll need to decide how you're going to respond to Jack's request."

Abby's gaze darted from the letter to her wheelchair. Desperate to anchor her spinning world, she folded the paper and stuffed it in her jeans pocket. "I need my ride." After Amanda moved the chair close, she maneuvered her body from the sofa then wheeled straight to her room. Dusty followed, her tail tucked. Abby closed the door, pulled her phone from her other pocket, and pressed Tommy's number. Dusty laid her head on her lap and seemed to study her.

Tommy answered, "Hey."

"Can you come over, like right now?"

"Are you okay?" His tone hinted of concern.

Not even close. "My father wants me to visit him in Baltimore."

"I'm on my way." Tommy ended the call.

Abby closed her eyes and stroked Dusty's muzzle while remembering her father's shocked expression that morning in Hilltop Inn's dining room when he realized she was his daughter. Did he know she'd been in an accident and was confined to a wheelchair?

After opening her eyes, Abby removed the letter from her pocket then dropped it into her desk drawer. She had twenty-four hours to decide her next steps.

Chapter 30

The morning before Thanksgiving, apprehension awakened Wendy before dawn. To avoid waking Chris, she slipped out of bed and tiptoed from the bedroom to the great room. Today she would follow Brent's instructions and give Zach the letter his mother had written to him.

Following the scent of freshly brewed coffee, she ambled to the kitchen, switched on the under-the-counter lights, and poured herself a cup. After adding sweetener, she settled on a stool at the counter. During the past few days, Zach's mood had soured, most likely from cell-phone withdrawal. Depending on his behavior through the weekend, Chris agreed to consider taking him off probation and returning his phone.

Wendy sipped her coffee while eyeing the letter she'd placed on the counter last night after Zach headed downstairs to his room. She drew on her sense of right and wrong to avoid reading the letter ahead of time. All she could do was hope his mother's words would comfort rather than upset him.

Duke padded in from Ryan's room and stretched out on the floor beside her. Funny how the loyal dog had taken on the new role as Ryan and Cindy's companion and protector. Maybe a puppy would improve Zach's mood. Wendy made a mental note to broach the subject with his father.

Responding to footsteps, Wendy glanced over her shoulder. "I hope I didn't wake you."

"You didn't." Chris poured a cup of coffee then sat beside her. "Are you still worried about Zach's response to his mother's letter?"

Wendy nodded. "Especially after he told us how he felt about his dad. I still don't understand why Brent wants Zach to read the letter today instead of on his birthday?"

"Maybe we'll understand after he reads it."

"Do you think we should give him the letter before or after he eats breakfast?"

"After. Since he doesn't have to go to work today, he's likely to sleep 'til noon." Chris set his coffee on the counter then leaned close and reached for Wendy's hand. "Before our little guy and gal wake up, why don't you and I go back to bed?"

Wendy flashed a flirtatious smile while summoning her best Southern accent. "What does my favorite lawyer have in mind?"

Chris winked while helping her climb off her stool. "An offer you won't want to refuse."

"Hmm." She let her fingers trail up his arm. "Are you talking about dessert before breakfast?"

"Oh, yeah."

Four hours after returning to their room, Wendy placed Cindy in her baby swing while Chris sat on the sofa watching cartoons with Ryan. "Should we go knock on Zach's door?"

Chris shook his head. "Better to let him wake up on his own."

"I suppose you're right." She settled on the other side of Ryan, doing her best to focus on the cartoon.

Five more minutes passed before Zach climbed up from the terrace level. Wendy popped off the sofa. "Good morning, are you hungry?"

"I guess."

"Would you rather have breakfast or lunch?"

"Doesn't matter."

"Why don't you join the guys while I fix all of us grilled cheese sandwiches."

"Okay."

Pleased he didn't say whatever, Wendy hastened to the kitchen and began preparing their lunch. Should she give Zach the letter as soon as they finished eating or wait a few minutes? If she waited, she'd risk him heading back downstairs to his room. She placed the sandwiches on the griddle then filled glasses with ice and water. When finished, her focus drifted to the envelope on the counter. Wendy flipped the sandwiches. Had Brent told his children their mother had written them each a letter? If he hadn't, how would Zach react?

Wendy set the water on the table then filled a sippy cup with juice before plating the sandwiches. "Lunch is ready."

Ryan climbed off the sofa and headed straight to the table. Wendy lifted him onto his booster seat while Chris and Zach settled at their places. Following a blessing, Chris took a bite. "It was nice of Tommy's dad to give the crew a few days off."

"I guess." After wolfing down his sandwich, Zach pushed his chair away from the table. "Can I go back to my room now?"

"Not yet." Wendy glanced at Chris. He nodded. "Before you leave we have something to give you." She headed to the counter, returning with the letter in her hand. "Are you aware your mother wrote letters to everyone in our family?"

Zach shook his head.

Wendy placed the envelope on the table. "This is her letter to you."

Zach remained motionless, his eyes focused on Wendy. "Do you remember the first question I asked you the day we met?"

Wendy nodded. "You wanted to know why our mother threw me away."

"Growing up, there were lots of times when I thought she wished she'd never had kids. When you told us she'd left you with a neighbor to become a professional singer, I knew I'd been right." His focus seemed to drift to the envelope. "Before she died she treated us different, like she felt guilty or something."

Wendy swallowed the lump rising in her throat when a painful memory surfaced. Sitting on a bench beside her sister under The Gaylord Opryland glass dome. While fingering the ruby ring encircled with diamonds Cynthia had given her, Kayla said "a mother can't show love she doesn't feel."

Wendy blinked, while struggling to find her voice. "Our mother loved you the best way she knew how." Zach's eyes met hers for a brief moment. Did he believe her? "Do you want to read her letter in private?"

Zach hesitated for a moment then grabbed the envelope and rushed out to the back deck. Duke followed and sat on his haunches beside the door.

Chris leaned back. "At least now we know Cynthia is another reason for your brother's anger."

"He failed to warm up to her during her final days. I think Zach's struggling with deep-seated guilt." Wendy pushed her half-eaten sandwich aside. "If he doesn't come back inside in five minutes, you should check on him."

Chris nodded toward Duke. "Our trusty guard dog is keeping watch. He'll let us know if we need to rescue Zach."

Five minutes passed with Duke remaining on guard duty.

Wendy carried the dishes into the kitchen while Chris and Ryan returned to the sofa. Five more minutes passed. Why was Zach taking such a long time to come back inside? She loaded the dishwasher. Had Cynthia's letter heightened his anger?

The deck door eased open. Zach plodded toward the sofa, gripping the letter in his right hand. "Can I have my phone back for an hour? I need to call my dad."

"I'll get it for you."

When Chris headed to their bedroom, Wendy moved toward Zach. "Are you okay?"

He nodded; however, his eyes seemed to carry the weight of unspoken words..

Chris returned with his phone. "You can keep it until tomorrow morning."

"Thanks." The letter slipped from Zach's fingers and fluttered to the floor. His chin dipped for a moment before he turned and headed to the stairs.

Wendy retrieved the letter then dropped onto the sofa. Chris sat beside her. "He left this for us to read.

Chris nodded.

Wendy gripped the letter in both hands, holding it so they could each read silently.

My Dearest Darling Zach,

Twelve years ago today, you warmed my heart when you first called me Mama. You were such a smart little boy, driven by curiosity and adventure, much like your father. He was over the moon the day you were born.

One of my deepest regrets was failing to be the mother you deserved, which was why during my final few months I poured every ounce of energy into making up for all those lost years. I don't blame you for resisting. I hope one day you will find it in your heart to forgive me while knowing you are deeply loved, not only by me and your dad, but more importantly by God.

While my family gathered around me during my final hour, I finally understood that bringing you and your three sisters into this world was my reason for being. For that moment I will be eternally grateful.

Wendy sniffled while tears pooled and trickled down her cheeks. She pulled a tissue from the decorative box on the end table and dabbed the tears before continuing to read her mother's letter.

If you are holding any grudges toward your father, please know that he has always loved you with all of his heart. Also know that my ambition and desire for a luxury lifestyle are why he poured so much of himself into his music and work. Now more than ever, you need each other as the loving father and son you were meant to be.

While you continue to grow into an amazing man full of potential, know that I'll be watching over you, cheering you on and rejoicing in every success.

All my love forever,

Mom

Chris slid his arm around Wendy's shoulder, pulling her close. "Zach will be okay."

"We all will." Peace flowed over Wendy like gentle rain washing dust from the air, leaving everything fresh and new.

Chapter 31

Moments after awakening, Amanda opened her bedroom blinds revealing the cloudless sky ushering Thanksgiving morning into Blue Ridge. Today was one of the few days the only businesses remaining open were restaurants, hotels, and inns. She donned her robe and slipped her phone into her pocket then headed down the hall toward the aroma of bacon and spices. Theo, secured in his high chair, stuffed a slice of banana into his mouth. Dusty sprawled beside him waiting for whatever tasty morsels found their way from his tray to the floor. After patting the baby's cheek, Amanda stepped into the kitchen. "Let me guess. Chocolate chip pancakes and crispy bacon."

Morgan stirred chips into the batter. "Awesam family's traditional Saturday morning and holiday breakfast."

Sierra laid bacon slices onto a microwave plate. "A tradition I'll continue to carry on after Theo and I have our own place."

After filling her favorite mug with coffee then adding creamer and sugar into her morning caffeine fix, Amanda sidled beside Morgan. "Although you plan to spend Christmas in New Orleans with Kevin's family, I'm glad you're spending Thanksgiving with me."

"I hope you're not too upset about Savannah and Dereck joining us."

"I'll make the best of the situation." Amanda stepped away. Had Linda and Keith invited Gary to celebrate the holiday with their family? Dismissing the random thought as an unwarranted stab of guilt, Amanda leaned against the counter. "Is Abby joining us for breakfast?"

Morgan shook her head. "Tommy picked her up a few minutes ago."

"Too bad, considering the chocolate pancake tradition began with her."

"Abby and Tommy are preparing a Thanksgiving meal for the families staying at the crisis center before they head over to Erica and Brad's. As of an hour ago, she still hadn't decided how to tell her mother about Jack's letter."

"For good reason. Based on everything Erica has told us about him, he can't be trusted."

"Maybe he's changed." Sierra set the bacon in the microwave. "People sometimes do, you know."

Amanda studied Sierra's expression. "Are you talking about Dereck?"

She shrugged. "He called a few minutes ago. He'll head this way after he visits his brother in prison."

Morgan poured batter onto a square griddle. "Speaking of prisoners, has anyone heard from Gunter lately?"

Amanda rolled her eyes. "First Jack and now Gunter. Talk about a couple of downers."

Morgan glanced over her shoulder. "I'm curious. That's all."

"Sorry for the snarky comment. To answer your question, following Gunter's last letter to Wendy, none of us have heard a peep from him. Which hopefully means he finally understands we don't ever want anything to do with him. On to a more pleasant conversation. When's Kevin arriving?"

"About an hour from now with a complete Thanksgiving dinner. All we'll have to do is warm everything up." Morgan pointed to the counter. "Except for the freshly-baked pumpkin pie Millie brought over a few minutes ago."

"I knew I smelled cinnamon and nutmeg." Amanda sipped her coffee.

Sierra set the microwave timer. "Mom always baked three pies for Thanksgiving. Pumpkin, sweet potato, and apple. We kids were happier when our trailer smelled more like a bakery than a not-so-clean, rundown tin can."

Morgan flipped the pancakes then glanced at Sierra over her shoulder. "I assume your mom likes desserts."

"If you met her, you'd know she's a big fan of any food loaded with sugar. I suppose eating distracts her from the harsh realities of living off welfare. At least Dereck is taking more responsibility for his future." Sierra paused, her brows drawing together. "Even though I invited him to spend the day with us, I still don't want him to become a permanent part of Theo's life."

Amanda eyed Sierra while gripping her mug in both hands. Was it her imagination, or did her declaration seem a bit too forced? "You were nice to invite him."

"He *is* Theo's father."

Startled by the ping in her pocket, Amanda set her mug on the counter and pulled out her phone. She stared at the message from Gary wishing her a Happy Thanksgiving. Confused, her finger hovered over the screen.

Morgan moved close. "You're trying to decide how to respond to Gary, aren't you?"

Amanda turned her phone face down, hoping Morgan hadn't seen her screen. "What makes you think the message is from him?"

"Lucky guess, which you just confirmed."

"Now you sound like Millie." Amanda pocketed her phone. "In case you're wondering, nothing has changed since you last asked about Gary. He's still nothing more than a friend."

"At least in your mind."

Amanda stared at her daughter. "What are you really trying to tell me?"

Morgan turned toward her. "Nothing except that you're a beautiful, intelligent woman, and Gary would be a fool to give up on you."

Sierra removed the bacon from the microwave. "I agree with Morgan."

"You're both sweet but wrong about Gary. He's okay with a relationship based on friendship." Had she at least sounded convincing? The look that passed between her daughter and Sierra made it clear they didn't believe her.

Morgan turned back to the griddle and transferred the pancakes to a platter.

Amanda released a sigh. No use arguing the point, especially since Gary—who had never included an emoji in a text—had ended today's message with a heart. Her daughter and Sierra might be spot-on about his intentions.

"I'll be back in a couple of minutes." Hoping she wouldn't add to their suspicions, Amanda retrieved her mug and returned to her bedroom. She pulled her phone from her pocket and stared at the heart. After carefully weighing her options, she typed "Happy Thanksgiving," followed by a turkey emoji. If her response didn't do the trick, refusing any invitations to join him for coffee would send a clear message.

Dismissing the momentary tug on her heart as hunger pangs, Amanda laid her phone on the dresser and headed straight to her chair at the dining room table.

Morgan passed her the platter. "Did you talk to Gary?"

"Let me ask you a question." Amanda transferred two pancakes and a slice of bacon to her plate. "Has Kevin ever added a heart to the end of a text?"

"Oh my gosh." Morgan's eyebrows shot up. "Gary texted you a heart emoji, didn't he?" She snapped her fingers. "I knew he wouldn't give up on you."

Amanda poured syrup on her pancakes. "Don't you think you're jumping to conclusions?"

"Not a chance. Now I have a question for you. How did you respond to Gary's text?"

Amanda hesitated. She might as well fess up, considering she'd painted herself into a corner. "With a turkey emoji."

"Are you kidding me?" Morgan shot Amanda an incredulous look. "A handsome, successful bank president who's crazy about you sends you a heart, and you respond with a turkey?"

Amanda stared at Morgan. Had one conversation with Savannah made her daughter forget that Preston's deception had destroyed her ability to trust another man? "Do you think he'll get the message?"

"He'll get the message, all right." Morgan swirled a forkful of pancake in a puddle of syrup. "Hopefully, he'll swallow his pride and continue pursuing you until you cave."

Amanda's focus shifted to her plate. If Morgan was right, she had no choice but to refuse any contact with Gary until he came to terms with reality, which raised one important question. Should she come up with some sort of an excuse to skip Keith's surprise birthday party? Except Linda had invited her, not Gary. Sensing Morgan was watching her, Amanda cut a piece of pancake. Best to show up and do her best to ignore any advances Gary might attempt.

Chapter 32

The mouthwatering aromas of roasted turkey, sweet potato soufflé, and pumpkin pie wafting through the crisis center kitchen did little to ease the tension headache holding Abby captive. In a few hours, she and Tommy would arrive at her mother's house, and she still had no idea how to break the news about her father's letter. Hoping to ease the ache, she washed down two over-the-counter pain pills with a sip of water.

Tommy eased beside her. "How's your headache?"

"I'll let you know when the pain meds kick in." She turned toward Autumn who was setting plates on the table to serve four adults, one big sister, and nine minor children. "Everyone will fit around the table like one big happy family."

"Even better." Autumn glanced around, most likely to ensure none of the children had wandered in. "No one will worry about getting beat up for saying the wrong word or overcooking the turkey."

One of the mothers standing close by nodded. "The curse of living with an abuser."

Out of the blue, the last Thanksgiving before Abby and her mom escaped from her father raced through her mind. As a Baltimore police officer, he had been on duty that day, pushing their meal to the Friday after. That morning he'd awakened in a foul mood, most likely from another hangover. Fifteen minutes after they sat down for dinner, he cursed then sent his plate crashing to the floor before storming out. At least that one time, he had exercised enough restraint to refrain from hitting his wife.

Tommy ambled beside Abby and reached for her hand, hinting he somehow knew her mind had gone to a dark place. "Your mother and Brad were kind to have this entire meal delivered."

"There will always be a special place in Mom's heart for women and children who have the courage to escape their abusers."

Summer wandered in holding hands with Bonnie, her new best friend. "After we eat, all us kids are gonna watch *Elf*. Know what his favorite foods are? Candy cane, candy corn, and syrup."

Bonnie giggled. "He left off candy bars."

Joyful chatter filled the kitchen while the rest of the children and mothers joined them. Pamela, the crisis center director, carried a plate of iced sugar cookies in a variety of holiday shapes. "Normally we would save dessert until after our meal. Since today is extra special, everyone can have one cookie before we eat." The children gathered around her, delighted with the special treat.

The pain in Abby's head eased when Tommy began cutting the turkey like a pro. "Where did you learn to do that?"

"Dad taught me." When finished he arranged the slices on a platter and carried it to the table.

Pamela stood at the head of the table while mothers, the children, and one big sister chose their seats. Following the blessing, she stayed to enjoy the meal with them while Abby and Tommy slipped out to the hall and turned toward the back door, leaving the lively chatter behind them.

After Tommy unlocked the door, Abby wheeled down the ramp then onto the sidewalk. She had ten minutes to decide whether or not to tell her mother about Jack's request.

Grateful for the balmy temperature following the cold snap, Erica carried her mug out to the covered deck spanning the full length of the house. While breathing in the fresh fall air, she set her phone on the coffee table then settled on the sofa facing the wooded backyard sloping down to the railroad track. Flames flickered in the fireplace anchoring one end of the space. A lighted garland adorning the mantel created a festive atmosphere, along with a live Christmas tree strung with hundreds of miniature colored lights. A squirrel skittering across the railing stopped ten feet away and eyed her as if questioning why she had invaded his domain.

Brad strode out, sending the pesky critter scampering away.

"I'm surprised you walked away from the football game."

"I'll wait for the guys to arrive to continue watching." He sat beside Erica and slid his arm around her shoulders. "This is our first Thanksgiving as a married couple—a year and a half after the day I first met you at Hilltop Inn."

"Wendy, Amanda, and I were newcomers, which is why we relied on Millie to come up with our grand-opening guest list. When she first mentioned your name, she described you as movie-star handsome." Erica nudged Brad's ribs. "She also claimed if she were thirty years younger, she would have had her eye on you."

Brad chuckled. "Good thing we were born decades apart. Along with Millie and her husband, my parents were frequent guests at Eleanor's dinner parties. They would have loved you as much as they loved my wife."

Grateful the mention Jan no longer gave her pause, Erica placed her hand on Brad's thigh. "What was your mother's favorite Thanksgiving dessert?"

"Hands down, plum pudding with hard sauce. Which I found a strange name given it was similar to fruitcake, and the sauce was mostly butter and sugar. Guess it was the brandy that qualified the description. Anyway, she always saved a little for the next morning. Did your mom have a favorite?"

"Most of our meals came from the local food bank. Except Christmas and Thanksgiving when Mom managed to come up with enough money to buy a turkey and bake pies. Our next door neighbor, Ms. Ginger, always gave us iced sugar cookies in all sorts of holiday shapes...." Erica's voice trailed off.

"Is she the same neighbor who explained how the women in your family ended up as casualties of generational poverty?"

Erica nodded. "The day my mother almost died from her addiction."

Brad squeezed her shoulder. "Ms. Ginger was right about you being destined to break the cycle."

"I like to think if my brother had survived that drive-by shooting, he also would have made something of himself." Erica paused for a long moment. "Even though Jack turned out to be an abusive husband, marrying him was my ticket out of the ghetto. Before he checked into Hilltop Inn last year, he had no idea where Abby and I lived. Considering his fiancée dumped him after we helped her accept the truth about his abuse, I doubt we'll ever hear from him again."

"One thing I've learned as a coach and principal is when teenaged bullies are confronted by someone bigger or smarter, they almost always back down—proving at the core they're cowards."

Erica leaned forward to lift her pinging phone off the coffee table. "A text from Tommy's mother. She's bringing a pecan pie."

"Inviting his parents to join us for dinner was a nice gesture."

"When Tommy stayed by Abby's side after her accident, Aletha finally admitted that her son and my daughter weren't too young to fall in love. Since then she and I have become friends. One of these days we'll end up as in-laws."

"Chances are I'll walk Abby down the aisle before either one of my sons takes the plunge."

"I'm looking forward to one day meeting Jimmy's brother, Bobby, and learning what it's like to live on an aircraft carrier."

"From the time he was a little kid, he wanted to fly helicopters. Now he pilots a chopper designed for anti-surface warfare. One of my sons fights fires; the other fights enemies. Both dangerous jobs." Brad's tone hinted of weariness. "All I can do is pray for God to keep them safe."

Erica squeezed his thigh. "In reality, I suppose that's the best any parent can do." The hum of an engine announced a car pulling up to the garage. "Which guests do you suppose are the first to arrive?"

"Good question." Brad pulled his arm away from her shoulders and strode to the end of the deck. "It's Abby and Tommy."

"I'll welcome them." Erica rushed inside to the foyer, pulled the front door open, and stepped onto the porch. Tommy pushed her daughter's wheelchair up the ramp they had installed, despite Abby's resistance, then into the foyer. "How'd everything go at the crisis center?"

"When we left everyone was having a good time, thanks to your generosity."

"We plan to provide Christmas dinner as well."

Brad strode over and clapped his hand on Tommy's shoulder. "Are you ready to watch some football?"

"Oh, yeah."

Erica eyed Abby's white-knuckle grip on her wheelchair's hand rim. Something was bothering her daughter. She forced a tight smile. "While our guys plant themselves in front of the television, why don't you and I enjoy eggnog out back."

Abby glanced up at her. "Sounds good."

Erica rushed to open the French doors. "I'll join you in a minute." While Abby wheeled out to the deck, she headed to the kitchen anchoring one end of the great room. Had something happened at the crisis center or at rehab? Eager to find out, she filled two mugs and carried them outside. Surprised her daughter had managed to maneuver from her chair to the sofa without moving the coffee table, she handed a mug to her daughter then sat beside her. "Millie's recipe."

Abby stared into her mug as if the eggnog might offer answers it had no right to hold. "Something happened you need to know about."

A prickle of dread slid down Erica's spine. She set her mug on the coffee table, the clink louder than it should've been. "I'm listening."

Abby's fingers tightened around the handle before she slipped a folded sheet of paper from her pants pocket. "This came in the mail yesterday." She held it out, her hand trembling just enough to notice.

Erica unfolded the paper, her gaze leaping straight to the signature as if it burned through the page. Her breath caught. Each word felt like an intrusion—calculated, self-serving, cruel in its presumption. How could Jack possibly believe he had earned the right to speak of reconciliation? Of fatherhood? By the time she reached the end, her hands shook with the effort it took to avoid ripping the letter apart and scattering the pieces like ash.

She forced herself to inhale. Exhale. With deliberate care, Erica folded the paper and set it on the coffee table, as though distance alone might dull its sting. "What are you going to do?"

Abby's eyes fixed on something far beyond the room. "Every day I talk to women who believed the men who hurt them would change." Her voice softened, weighted with experience. "I wonder if any of them ever truly do." She turned back to Erica. "Did Jack ever hit you when he wasn't drinking?"

The question landed hard. Erica pinched the bridge of her nose, memories pressing in—raised voices, slammed doors, the constant calculation of what might set him off. "Although I'm not a hundred percent sure..." Her hand fell to her lap. "I don't think he did."

Abby swallowed. "How do you think I should respond, Mom?"

The answer clawed at Erica's throat. She wanted to protect her daughter the only way she knew how—by saying never, by saying run, by saying trust him and you'll regret it. Deep down she understood the choice could never be hers. Meeting Abby's eyes, she spoke softly. "Carefully consider your options, then follow your conscience, sweetheart."

Abby exhaled, the sound weary. "Seems I have a lot to think about."

"Yes, you do." Erica reached out and patted her daughter's knee, hoping she would reject Jack's request.

Abby's expression shifted—lighter, almost shy. She covered Erica's hand with her own. "Now that I've dropped something so heavy on you, I have something good to show you. Stand up. Right in front of me, and hold out your hands."

"All right." Erica rose, a fragile hope blooming in her chest as a soft smile curved her lips. She hardly dared to believe.

Abby clasped her hands while rising to her feet. Her brows knitted together in fierce concentration, as though the rest of the world had gone quiet. She released her mother's grip and took one step. Then another. "By Christmas, with braces I'll be strong enough to walk across a room."

Tears spilled down Erica's cheeks as unrestrained joy rushed in. She pulled her daughter into her arms, her heart lifting in gratitude as she silently thanked God for giving her hope and healing her child—body and spirit.

Chapter 33

Thanksgiving morning Wendy awakened more refreshed than she'd been since Zach arrived. Last night after carrying on a lively conversation during dinner, her brother had joined them to watch *A Charlie Brown Christmas* with his nephew sitting beside him. She glanced at Chris, still asleep. After she'd tucked Ryan into bed, Zach stayed in the den and watched *Die Hard* with Chris, making him the coolest brother-in-law on the planet.

Her heart warmed, Wendy donned her robe then headed to the kitchen and poured a cup of coffee while the sun painted shades of pale pink and blue across the sky. She turned toward Chris ambling in. "I hope I didn't wake you."

"You didn't." He kissed her cheek then poured himself a cup. "Zach's coming up to help me fix you breakfast."

Wendy tilted her head. "What did I do to deserve such a special treat?"

"You didn't object to us watching what a lot of guys call a real Christmas movie."

"While you two were focusing on the mayhem, I found *When Harry Met Sally* on the internet. Now I understand what Linda meant about setting the stage for Amanda and Gary to get back together. Although it will take a lot more than one party to heal Amanda's broken heart."

Zach wandered up from the terrace level. "Why's her heart broken?"

"She discovered that years ago her husband had fathered a child with another woman. That child who's now twenty three years old moved here to Blue Ridge a few weeks ago."

"Bummer."

Chris grinned. "With your sister, Erica, Millie, and Mom scheming, Amanda will eventually recover from the shock."

Wendy patted Chris's cheek. "What you call scheming, darling, we consider a romance intervention."

Chris chuckled. "The perfect subject for a country music song."

"And a Hallmark movie. Now for this morning's most important question. What are you guys planning for breakfast?"

"Pancakes and bacon."

"Sounds delish. I'll wake our babies while you two take on kitchen duty."

Hours after enjoying each other's company around the table, Chris pulled onto his parents' driveway. "Time for another Armstrong Thanksgiving complete with football and all the trimmings."

After Chris unbuckled Ryan from his car seat and Wendy lifted Cindy's carrier from the cradle, Zach climbed out from the third row. "Dad and my sisters are gonna spend the day at Gaylords and go to the ice show. Mostly for Riley."

Wendy moved beside Zach. "Do you miss being with your Nashville family?"

"Kinda, especially after talking to Dad last night."

Chris held Ryan's hand while they made their way along the sidewalk to the front porch. "In a few more weeks, you'll head home."

"Then I'll miss you guys."

Chris nudged Zach's arm. "You know you're welcome to come visit us any time."

Zach nodded. "Yeah, I know."

Wendy's heart was full while they walked into the foyer and headed to Linda and Keith's great room. Lively chatter mingled with a sports announcer's recap of the last play while Chris's sister, Allison, greeted them with hugs. "Turkey and football. Thanksgiving traditions at the Armstrong home."

Ryan scurried toward his year-old cousin Ellie on her playmat, while Chris and Zach joined Keith and Allison's husband Mark in front of the television.

Wendy followed Allison into the kitchen and set Cindy's carrier on the island.

Susan loosened the blanket around her great-granddaughter. "I always find it amazing how babies are able to sleep through all sorts of commotion."

"I fed her before we left home, so she'll sleep for a couple more hours." Wendy sniffed the mouthwatering aromas of poultry seasoning and pumpkin pie spices. "Everything smells delicious."

"Thanks to my mother-in-law's culinary talent." Linda removed a bottle of prosecco from the wine chiller. "She's been cooking up a storm since noon. Hanging out with Millie has inspired her to volunteer for kitchen duty."

"Only for Thanksgiving." Susan climbed onto a stool. "Millie and Bernie agreed to cater my New Year's Eve party."

"I'm surprised after all these years, you've decided to host another big event." Allison's eyebrows shot up as if the light had suddenly come on. She snapped her fingers. "I finally get it. You want to recreate the scene from one of Mom's favorite movies when Harry races through the streets of New York to tell Sally he wants to spend the rest of his life with her."

A sly grin curled Susan's lips. "Linda and Erica are responsible for making sure Amanda and Gary both show up."

Wendy pictured Erica attempting to convince Amanda to attend the party she'd no doubt know was a set up. "Which could end up a huge challenge when Amanda believes the mystery club came up with the idea."

"Outsmarting two people as smart as Amanda and Gary won't come easy." Linda filled flutes with peach nectar and prosecco. "Bellinis and conversation for us ladies. Beer, soft drinks, and football for the guys." She pushed a glass to Wendy. "Zach seems to be in a good mood. What happened to turn him around?"

"Yesterday he read the heartwarming letter his mother wrote to him before she passed on." She shared tidbits.

Linda pressed her hand against her chest, her eyes on Wendy. "What a beautiful gesture. You're blessed to have found Cynthia in time."

"I wish I hadn't waited as long as I did." Wendy wrapped her fingers around her flute. "Anyway, Kayla and Riley will read the letters she wrote to them on their birthdays."

Susan took a sip of her bellini. "I believe I might borrow Cynthia's idea. Considering I plan to stay around for many more years, I'll have plenty of time to decide what to write."

The doorbell rang, followed by Gary walking into the kitchen. "Hello, ladies." He handed Linda a bouquet of flowers then set a bottle of wine on the island.

"The flowers are gorgeous and the wine perfect." Linda removed a beer from the fridge and handed it over. "The guys are in football mode."

"I'll join them."

While arranging the flowers in a vase, Linda turned her back toward the men. "Gary took a long time to recover from his wife cheating on him. If Amanda shuts him out of her life, his heart won't heal a second time."

Wendy reached across the counter and touched Linda's arm, praying her next words would prove true. "Given enough time, I believe Amanda will learn to trust again. Plus, I'll do my part in a few weeks when Amanda, Erica, and I check into the Blue Ridge Inn for our second annual Victory Sorority Sister gathering."

"I hope all of our efforts pay off. Especially since Amanda and Gary are perfect for each other." Linda ran her finger around her flute's rim. "If you could have seen how well they worked together during Keith's campaign...the way Gary looked at Amanda with pure admiration. It took him a while to win her over. Now a lot of people around town consider them a couple."

Allison aimed her glass at her mother. "Such is life in a small town where everyone knows everyone, which reminds me. I met Savannah Landry at the salon yesterday. Britany couldn't work me in, so she cut my hair."

Wendy's brows arched. "Did she say anything about Amanda, or why she moved to Blue Ridge?"

Allison shook her head. "She wasn't the chatty type. Still, it's only a matter of time before people find out her connection with Amanda."

Susan nodded. "One more reason we need to ensure our efforts to reunite Amanda and Gary are successful."

Following another doorbell chime, Regina ambled in and set a bottle of Champagne on the island. "Thanks for inviting me to spend Thanksgiving with you."

"You're family. Of course, you're welcome to join us for Christmas as well." Linda moved the Champagne to the fridge. "Would you prefer beer or a bellini?"

"A beer will hit the spot." Regina climbed onto a stool. "I'm not one to gossip, but have you ladies heard the latest rumor?"

Linda handed her a beer. "Are you talking about Crystal Bullock's plan to sue Richard Watson for false imprisonment?"

Regina nodded. "Keith told you, didn't he?"

"Last night. Crystal was smart to hire you to fight for her."

"By the time the trial ends, I'll have Watson on the hook for enough money to set Crystal up for life."

Allison snickered. "Talk about another small-town drama."

"One fact is certain—" Linda refreshed her drink. "The new year promises more than a little excitement."

Chapter 34

By three-thirty a swarm of butterflies had taken up residence in Amanda's chest. While Morgan and Kevin warmed up the Thanksgiving dinner, she set the table designed for six with Theo's high chair sandwiched between two chairs. Everyone would certainly be elbow to elbow during the entire meal.

While Sierra finished creating a centerpiece with miniature pumpkins, greenery, and candles, Morgan glanced at her watch hinting that Amanda wasn't the only one struggling with anxiety. Sierra and Amanda both froze the moment the doorbell chimed, sending Dusty scampering to the foyer.

At the second ring, Morgan rushed in from the kitchen with Kevin following close behind. "While you two stand here gawking at each other, I'll greet our first guest." She brushed past them, returning minutes later with Savannah by her side. "Meet my husband, Kevin."

He smiled while extending his hand. "It's a pleasure."

Savannah accepted, her lips tight, her grip brief before she withdrew her hand. "Likewise."

Morgan placed her hand on Savannah's arm. "You've met Mom and Sierra."

"I have." Savannah handed Amanda a gift bag, their eyes meeting for a brief moment. "A little something to thank you for allowing me to celebrate with your family. It's okay if you wait and open it later."

"Thank you." Amanda lowered the bag to her side while Savannah slipped out of her coat revealing a long-sleeve, pale teal sweater dress.

"I love your outfit." Morgan looped her hand around Savannah's elbow. "Come on in the kitchen, and I'll pour us some wine."

Ignoring her curiosity, Amanda set the gift bag on an end table without peeking inside then dropped onto the sofa.

Sierra followed and sat beside her. "You were sweet to allow Savannah and Dereck to join us."

"As if I had a choice."

"You could have told us to uninvite them. After all this is your house."

Regretting her snarky comment, Amanda patted Sierra's arm. "While you and Abby live here, this is as much your home as it is mine."

"I'll always be grateful to you and Erica for taking me in."

"You know you're part of our family now, don't you?"

"I do. If my next custody hearing goes my way, I'll begin looking for my own place with a yard, so I can buy Theo a puppy."

The doorbell chimed the same moment Theo's babble made it clear he'd awakened from his afternoon nap.

Amanda touched Sierra's arm. "Do you want me to answer while you take care of your son?"

"Do you mind?"

"Not at all."

"All right then." Sierra scurried toward her room while Amanda made her way to the foyer. She hesitated a moment then pulled the door open.

Dressed in black jeans, a long-sleeve blue dress shirt, and a tie, Dereck handed her a foil-wrapped plate and a bouquet of flowers. "The pie's from Sierra's mother. The flowers are from me."

"They're lovely. Thank you." Amanda stepped aside. "Come on in and meet the rest of our guests." After leading the way to the kitchen and making the introductions, she arranged the flowers in a vase then set them on the table beside the gift bag.

Dereck followed her, settling on a club chair beside the fireplace. His slumped shoulders hinted he felt more than a little awkward.

Amanda sat on the sofa. “How’s your job going?”

“Good.” He nodded toward the Christmas tree in the corner. “Me and Jay never decorated our trailer for Christmas.”

“How’s your brother holding up?”

“Okay, I guess.” Dereck fell silent for a long moment. “Jay’s where he belongs.”

Surprised by the comment, Amanda nodded. “Hopefully when his sentence ends, he won’t return to a life of crime.”

“Most parolees go back to doing what got ‘em arrested in the first place.”

“Maybe your brother will be the exception.”

Sierra walked in carrying Theo dressed in a button-down dress shirt, a navy vest, and matching pants. She moved beside Dereck. “I’m glad you’re joining us.”

“Me too. Theo looks real cute all dressed up.”

“I bought the outfit yesterday with money you gave me. Do you want to hold him?”

Dereck hesitated, seemingly a bit uneasy. “You don’t mind?”

“I wouldn’t have offered if I minded. After all, you are his father.” Without waiting for a response, Sierra placed Theo on his father’s lap then settled on the other club chair.

Dereck fingered Theo’s bare foot. “Does he talk?”

“Not yet, but he’s real smart, so he’ll probably say his first word early next year.”

Morgan and her sister strode in carrying glasses of white wine. Savannah handed a glass to Amanda while Morgan gave one to Dereck and the other to Sierra. "Even though you're a couple of years from legal age, today's special."

Kevin followed. "If we were in Italy, she'd be legal."

Sierra's head tilted, her eyes wide. "Have you been to Italy?"

"Twice with my family, once as a graduation trip with my high school pals."

"Someday I want to take Theo on a trip to another country."

Amanda clenched her fingers tight around her wineglass while paying close attention to the actors playing their roles in the drama going on around her. Morgan sat on the middle cushion with Savannah beside her. Kevin stood beside the fireplace with his right foot planted on the hearth.

While the conversation focused on fun places to visit, Sierra appeared to keep a close eye on Dereck who seemed a bit more comfortable holding his son on his lap. Amanda sipped her wine. Was Sierra having second thoughts about allowing her son's father into their lives? What about Savannah? Had she accepted Morgan's invitation hoping Amanda would change her mind about forming a relationship?

Amanda fidgeted as she crossed one leg over the other. Would she ever be able to be in the same room with Preston's other daughter without feeling deceived? Maybe she should have opted out of dinner and volunteered to help Millie serve the family staying at Hilltop Inn. Except Morgan would have balked at her taking the coward's way out. Besides, if Preston's daughters bonded, at some point she would be forced to accept Savannah into their family.

Following another sip of wine, Amanda's thoughts drifted to Gary's last text punctuated with a heart emoji. Was he spending the day with Linda and Keith's family? Were the guys watching football or playing pool? Did Gary keep popping into her head because she struggled with guilt over ending their relationship? Maybe she should come up with a logical reason to skip tomorrow's surprise birthday party. Not an option. She had to go, if for no other reason than respect for Linda and Keith.

Morgan turned toward Savannah. "How's your new job going?"

While listening to Savannah's response, Amanda's focus shifted to Kevin. Was it her imagination, or did he seem a bit preoccupied? Morgan hadn't mentioned either of their jobs since she'd arrived. Did her silence mean good or bad news?

Responding to a kitchen timer, Morgan lifted off the sofa. "Time to carve the turkey."

"I'll help." Amanda trailed behind her daughter. She paused beside the dining room table, eyeing the new addition before joining her daughter. "Who added the place cards?"

"I did, so no one will have to worry about where to sit." Morgan removed the turkey from the oven. "Don't act surprised when you discover I've seated you between me and Savannah."

"Have you thought about how she might react?"

"I already told her."

"And?"

Morgan lifted the turkey onto a cutting board. "She didn't object."

Amanda removed two casserole dishes from the oven, the heat flushing her face. "Just because she didn't say anything doesn't mean she's comfortable with the arrangement."

"Maybe after we share a meal together, you'll at least consider accepting her into our family."

Amanda paused. "Is that why you invited her?"

"The main reason I asked Savannah to join us was to help ease the pain of losing her mother." Her tone softened. "I'll consider any other progress an added bonus."

Amanda exhaled slowly. "Clever move."

Morgan kissed her cheek. "I thought so."

Ten minutes after Kevin walked in to carve the turkey, everyone found their places around the table. Dereck secured Theo in his high chair between his seat and Sierra's. Savannah hesitated for a brief moment before settling at her assigned place beside Amanda, her posture guarded.

After Morgan directed everyone to join hands for the blessing, Amanda grasped Savannah's trembling fingers. She stiffened, then slowly relaxed as Amanda gave a gentle squeeze. When Savannah closed her eyes, Amanda did the same.

While Kevin offered thanks, the weight of the moment settled deep in Amanda's chest. No matter how painful Preston's deception had been, both of his daughters deserved a place at her table—and, for tonight at least, in her heart.

Chapter 35

Following the guests' request for a family-style Thanksgiving feast rather than a plated dinner, Millie arranged formal serving dishes on Hilltop's kitchen island. "Little did I know when I helped Eleanor prepare her dinner parties that I'd become a professional chef, or that one of my servers would be a former cop."

Gordon wiped a smudge off the island counter top. "I show up wherever duty calls."

Millie set the appropriate serving utensil beside each dish. "I'm glad you're here because there's something strange about this family."

"Don't pay too much attention to Millie's comment, Gordon." Bernie removed a Dutch apple pie from the oven. "Since taking on the role of our mystery club leader, her suspicions have been on overdrive."

Millie pointed a serving spoon at Bernie. "When you see the head of the family we're catering to, you'll see what I mean. He looks like a mobster straight out of *The Godfather*, and he lives in Chicago."

"Talk about an overactive imagination." Gordon plucked a cookie off the plate Millie had set out. "I'm surprised you're familiar with that old classic."

"They were some of Rupert's favorites, which is why I've watched all four movies more than once."

"Your husband had good taste in movies and in women."

"Careful, detective, or my assistant chef might think you're flirting with me."

"Too late." Bernie removed a second pie from the oven. "In case you haven't noticed, everyone in our little club is having a ball watching you two carry on."

"Which proves old people are easily amused." Millie rolled her eyes before facing Gordon. "I'm counting on your experience to size up our guests."

"Let me get this straight. You want me to go undercover as a waiter to spy on a family that's paying a hefty price for your services as their personal chef?"

"You really are a smart detective."

"Forget the flattery. The assignment you're suggesting requires a lot more than you're paying me."

"In the event you've forgotten—" Millie propped her hands on her hips. "You volunteered to help."

An amused grin deepened the wrinkles around Gordon's eyes. "I've learned you're a little dangerous when you put your hands on your hips, Chef Millie. Makes people agree to do things they know they shouldn't."

"Are you saying if I give you a bonus, you'll play detective?"

"Well now, that depends on what sort of bonus you have in mind."

"I see." Millie lowered her hands to her sides. "How about a week's worth of desserts?"

Gordon laughed. "Believe me, it would have taken a lot more than sweets to bribe James Bond, but I'll go along if for no other reason than to humor you."

Bernie removed homemade cranberry walnut sauce from the fridge. "Why whenever you two are around do I feel like I'm a character in an old-folks romantic comedy?"

"Because you are," Millie and Gordon responded in unison triggering a bout of laughter.

Millie removed a pitcher of mocktails from the fridge then handed Gordon two bottles of chardonnay and a corkscrew. "Now that we've established the real reason you're here, it's time for you to help me serve pre-dinner drinks to the questionable family."

"I'll go along." He uncorked the wine. "Fair warning. If I spill wine on your guests, I'll blame your training."

"What training?"

"My point exactly." Gordon followed Millie to the living room where eight adults and six children—all dressed to the nines—had gathered.

After helping Gordon fill glasses she had placed on an end table, Millie served the first to the head of the family and his wife. "We're delighted you've chosen to celebrate Thanksgiving with us, Mr. and Mrs. Giordano." She emphasized the last name hoping to prove the validity of her suspicion. "My friend, Mr. Davenport, is helping me today. He's a retired police detective."

"No kidding?" Mr. Giordano tipped his glass toward Gordon. "I'm a retired police chief. The tall man standing beside the hearth is my son who owns a prestigious law firm. He's the real brains in the family."

Millie's eyes darted from the father to the son. Who would've thought?

Gordon cleared his throat hinting at a struggle to swallow a laugh. He extended his hand to the senior Giordano. "It's always a pleasure to meet a fellow officer. You've chosen the perfect place to celebrate with your family. Chef Millie is an award winner."

"We know." Mrs. Giordano smiled up at Millie. "I read about your accomplishments on the inn's website, which is why we've chosen to dine here."

Recovering from a momentary bout of speechlessness, Millie squared her shoulders. "My partners and I always aim to please." After serving the remaining glasses of wine to the adults and mocktails to the children, she returned to the kitchen.

Gordon followed, closing the door behind him. He slid onto a stool grinning from ear to ear. "One fact is certain. The first dessert you prepare for me should be humble pie."

Bernie laughed. "Good one, Gordon."

Resisting the urge to prop her hands on her hips, Millie kept her arms glued to her side. "You have to admit Mr. Giordano looks more like a Mafia guy than a police chief, and who's to say he's telling the truth?"

Gordon reached for a cookie. "The worst criminal I ever nabbed looked like an innocent choir boy."

Millie pursed her lips. "One of these days, my suspicions will lead our little group to crack a real case wide open."

Gordon swallowed a bite of cookie. "If I'd had this much fun on the job, I might not have retired. Although I would have missed out on solving mysteries with the most entertaining gang of wannabe detectives in the country." He winked at Millie. "Led by the most fascinating woman I've ever met."

"One more compliment, and I'll owe you two weeks of desserts."

"I'm counting on it."

"In case you two haven't noticed—" Bernie pointed to the microwave clock. "It's time to stop flirting and help me serve our guests."

Gordon saluted. "I'm on it."

After transferring the meal to serving plates, they carried them to the table. While the family meandered in and chose their seats, Gordon uncorked a bottle of zinfandel. Millie's eyes followed him while he filled the first adult glass. All those years ago when they were high school students, she'd admired him from afar, never in her wildest dreams imagining he would one day call her fascinating. If he had paid even a smattering of attention to her, maybe she wouldn't have ended up in an affair with the traveling salesman.

Millie blinked when she noticed Bernie staring at her with a sly grin. Attempting to ignore the sudden onset of heat warming her cheeks, she headed back to the kitchen.

Bernie followed and refreshed her coffee. "He is a good-looking man."

"Mr. Giordano?"

Bernie faced her. "You know I'm talking about Gordon."

"What's your point?"

"No point, just an observation."

Gordon returned. "Now that our guests are served, we have time to celebrate before dessert." He pulled the cork from the bottle of Champagne he'd brought and filled three glasses, handing one to Bernie, another to Millie. He tapped his glass to theirs. "Cheers to new friends who have made moving back to my hometown far more enjoyable than I imagined." His eyes met Millie's. He winked. "Especially you."

"If you're not careful, Gordon, my assistant chef might think you're sweet on me."

Bernie aimed her glass toward Millie. "Too late, everyone already knows."

Millie's eyes remained locked on Gordon. "I suppose I can't blame him. I *am* irresistible after all."

Gordon grinned. "Irresistible, huh? I'll let you prove it, beginning with dessert after we finish serving our guests. Oh, and Bernie can stay as our chaperone."

Millie clicked her glass to his. "Prepare to be amazed."

Chapter 36

Early Friday evening Wendy stood in their closet eyeing the clothes on her side.

Chris leaned against the doorframe, smiling. "Still can't decide what to wear?"

"I talked to Donna before you walked in. She and her boys left Atlanta a half hour ago, which will have them arriving at the inn smack dab in the middle of the surprise party."

"Not the best timing, considering Hilltop's entire staff will be celebrating Dad's birthday at Susan's."

"Which is why Amanda will leave a key and the inn's phone with Sierra. Donna will text me when they arrive." Wendy lifted a silky gold, off-the-shoulder top off the rack. "How about this with dressy white jeans?"

"Perfect."

Wendy slipped the top over her head then donned the jeans. "After a full day at the aquarium and a long drive, Donna's looking forward to going to bed early. We'll pick them up at eight tomorrow morning and take them to breakfast then on a train ride. Is Zach upset about Regina coming over tonight to babysit?"

"He's relieved we didn't ask him to take care of Ryan and Cindy. He said, and I quote, 'no way I wanna mess with dirty diapers.'"

"We could take him with us."

"I offered. Now that he has his phone back, he'd rather stay here and catch up on his games. Besides, he'll have a good time with Regina. Since he's been studying at our office, they've become friends."

"I'm still surprised she agreed to babysit, especially since she never had children." The doorbell chimed. "Your law partner has arrived." Wendy rushed through the great room and opened the front door. "Thank you for agreeing to stay with our babies."

Regina grinned. "I can't think of a better way to spend a Friday night."

Zach ambled over holding Ryan's hand. He fist-bumped Regina. "What's up?"

"For the next few hours, you and I are partners."

"Cool, as long as you have diaper duty."

"You've got it." Regina bent down to Ryan's level. "We're going to have a fun time tonight."

Wendy smiled at Chris confirming his decision to engage his law partner. After giving Regina instructions, she slipped into her coat and followed Chris to the garage. During the drive Wendy eyed the passing scenery while mentally reviewing tomorrow's schedule. When they arrived at Susan's home, she pocketed her phone so she wouldn't miss Donna's text.

Chris grabbed the gift from the back seat then opened her door and helped her step out of the car. "Time to celebrate a birthday and play the role of audience in Susan and Millie's get-Amanda-and-Gary-back-together drama."

Moments after donning a teal long-sleeved, cowl-neck sweater over black pants, Amanda lifted Savannah's gift off her dresser. She swallowed the lump in her throat while fingering the crystal Christmas ornament in the shape of Georgia. Its red stone indicated Blue Ridge, and the words underneath read, 'home is where the heart is.' The way Preston's daughters enjoyed each other's company yesterday during dinner continued to tug on her heartstrings. She carried the gift to the den and hung it on the tree. Even if she couldn't forgive Preston, shouldn't she at least invite Savannah to join the family at Hilltop Inn Christmas morning? Another decision for another day.

Sierra strode in from her room. "Nice ornament. Did you buy it?"

Amanda shook her head. "It's the gift from Savannah."

"She seems really sweet." Sierra paused. "I hope you don't mind that I accepted her invitation to meet for lunch during the Christmas holidays."

"Who you choose as friends is your decision." Amanda stepped away from the tree. "Hilltop's key and phone are on the dining room table. You should expect Wendy's stepmother to arrive in a couple of hours."

"I'll take good care of them."

"I know you will." Amanda grabbed her purse, keys, and Keith's gift then rushed to her car before she had a chance to change her mind. Her pulse accelerated with each passing mile. She and Gary were the real stars of tonight's drama. She tapped her fingers on the steering wheel. Hopefully by the time the party ended, everyone involved in the scheme would understand their efforts were pointless.

Amanda parked across from Susan's two-story brick home the same time Chris opened the car door for Wendy. "It's showtime." She plucked the gift bag off the passenger seat, climbed out, and caught up with them at the front porch. "Does Keith have a clue about the surprise?"

"He'll know when he sees all the cars." Chris held the door open.

Amanda followed Wendy into the two-story foyer illuminated by an elaborate chandelier. Her eyes drifted from the formal dining room on the left where Allison stood in front of the window to the elegant living room displaying a Christmas tree with a gold and white motif on the right. "Your grandmother has elegant taste."

"The front part of the house is her influence; the back is my grandfather's." Chris led them toward voices and background music drifting from the combo kitchen and den spanning the full length of the house.

"I see what you mean." Amanda glanced around the casual space befitting a country lifestyle. Gary stood beside the fireplace chatting with a couple she didn't recognize. Had he noticed her?

Susan strode over. "We're delighted you could join us to celebrate my son's birthday."

Swallowing the snarky remark threatening to roll off her tongue, Amanda handed Susan the gift. "Your home is lovely."

"My husband and I built this house two years after he established the Armstrong law office. Years of wonderful memories live here with me." She looped her arm around Amanda's elbow. "Linda and Keith are on their way over."

"I'm surprised you didn't ask guests to park away from the house."

"My son knows I invited a few special guests to help him celebrate."

Amanda leaned close while eyeing Millie and Gordon chatting with Erica and Brad. "You know I'm onto the mystery club's conspiracy."

"Of course I do, dear. So is Gary."

Millie sauntered over and handed Amanda a glass of wine. "In the event you're wondering what happened to our competition, it's still on."

"If you're referring to your who-lands-a-guy-first bet, I'm declaring you the winner."

"Sorry, honey. You can't forfeit until one of us officially snags a guy." A sly grin curled Millie's lips. "The competition is very much alive, and despite Gordon's fascination with me, I'm betting on you crossing the finish line first."

Amused by Millie's playful tone, Amanda mirrored her smile. "You're obviously delusional. Although I appreciate your sense of humor."

Allison rushed in from the front of the house. "Quiet, everyone. Mom and Dad are walking up the sidewalk."

From the corner of her eye, Amanda caught sight of Gary heading in her direction. He stopped beside her. Amanda inched away while forcing her attention to the guest of honor who entered to applause and shouts of happy birthday.

"I wasn't sure you'd show up." Gary's voice was low.

"Keith's my friend. Why wouldn't I?"

"Because we both know the real reason Susan and Millie planned this party was to put us together."

Amanda breathed in the subtle scent of the cologne Gary had worn the night he cooked dinner at his condo—the night she'd finally stopped lying to herself about what she felt for him. Standing this close now with his arm brushing her shoulder made her chest tighten. It took effort to draw a steady breath, to remind herself she was still standing, still in control.

He leaned closer, his voice still low. "Considering we're key characters in this drama, how do you suggest we act?"

Millie's bemused smile forced Amanda to inch away from Gary. "We should wish Keith a happy birthday and then mingle with the other guests."

"All right." He leaned in again, his tone unmistakably serious. "Before the party ends, you and I need to talk. Alone."

Her pulse quickened. "How do you suggest we pull that off without starting wild rumors?"

"Leave the details to me."

Linda strode over, her presence filling the space between them. "Thank you both for coming." She placed her right hand on Amanda's arm, her left on Gary's. "A party for Keith wouldn't be complete without his amazing campaign partners."

Could she be any more obvious? Amanda swallowed the sharp reply pressing against her tongue.

Linda released Gary. "Why don't you go hassle the birthday boy while Amanda and I check out Millie's appetizers?"

"I'm on my way."

Linda's gaze lingered on Amanda. "You look fabulous in that shade of teal. Based on Gary's expression, he agrees."

Enough with this charade. Amanda squared her shoulders. "You can stop pretending. Gary and I both know the real reason Susan planned this party."

Linda's smile softened. "You're an intelligent, strong-willed woman." She withdrew her hand. "Please don't let the past destroy your chance at happiness."

Amanda blinked, emotion catching her off guard. How could someone who'd never had her world implode understand the cost of hope? "I appreciate how much you care, Linda. I truly do, and I'll always value your friendship." Her throat tightened. "But Gary deserves a woman whose ability to trust hasn't been crushed."

Linda's smile faltered, concern dimming her eyes. "Gary's one of the most trustworthy men we know."

Erica appeared beside them, her timing merciful. "Susan and Millie outdid themselves tonight."

"Indeed they did." Amanda felt the tension ease just enough to breathe. "Linda and I were headed to sample Millie's appetizers." She looped her arm through Erica's. "Come join us."

They gathered at the kitchen island where laughter and conversation rose around them. Amanda chatted with Bernie, tasted Millie's food, and played her part—smiling, nodding, avoiding Gary with practiced precision. An hour slipped by before she noticed Wendy lingering at the edge of the group, her shoulders rigid, her brows pinched as she stared at her phone. She checked the screen, looked away, then checked again as if willing it to change.

Amanda stepped closer. "Everything okay?"

Wendy's gaze flicked up, then back down. "I haven't heard from Donna since she and the boys left Atlanta." Her thumb tapped the edge of the phone. "They should've reached the inn by now."

"Chances are they ran into a Friday traffic jam along the way." Amanda rested her hand on Wendy's arm. "Or they stopped to eat."

"I suppose that makes sense." Wendy nodded, but the movement was quick and unconvincing. She slid the phone into her jeans pocket, then pressed her hand over it, as though she might feel a vibration. Her eyes scanned the room. "I'm going to watch Keith open his presents." She glanced one more time at her pocket before walking off, leaving Amanda alone by the glass door.

Gary appeared at her side. "Everyone's focused on Keith. No one will notice us slipping out."

Amanda hesitated then nodded. She let him guide her onto the deck toward the outdoor hearth where flames curled around the logs. A chill brushed her skin. Gary shrugged out of his jacket and draped it over her shoulders. His arm remained wrapped around her as though it belonged there.

Her heart pounded. "Why did you add a heart emoji to your Thanksgiving text?"

He smiled softly. "Why did you add a turkey to your response?"

"To send a message."

"Same reason for the heart." He drew her closer. "The moment you walked in tonight, I realized I love you too much to pretend friendship is enough."

The warmth of his body and the steady rise and fall of his chest threatened to unravel her resolve. "You've been nothing but good to me, Gary." Her voice trembled. "But the men I trusted—believed in—broke my heart."

"I intend to prove I'm worthy of your trust and your love."

Amanda leaned into his warmth, shivering when unease threaded through her comfort. She wanted to trust him—wanted the promise of patience to be enough—but uncertainty pressed in, heavy and insistent. Healing wasn't a single step forward but a long winding path she hadn't yet learned to navigate. A log split, sending sparks dancing into the night. Amanda swallowed hard. "Maybe one day I'll find the courage to trust again. For now all I can do is breathe without falling apart."

His hold tightened, protective and patient. "Then I'll wait for as long as it takes."

Thank you for reading Fragile Hearts. I hope you're enjoying reading this series as much as I'm enjoying writing it. The series continues with book 9, Road to Forgiveness, which will publish June 2026.

If you aren't one of my newsletter friends, I'd love to send you a link to my only standalone novel, Jenny's Grace. To sign up go to https://www.subscribepage.com/pat-nichols-newsletter

Afterword

Sometimes it's hard to believe my author journey began twelve years ago and my first book published in 2019. Pursuing a career as an author nine years after retiring from the corporate world proves it's never too late to follow your dreams. I have met so many wonderful new friends and reconnected with friends from the past. I am especially grateful for those who are traveling with me on my journey.

My editor and dear friend, Sherri Stewart, who's also a multi-published author, has edited every Blue Ridge series book. She knows my characters as well as I do. Elaina Lee has designed all sixteen of my current covers.

My beta readers, Pat Davis, Carlene Dunn, Bev Feldkamp, Kitty Metzger, Kathy Warner, CJ Bruce, Zanase Duncan, and Lynn Worley give me excellent feedback from readers' perspectives. My Word Weaver friends provide feedback from authors' perspectives. My dedicated launch team members are the first to read and post reviews. My newsletter friends and readers' loyalty always make my heart sing.

A special thanks to my high-school-sweetheart husband, Tim, for smiling when I talk about my characters as if they lived outside my head. I'm grateful to my entire family for their encouragement and patience when I share my newest plot twist.

Above all I'm grateful to God for His amazing grace, His Son my savior, and for the gift of eternal life. I know one day I will spend eternity with loved ones who have passed on.

www.ingramcontent.com/pod-product-compliance
Lightning Source LLC
LaVergne TN
LVHW091302150826
845673LV00006B/1504
9798991241151